PHILADELPHIA NOIR

PHILADELPHIA NOIR

EDITED BY CARLIN ROMANO

AKASHIC
BOOKS

Published by Akashic Books
©2010 Akashic Books

Series concept by Tim McLoughlin and Johnny Temple
Philadelphia map by Aaron Petrovich

ISBN-13: 978-1-936070-63-3
Library of Congress Control Number: 2010922722

First printing

Akashic Books
PO Box 1456
New York, NY 10009
info@akashicbooks.com
www.akashicbooks.com

ALSO IN THE AKASHIC NOIR SERIES:

Baltimore Noir, edited by Laura Lippman
Boston Noir, edited by Dennis Lehane
Bronx Noir, edited by S.J. Rozan
Brooklyn Noir, edited by Tim McLoughlin
Brooklyn Noir 2: The Classics, edited by Tim McLoughlin
Brooklyn Noir 3: Nothing but the Truth
edited by Tim McLoughlin & Thomas Adcock
Chicago Noir, edited by Neal Pollack
D.C. Noir, edited by George Pelecanos
D.C. Noir 2: The Classics, edited by George Pelecanos
Delhi Noir (India), edited by Hirsh Sawhney
Detroit Noir, edited by E.J. Olsen & John C. Hocking
Dublin Noir (Ireland), edited by Ken Bruen
Havana Noir (Cuba), edited by Achy Obejas
Indian Country Noir, edited by Sarah Cortez & Liz Martínez
Istanbul Noir (Turkey), edited by Mustafa Ziyalan & Amy Spangler
Las Vegas Noir, edited by Jarret Keene & Todd James Pierce
London Noir (England), edited by Cathi Unsworth
Lone Star Noir, edited by Bobby Byrd & John Byrd
Los Angeles Noir, edited by Denise Hamilton
Los Angeles Noir 2: The Classics, edited by Denise Hamilton
Manhattan Noir, edited by Lawrence Block
Manhattan Noir 2: The Classics, edited by Lawrence Block
Mexico City Noir (Mexico), edited by Paco I. Taibo II
Miami Noir, edited by Les Standiford
Moscow Noir (Russia), edited by Natalia Smirnova & Julia Goumen
New Orleans Noir, edited by Julie Smith
Orange County Noir, edited by Gary Phillips
Paris Noir (France), edited by Aurélien Masson
Phoenix Noir, edited by Patrick Millikin
Portland Noir, edited by Kevin Sampsell
Queens Noir, edited by Robert Knightly
Richmond Noir, edited by Andrew Blossom,
Brian Castleberry & Tom De Haven
Rome Noir (Italy), edited by Chiara Stangalino & Maxim Jakubowski
San Francisco Noir, edited by Peter Maravelis
San Francisco Noir 2: The Classics, edited by Peter Maravelis
Seattle Noir, edited by Curt Colbert
Toronto Noir (Canada), edited by Janine Armin & Nathaniel G. Moore
Trinidad Noir, edited by Lisa Allen-Agostini & Jeanne Mason
Twin Cities Noir, edited by Julie Schaper & Steven Horwitz
Wall Street Noir, edited by Peter Spiegelman

FORTHCOMING:

Barcelona Noir (Spain), edited by Adriana Lopez & Carmen Ospina
Cape Cod Noir, edited by David L. Ulin
Copenhagen Noir (Denmark), edited by Bo Tao Michaëlis
Haiti Noir, edited by Edwidge Danticat
Lagos Noir (Nigeria), edited by Chris Abani
Mumbai Noir (India), edited by Altaf Tyrewala
Pittsburgh Noir, edited by Kathleen George
San Diego Noir, edited by Maryelizabeth Hart

PHILADELPHIA

Chestnut Hill

76

1

Frankford

East Falls

Narberth, PA

95

Strawberry Mansion

Fairmount

Fishtown

676

West Philadelphia   University City

Old City

Rittenhouse Square

South Street

Bella Vista

Grays Ferry

DELAWARE RIVER

76

South Philadelphia

NEW JERSEY

95

676

SCHUYLKILL RIVER

95

TABLE OF CONTENTS

PART III: THE FAKER CITY

PART IV: THOSE WHO FORGET THE PAST . . .

INTRODUCTION

C'mon, Ben Franklin and *noir*? The Framers and *noir*? George I-Cannot-Tell-a-Lie Washington and *noir*? According to the national mythology, and even our local creation tale about William Penn's "Greene country towne," *Philadelphia Blanc* makes a more sensible title for a volume of local stories than *Philadelphia Noir*. This, after all, is where all of America's greatness and goodness and idealism began.

Betsy Ross dangling a cigarette from her lip? Abigail Adams two-timing John with a local punk?

You could say that was then, and this is *noir*.

But you'd be wrong. Read any of the eighteenth-century scholars who love colonial Philadelphia more than their own parents or kids, and you know that some pretty bad *defecation* was going down in our cobblestoned streets back then, and it got even worse.

By the 1830s and '40s, Philadelphia's antiblack and anti-Catholic riots guaranteed a steady number of bashed heads and windows. Readers innocent of the real Philadelphia may want to consult historian Gary Nash's fine *First City* (University of Pennsylvania Press, 2002), and learn of our antebellum street gangs, "the Moyamensing Killers, Gumballs, Bloodtubs, Scroungers, Hyenas, Bedbugs, Swampoodle Terriers, Nighthawks, Flayers, and Deathfetchers."

You've only heard of the Phillies?

When local officials expanded Philadelphia in 1854 by merging its two square miles with the hundreds of small towns around it—creating the 135-square-mile municipal behemoth it remains today—the move came largely out of desperation, the need to control a crime scene gone wild.

And how far we've come! Nash's colorfully named gangs are the spiritual ancestors of today's "flash mobs"—hundreds of no-goodnik, dumb-as-a-doornail teens (with, we suspect, not-so-hot grades), who congregate somewhere in Center City at the flash of a global Twitter message and start beating the crap out of normal passersby.

Yes, it sometimes happens in Philadelphia, City of Brotherly Love, not far from Independence Hall and the Liberty Bell.

America's first great city, first capital, and first industrial metropolis contained from the beginning the mix of poor workers and elite culture, of ethnic enclaves and religious intolerance, of easy skullduggery and flesh-pot possibilities, that led Lincoln Steffens in 1903 to famously rule it "corrupt and contented." Colonel William Markham, deputy governor of Pennsylvania from 1693 to 1699 (and William Penn's cousin), was the first official on the take, hiding pirates at one hundred pounds a head, including Captain Kidd himself. We've had many similarly devoted public servants since.

In the early innings of the twenty-first century, Philadelphia needs no PR help as a *noir* town, not when some of our own best and brightest call us "Filthydelphia" (and not just for the residents who take jump shots at garbage cans and miss). Remember Brian De Palma's *Blow Out* (1981), with John Travolta smoothly recording vehicular murder on Lincoln Drive? And *Witness* (1985), with its affront to Amish decency in the Men's Room of 30th Street Station?

Creepy stuff happens here. The city's attractions, aside from Independence Hall, the National Constitution Center, and standard guidebook stuff, include more dope joints, brothels, larceny lairs, and related dens of iniquity than Fodor, Frommer, and Fielding could handle even if they pooled coverage (that is, if they ventured into the alternate reality that bourgeois travel guides consider hands-off). Actually, even some of the guidebook stuff is pretty dark. Try the Mutter Museum, with that tumor extracted from President Grover Cleveland's jaw, the liver shared by the original Siamese twins. How about the barely furnished Edgar Allan Poe House, with the basement from "The Black Cat"?

Philadelphia *noir* is different from the mood, the sensibility, the dimensions, of *noir* encountered in more glamourous American cities. With the national spotlight long since gone—the federal government fled to Washington, the national media navel-gazing in New York, the glitter of the movies permanently in L.A. (even if M. Night Shyamalan fights for our spookiness)—we don't live a noble, elevated kind of noir. In D.C., that dead body may belong to a senator. In New York, the gumshoe following the scent may find himself suddenly face-to-face with international intrigue. In Philadelphia, we do *ordinary noir*—the humble killings, robberies, collars, cold cases that confront people largely occupied with getting by.

How, after all, would you expect normal Philadelphians to operate when this way lies the house where Thomas Jefferson wrote the Declaration, and that way offers some smelly street bum doing his business on the sidewalk? We negotiate our lives between *Philadelphia Blanc*—the city with more higher-ed institutions than any in the country, a sterling concentration of medical and pharmaceutical professionals, an arts tradition that boasts the nation's oldest theater, an exhaltation of delicate virtuosi at the Curtis Institute of Music—and *Philadelphia Noir*. In the latter town, a Starbucks barista gets beaten to death on the subway for sport, a lawyer gets gunned down at his regular ATM machine, and two Chinatown officials bite the dust when a maniacal speeder barrels into them by the Immigration Services building.

You can get cut or smashed at any moment in Philadelphia—see Duane Swierczynski's taut "Lonergan's Girl," or Aimee LaBrie's caustic "Princess." It's a city where pretend glamour falls apart fast, as in Jim Zervanos's sly "Your Brother, Who Loves You," a city where the frustrated tumble into bad choices like Laura Spagnoli's Beth in "A Cut Above." (Readers who follow Philadelphia's tabloid tales will recognize familiar elements in Zervanos's slumming TV news anchor, and Spagnoli's credit-card swiping couple.)

Violent crimes in Philadelphia often prove matter-of-fact and of the numbskull sort—the kind of feats by fabulous losers that the narrator of Diane Ayres's wry "Seeing Nothing" deals with, that Dennis Tafoya's Jimmy Kelly profits from in "Above the Imperial." The saddest kind resemble a type of destiny, one captured in the desperation of Solomon Jones's breakneck "Scarred," Asali Solomon's subtle "Secret Pool," and Keith Gilman's tragic "Devil's Pocket," where good deeds do not go unpunished. It doesn't matter, in Philadelphia, whether you're Irish or Italian, Jewish or Black, Latino or Polish, Korean or a hundred other things. It won't help if you think salvation lies in escape to the privileges of the Main Line, as does Meredith Anthony's wannabe suburbanite in "Fishtown Odyssey," or that safety can be preserved in the quiet deceptions of a bordertown like Narberth, as the shifty psychiatrist of Halimah Marcus's "Swimming" seems to believe. Shit can happen at any time.

Per capita, Philadelphia matches any city, weirdo incident for weirdo incident. But we trump everyone on history. In this volume you'll see that a few top writers who know the city best—the kind who can tell you that Schuylkill means "hidden stream," and that "Mummers" are "people with masks" (okay, with sequins and feathers too)—wind up decades or hundreds of years in the past when asked to channel their inner *noirista*. Cordelia Frances Biddle's cocky stroller in "Reality," Cary Holladay's eerie bartender in "Ghost Walk," the neutral narrator of Gerald Kolpan's "The Ratcatcher"—all experience the Philadelphia truism that if you think you've got local history under control, you don't.

With apologies, you won't find the obvious here. Having served as literary critic of the *Philadelphia Inquirer* for twenty-five years, and written more stories on "Philadelphia literature" than anyone living, I thank my contributors for their very limited references to hoagies, cheesesteaks, water ice, soft pretzels, and waitresses who call their customers "Hon." There's no glimpse of Claes Oldenburg's *Clothespin* or the rowers by the Waterworks, and only one passing mention of *Rocky*. Truth is, we don't talk much about those things. We just live our lives.

Carlin Romano
Philadelphia, PA
August 2010

PART I

CITY OF BURSTS

PRINCESS

BY AIMEE LABRIE
South Philadelphia

I t's Saturday at three a.m. and I'm coming off a hellish shift at Ray's Happy Birthday Bar. It's pouring rain, no taxis in this part of town, and the 23 bus runs about every two hours now. My feet hurt from standing and my mood is black after spending most of the night serving a crowd of out-of-towners—a group of prickish frat boys slumming it and cracking racist jokes. I let them get good and drunk, even send a few shots of Jack their way, and then, when one of the jerk-offs slaps his Am Ex on the bar, I add $100 to the tab.

I know they are too drunk and too cocky to eyeball the final tally. Good thing, too, because they leave behind a five-dollar tip and some change. When one of them asks for directions to Washington Avenue to hail a cab to Center City, I send him south instead of north, deeper into darker territory not so friendly to their kind. But hey, they said they were looking for an authentic Philly experience. I am just making sure they get what they asked for.

So, I'm standing at the curb, weighing my options, when a car pulls up, splashing filthy rain water over my sneakers.

Now, I know better than to jump into a car with a near stranger, but it's raining hard, in the way only a summer night in Philadelphia can deliver—appearing out of nowhere, flooding the sidewalks, sending Styrofoam cups and discarded cheesesteak wrappers from Pat's careening in a river of water down the curb. Lightning cracks the sky like the end of the world is right around the corner. And I see from his crag-nosed profile that I do sort of know this guy—he's the uncle of a kid I used to sleep with. Uncle Tony (one of many Uncle Tonys in this part of town). And a former regular at Ray's before Lou, Ray's son and the owner, banned him from setting foot in the place ever again.

He sits in his big maroon Chevy Cadillac, a fat man with a salt-and-pepper crew cut wearing a too-big, shiny Eagles T-shirt. The passenger window rolls down. "Hey, doll," he says. "Get it the car. You're soaked." I hesitate. "Holy Mary, Mother of God, don't be stupid. It's not like I'm some douche bag from Trenton you never met before."

I check the street again. The back of my T-shirt smells like a cigarette butt after eight hours of serving cheap beer and shots. It sticks wetly to my back. What the hell. I get in the car. He has the heater running full blast, which I appreciate. The interior is a deep plush maroon and stinks of stale cigars and cheap cologne. "You South?" he asks.

"Yeah, just drop me at 8th and Morris, and I'll hop out." A rosary hangs from the rearview mirror with a sad-looking Jesus dangling forlornly on the end.

"Hey, let me ask you something." The car idles. "You hear what happened to my nephew Johnny?"

I shake my head. I haven't seen or thought of Johnny in a couple of weeks, not since I kicked him out of my bed.

"Smashed by the 147. No helmet, not that it woulda mattered. Run him over while he was on his bike. F-ing SEPTA buses." He drums his pudgy fingers on the steering wheel. "No chance even for any last words."

"Jesus, sorry, Tony." Too vain to wear a bike helmet. I am starting to remember more about Johnny now. His long curly hair was one of his best features. Though I could be remembering one of the others. They blur together after a while.

"Yeah, well, what can you do?" Uncle Tony doesn't seem that busted up about it. "He left his journals behind though. You ever read them?"

"No." I am starting to think it's time for me to take a pass on the ride and be on my way.

"He ever talk to you about a key? He leave one at your place? I'm wondering, because in his journals he hints a lot about where this key might be. It's the one that opens that garage across the street. Where he stores his bikes, right?" The car begins to feel a little too warm. I see that I've made a mistake accepting this ride. Maybe a big one.

I grab the door handle. The automatic lock clicks shut. "I don't know what you're talking about, you lunatic. Let me out of here." I remember now why Lou banned him for life from the bar. He'd started a brawl one night about the lack of paper towels in the men's room. After getting no response from Lou, he hurled a bar stool at the big-screen TV behind the bar. He missed the television, but busted the neon Bud Light sign. That was his last night at Ray's. He was crying and wailing, "But I'm a Mummer!" when they tossed him out onto Passyunk Avenue.

"Listen, just tell me where the key is and I'll take you home like I said," he pleads.

I reach in my purse to take out my pepper spray. He lunges forward, and, for a second, I think maybe he's going to kiss me. He takes my face in both of his hands and whacks my head hard on the dashboard. Then it's lights out.

I wake up to the tickle of something licking my ankle. I'm sitting on a cushioned chair with my hands tied behind my back, feet bound together by what looks like a dog leash, and duct tape covering my mouth. The something washing my foot is a fat brown dog, one of those pugs with the curly tails and popped-out eyes. It wears a fancy pink collar. I jerk my leg. The dog looks up at me, eyes rolling stupidly and blackish tongue hanging out of the side of its mouth.

At least my clothes are still on; all except for my shoes.

I struggle against the ties and look around. I've descended into the middle of South Philly grandmother-land. My best guess is that it's Tony's mom's house. It's an old-school Italian living room with thick, pink shag carpet, a blue leather sofa and matching armchair covered in plastic. The surfaces are decorated with doilies and throw pillows with fluffy white kittens stitched in needlepoint, along with afghans, Virgin Marys, and multiple Jesuses—Jesus and a lamb, Jesus on the cross, Jesus flashing the peace sign and looking like a hipster. The best is a picture featuring the holiest of holy—Jesus, John F. Kennedy, and Pope John Paul II. How they got the three of them together for that photo op is anybody's guess. Underneath it all is the trapped-in smell of old lady. Part Jean Naté body wash, part pancake makeup, and part getting closer to death. No wonder Johnny never brought me here. He had mentioned he was crashing at his gran's for a while, but didn't say he was living with an old-fashioned stereo as big as a spaceship, giant fake flowers in an even bigger shiny vase, and a crappy oil painting of the family hanging in a gold frame above the couch: Grandma, Tony, and Johnny. Another unholy trinity.

I've got to make sense of this somehow before the lunatic returns. I am starting to recall a little bit more about Johnny.

I don't usually chat up customers, but Wednesdays are slow at Ray's. He wore low-slung jeans and a white T-shirt that stretched tight across the muscles of his chest and back.

I was new to the joint—the first female bartender, but I didn't need to prove myself. Lou, Ray's son, was a friend of my dad's. I just wanted a job where I could get paid in cash and stay off the radar of the IRS for a while.

He looked just like all the white, angst-filled hipster dudes you see there or at the Dive or Pope's—in their grungy T-shirts from Circle Thrift and skinny girl jeans with one leg rolled up so that they can get around the city on their beat-up, expensive vintage bikes. Chain wallets, ironic tattoos, and multiple piercings. I can't say that he was any different, except he said "please" and "thank you" when I set the PBRs in front of him and he was writing in a red spiral notebook—like the kind you'd use in high school. His wrote feverishly and I imagined it was a screenplay about a misunderstood twenty-something, or a proposal to City Council for a more sustainable Philly, or song lyrics for his Flaming Lips sound-alike band so that **they** could get another gig at Johnny Brenda's.

We started talking about what he was writing. He had a rough voice, the voice of a smoker who'd picked up the habit with a vengeance in junior high, though he couldn't have been too far into his twenties.

He told me he'd always kept a journal. "I know, I'm a pretentious prick. No poetry though," he added. I asked him what he wrote about. "Deep, dark secrets," he said. He didn't look like he'd lived long enough to have anything worth hiding, so I figured he was making shit up. "I write descriptions about places. Like this dirty little bar and that old man over in the Elvis shirt with his head on the table. I wrote a paragraph about you." He read it to me. He was generous.

I took him home to my latest cheap house on one of those narrow one-way streets without trees—this shitty apartment next to the JC Chinese restaurant. I go to sleep and wake up smelling chop suey. It's the kind of street where you hear Mexican music playing and jacked-up cars revving at all hours. I don't mind. I usually sleep through anything, like a dead person. Junk lines my street—crushed Red Bull cans and empty Corona bottles, dirty diapers, and abandoned condoms. Like the rest of the city, South Philly changes from block to block and I happen to live on one where the shades are always drawn shut with yellow miniblinds and the windows sport signs reading, *Se cuarta a renta*. But the apartment is dirt-cheap and I have lived in worse places.

Johnny had a bike of course, and insisted on taking it inside with us. He didn't stay the night, which I appreciated. He came back to the bar the next night. I took him home again. He had a tongue ring, which I also appreciated. This went on for a while, not long, maybe three weeks, and always with that stupid Raleigh bike, and then one night when he wasn't at the bar, I brought someone else home and Johnny showed up at my door, ringing the bell again and again until I answered, and bleated, "But you don't understand. I love you!"

I told him to get real, get lost, and get a new dive bar to hang out in—try the Royal or Pope's—not Ray's anymore. He called me a fucking bitch. I pushed over his bike and he squealed like an adolescent girl, picked up the bike, and pedaled furiously away in his high-top Converse sneakers, never to be heard from again.

Except he *had* come back.

I consider my next move. I imagine the *Inquirer* headline: *Stupid Bartender Murdered by Moron*. As if on cue, the moron walks in.

Tony has changed into yet another Eagles jersey. He seems glad to see me awake. "Look, I don't like this any more than you, but I figured we'd get lots more done if you wasn't running loose." His eyes are bloodshot, but instead of smelling like booze, he smells like Old Spice.

He turns on the big-screen TV plastered next to the family portrait and turns it to the classics sports channel, the one that replays old football games where you already know how it all ends and who wins. "Now, I'm going to pull off this tape and it's going to hurt, so I'm sorry about that. Don't scream." He rips the tape off in one quick motion, taking half my lip with it. I scream. "You'll scare the dog!" he says. The dog is stretched out across the floor on its back, snoring. He pushes the volume up on the TV so that Howard Cosell's nasally voice booms out into the room. I am going to die listening to Cosell announcing a bygone two-point conversion. "My ma is down the shore, but she'll be back before too long, so we got to figure this out quick."

Maybe if I stall long enough, Granny'll rescue me. That's assuming she isn't an accomplice in whatever this mess is. I've seen plenty of these South Philly old ladies, sweeping up the sidewalk in front of the house early in the morning with their teeth still sitting in a jar by the bed. Cross them, and they'll cold cock you in a second with the broom or whatever else is handy.

Tony picks up a red spiral journal from the doily-covered coffee table. "Johnny wrote a lot about you. I just need to know where the key is. He writes that he's left it with someone he trusts. Well, I can't find it here, and believe me, I've looked under every doily and cookie jar in the place."

"I barely knew the kid. We maybe hung around once."

He frowns. "Oh yeah? Does this sound like you?" He flips to the middle of the book and reads a description of my apartment with the rusty kitchen sink and the rats scrabbling in the walls. He describes what I look like in bed and the color of the mole under my right arm. Tony snaps the books shut and pushes up the sleeve of my shirt. "What a coincidence! This shit about you goes on for pages and pages. I know Johnny told you something more about where the key is, didn't he? If I can find the key, I can get to the money, and if I get to the money, you got nothing to worry about."

In fact, Johnny may have mentioned a key of some kind. He was a Chatty Cathy. Problem is, I'm not much of a listener. Still, I would've remembered money talk.

"He wrote about you like you was his girlfriend," Tony says, waving the notebook under my nose.

"We were fuck buddies, that's it." His eyes flick to the Jesus on the wall. "We weren't going steady or anything. He didn't hand over his old high school letter jacket from St. Nick's. I don't know about any of this."

"You know the A&M garage across the street from Ray's? He keeps his bikes in that place. You know that?" I nod. "You ever wonder what else he might have tucked away in there? You ever wonder why he was delivering office paper at two in the morning?"

Working as a bartender teaches you pretty quick that people will eventually spill whatever it is that's gnawing at them. All you have to do is wait. And so I wait. And keep telling him that I don't know anything about a key. And wait some more. Repeat my innocence. Then shut my mouth, praying he doesn't beat the shit out of me or worse.

He paces the room. I notice he's not any wearing shoes, just long white athletic socks pulled up to the knees. I suppose we're both shoeless so the carpets don't get messed up. He explains the "sitch." Johnny was a drug courier—some of his friends were too, but he was the head honcho, the numero uno courier. The drugs were shipped from New Jersey to Johnny's storage place at A&M in bicycle frames. Johnny would then distribute the bikes to his other courier pals to take apart so they could peddle their wares to various eager customers far and wide across the City of Brotherly Love.

I am starting to have a little more respect for the dead kid.

Tony doesn't elaborate on his role. "I was just the connector, mostly, with these guys in Jersey. I never touched the bikes. I never even seen the bikes. I just arranged for the shipments. To tell you the truth, I had no idea what was really going on until the thugs in Jersey contacted me and told me." His voice is stiff, like one reserved for false testimony in court.

And then, it seems, Johnny got greedy—maybe he needed some new guitar amps or fancier pens—and he started keeping a portion of the proceeds locked away in the storage center along with the bikes. And then the Jersey guys, these "bicycle distributors," wanted to know where their money had gone. They didn't want to hear about how Tony couldn't get to it or how Johnny had taken the secret to his grave. They just wanted to get paid, and fast.

"They been here twice already," Tony says.

"What does your ma say about this?"

His thick, caterpillar-looking eyebrows fly up in surprise. "She don't say nothing. She just grinds up beans for coffee and gives them cake."

I don't believe him, but I don't say that either. I bet Granny's grown used to the perks the money brought in; the status she earned for the extra church tithes; maybe she even bought a few wigs made out of real hair or new plastic covers for the furniture.

"How about if I make you a deal? You let me out of here and we forget about this whole thing. I'll talk to Lou about you being allowed back in the bar. You know, we'll start with Tuesday-night karaoke. You can sing Johnny Cash or Britney or whoever the hell you want. But you gotta let me out of here first."

"They'll be coming back soon," Tony says. He actually wrings his hands, like an old lady. "And now I got you to deal with and no key and no money either."

"I'm telling you, I'll put in a good word with Lou. No problem. I bet he'd even help you out with the money if I ask him nice. And talk to these Jersey thugs. He's a popular guy. People love him."

Tony gives a big, long sigh. "Give me a second." He paces some more and then says, "You need anything? Like a glass of water?" I nod and he disappears into the kitchen.

The dog looks up at me as though we are old friends, then jumps on my lap, landing on my full bladder. Her collar jingles. It's an ornate thing with a name tag and other assorted doggie bling. She starts licking my face. "Get off!" I try to shake her from my legs.

From the other room Tony yells, "Get down, Princess!"

A church bell rings from some distant street, signaling the approach of dawn. I recall something else about Johnny.

Like every other hipster kid, his skinny, undernourished body was plastered with tattoos. Nothing too strange, no Tweety Bird or names of ex-girlfriends drawn in Gothic lettering. He did have an awful tattoo on his ankle though. I spotted it the first night because of his rolled-up pant leg. A dog. A pug, to be exact.

"What's that?" I'd asked.

"That's Princess," he said. "She holds the key to my heart."

I told him to stop talking like a Danielle Steele novel and take off his tightie-whities already. Which he did.

Tony comes back into the room, holding a glass of water etched with daisies. It looks as though he's reconsidered the situation. "Aw, shit. Aw, Christ. Look, I really just wanted to talk to you, but you bartenders are intimidating."

I make my face as blank as possible. He sets the water glass down very carefully on one of the doilies.

"Listen, you can think about it, but I have to pee," I tell him. "I have to pee right now and if you won't let me use the bathroom, I will piss all over this velveteen cushion. You know how hard it will be to clean? I bet these are antique chairs. I bet this fringe is from the old country. Irreplaceable. How would you explain that to your ma?"

He shrugs, trying to shake off his look of concern. "The dog coulda done it."

"That little thing?" The dog scratches itself, fancy pink collar jingling, and then begins grooming its private parts in earnest. "There is no way the amount I have to piss could come out of that runt. Trust me. I don't know what time it is exactly, but I would guess I haven't used the powder room in a good four hours."

He looks torn, but finally he begins to untie me. I wish the knots were in the front, so I could kick him in his fat face.

When I'm free, I say, "We'll work this out." I try to walk casually and not bolt for the door.

I close and lock the bathroom door. I figure I have about one shot at knocking him out. I search the room. A toilet plunger isn't going to do the trick and neither is a plastic lady torso whose skirts cover the extra toilet paper rolls. I could Aqua Net him to death or stab him in the eye with a bobby pin.

I catch sight of my face in the vanity mirror. I've got a nice purple shiner and a crust of blood on my upper lip. If I make it out of here, I'm going to treat myself to a real haircut, not one of those ten-dollar Chop Shop hatchet jobs.

Then I catch sight of it in the reflection of the mirror. A heavy-duty Virgin Mary statue with her hands outstretched as if she's saying, *Don't look at me. It's not my fault.* She's propped up in the bathroom window, surrounded by cotton balls and Max Factor makeup. Hail Mary, full of Grace. I tuck her under my arm.

Tony hovers outside the door. "Okay, listen, you'll talk to Ray then?" He sees what I'm carrying. "Hey, what're you doing? Put that back! Ma will kill you!" I walk into the living room. He follows. "No kidding, don't be smart."

I put a little distance between us and then, with the VM held out in front of me like a bat, I spin around and smack him as hard as I can across the head. The statue stays in one piece. His head does not. He gives a little "Oh" of surprise and touches his temple in disbelief. He staggers and bleeds all over the plastic on the furniture. He looks more horrified about the mess he's making than he does about losing his life.

When he sees the blood spill onto his Eagles shirt, his legs accordion and down he goes. I've never seen anyone bleed quite like that. We've had two guys drop dead at Ray's, but neither were bleeders. The cut isn't going to kill him, but it will buy me enough time to get out and make it to the storage space. I'm sure the money is there along with one or two of Johnny's stupid bikes. The Jersey jerks will get to Tony soon enough. Or his own mother when she sees what he's done to her living room.

Hey, I'm not a murderer, just an opportunist.

The Virgin Mary statue lies on her back on the pink shag carpet, staring up at the ceiling, still looking as if she's just an innocent bystander. Except she's not. In fact, she may have just changed my life. Now, I'm not going to start genuflecting and hanging out at the doors of St. John's. I don't believe much in that Catholic shit, but you never know. Maybe I'll even buy a Virgin Mary night light from the Italian Market after I get the money and move out of my shitty apartment on Morris and into a slightly less shitty one further west.

I take hold of Princess's collar—rabies vaccine, heart-shaped name tag, and a key. I remove it and slip it in my pocket.

I consider leaving the animal. It's not like she'd be much of a watch dog for me. She doesn't seem at all concerned that I cracked Tony in the head and he's now bleeding on the carpet.

I look at the dog and she looks back at me with her popped-out googly eyes. She wags her stubby tail half-heartedly as though unsure about the deal too. "You're not much of an accomplice," I tell her. I could dump her on the streets. Some sappy grandma would take her in. Or she'd get hit by a bus just like Johnny. "All right, Princess, let's go." I pick her up. "You can stay with me," I say. "For now."

SCARRED

BY SOLOMON JONES

Strawberry Mansion

Thunder clapped, and the street went black as if God had blown out the candles. A single flash of lighting streaked across the sky. After that, the only sound was the rain.

That kind of quiet was rare at 33rd and Cecil B. Moore, the North Philly corner where a hodgepodge of crumbling housing and new development met the orchestrated greenery of Fairmount Park.

Most autumn evenings, the corner rumbled with the sounds of the 3 and 32 buses, danced with the laughter of children at the water ice stand, and banged with the clatter of tools at the used tire shop. There was music to this corner, and the tunes went far beyond the rhymes of Li'l Wayne or the gospel of Kirk Franklin. The music had a distinctive rhythm, like the jazz of John Coltrane, who'd once lived a block away.

But just like Coltrane's house, the streets were empty and the rhythm was off, because the storm and the blackout had snatched the life from the streets, forcing everyone and everything indoors.

The occupants of the new lofts who'd arrived with the long-gone real-estate boom were huddled in darkness, just like their impoverished neighbors. As rain poured down and lightning flashed, their differences no longer mattered. They all waited nervously for the lights to come on, because somewhere deep down, they understood the power of the heavens.

But Richard and Corrine weren't afraid. In their rehabbed three-story home at the end of a ramshackle block, the only power that mattered was love. And heaven? Heaven was between them, in every whisper, every kiss, and every touch.

As the storm raged outside their window, the newlyweds welcomed darkness into a bedroom that overlooked the water ice stand. While neighbors shut their eyes against the blackout, the husband and wife christened their new home, joining themselves like instruments in a symphony of passion.

The driving rain struck the windows as they poured themselves into one another, and as their bodies gave in to the moment, their whispers of love became shouts of joy. The harmony reached perfection. The symphony climaxed and ceased. Then their voices faded into the blackness of the night, with gasps and shudders and moans.

Afterward, they lay in each other's arms, listening to the rain fall. Corrine reached up and twisted Richard's blond hair around her fingers. Even without light, she knew every part of his face. His pink lips were thin and sculpted. His jaw was square and strong. His blue eyes were set wide on either side of his sharply pointed nose.

Her features were the opposite: cinnamon-brown complexion, silky black hair, eyes brown and bottomless, skin the texture of a ripened peach.

They were an odd couple—the thirty-year-old white war veteran and the slightly older black nurse. At least it looked odd from the outside. But Richard never found it to be strange. They'd clicked the first time they met, when he saw her working in the physical therapy unit at the Philadelphia V.A. Medical Center.

He'd asked her out for coffee after finishing his appointment and they went to the hospital cafeteria to drink cappuccino and speak of their pasts. He told her that he was a Special Forces soldier whose third tour in Afghanistan had been cut short by a roadside bomb. She told him that her only brother—a twenty-one-year-old grunt who was barely out of boot camp—had been killed by a grenade in Iraq.

As the few minutes they'd intended to spend together stretched to hours, she told him that she hated working at the V.A. because of the misery and apathy she often found there. But she stayed in the hopes of helping other soldiers the way she wished she could've helped her brother. While doing a job she despised, she hid her pain from everyone around her; everyone, that is, except Richard.

He instantly recognized her grief because it mirrored his own. It was the same emotional pain he'd hidden when he'd seen his comrades gunned down near Kabul. It was identical to the pain he'd suppressed when he returned home and found himself isolated. It matched the grief he felt whenever he thought of his past. That's why it was so easy for him to see Corrine's hurt crouching behind forced smiles. He knew he had to make her pain go away.

For months, Richard and Corinne comforted each other, slowly drawing out bits and pieces of the things war had taken from them. Corrine told him that she'd lost her joy. Richard admitted that he'd lost his compassion. They both said they'd lost opportunities to love, and vowed not to lose one more.

Slowly they began to leave war behind. Richard allowed his military high and tight to grow out until his hair reached his shoulders. Corrine's sad demeanor gave way to an easy smile. Their whirlwind courtship led to marriage, and when they bought the house on the corner of 33rd and Cecil B. Moore, rehabbing it with their own hands, the imperfect neighborhood was just like their lives. It was somewhere between the horrors of war and the safety of peace. The direction they took from there would be up to them, or so they hoped.

On this night, as they lay in each other's arms, waiting for the blackout to end, they both realized that some things were beyond their control. These things included the scars they'd suffered in the past. They'd already dealt with the emotional ones, but for Richard, especially, some physical scars remained.

As Corrine lay in his arms, she reached for one such scar. It was ugly and purple, and it knifed down the left side of his powerful chest. When her slender fingers touched it and lingered there, Richard braced himself for the inevitable question.

"Where did this come from?"

"We've been over this, Corrine," he said, gently moving her hand away from the old wound. "It happened in the war."

"I know that, but—"

"Look," he said with an edge to his voice. "I told you about every fight we won, every guy we lost, and every civilian who died. The truth is, I don't remember where this scar came from and I don't know if I want to. But I do know I love you, and that should be the only thing that matters."

"You're right Richard. It's just that . . ."

"What? You think I'm hiding something from you?"

She lay back and ran her palm along his face, searching in the darkness until she found his eyes.

"Yes, I do," she whispered playfully as she wrapped herself around him. "And you're going to make me use everything I've got to get it out of you."

Richard leaned back and looked at her, trying to see her

face beyond the shadows. Then lightning flashed, filling the room with brilliant blue-white light. She smiled and he buried his face in her hair, whispering her name as only he could.

"Corrine."

She giggled and reached for him as the rain smacked against the windows. But just as their lips were about to touch, the soothing sound of the downpour was interrupted by shattering glass.

Corrine sat up in bed. "What was that?"

"I don't know," Richard answered, reaching down to grab his pants from the floor. "Stay here."

He got up and walked briskly down the hall. Then he descended the steps two at a time, his feet padding silently on the hardwood floor. When he entered the kitchen, he saw that one of the windows over the sink was broken.

"Probably the wind," he said to himself, and reached up into a cabinet for a candle.

He lit it and searched the cabinet. When he found the roll of duct tape he was searching for, a shadow crept across the wall. The shape of it was unmistakable. It was a man.

Richard didn't look up. Instead, he reached down into a drawer as his eyes darted back and forth across the room. He released the tape, wrapped his fingers around a kitchen knife, and hoped that he'd imagined what he'd seen. But when he turned around, he knew that it was real.

The man crashed through the kitchen door, lunging as Richard brought the knife down with all the force he could muster. The man yelped, like a dog, and stumbled back onto the counter as the blood from his wounded arm soaked through his shirt.

"Richard!" Corrine yelled from the bedroom.

"Stay there," Richard managed to bark out as he slashed

the man's cheek with a sideways stroke of the knife.

The man ducked when Richard swung the knife back in the other direction. His fist pounded Richard's kidney, knocking the breath from his body and forcing him back into a cabinet. The man rushed toward him. Richard gripped the knife with both hands and swung upward. The man grunted, and warm blood flowed from the ragged gash that extended the length of his stomach.

A second passed, then two. Richard's heart beat wildly. The weight of the dead man pressed against him, pushing him into the cabinet as the blood saturated his clothes. The wind moaned and whisked through the broken glass in the kitchen. The rain fell in a thousand tiny drumbeats, tapping out its own timeless percussion.

As Richard pushed the man's body to the floor, another sound tore through the house, biting into him like nails against a blackboard. The sound was Corrine. She was screaming.

"Help me!" she shrieked, and the wind seemed to fade into the echo of her voice.

Richard turned and ran toward the bedroom, slipping on the blood-soaked linoleum of the kitchen floor. He ran, pushing himself toward the sound of his wife screaming. He ran, forgetting the body that lay in his kitchen, the pain shooting from his side, the blood covering his hands. He had only to get to Corrine. And when he did—when his feet had carried him up the steps and into the bedroom—all he could see was a shadow in the darkness, straddling his wife as she struggled to free herself from its grip.

Richard charged into the room, slashing into the back of Corrine's assailant with the knife. The man rolled onto the floor, arching his back against the pain when Richard brought the knife down again. Corrine joined the fray, her tiny fists striking the man's head angrily. Richard pushed her away and raised the knife high into the air—a madness playing in his eyes as he delivered the killing blow.

A split second passed. Then something whistled through the air. Richard was momentarily blinded by a white flash of light as a burning sensation gripped the back of his leg. He dropped the knife and grabbed at the bullet wound, then turned around to see yet another shadow coming toward him.

Corrine screamed when the shadowy figure aimed a gun with a silencer. There was another whistling sound. This time, the heat glanced Richard's shoulder. He reached for Corrine. There was a final silenced shot, and as the shooter lowered his weapon and retreated down the stairs and into the windswept rain, Corrine's blood spilled onto Richard.

He wrapped his arms around his wife, and as her eyes went vacant, Richard's mind went to a place he thought he'd forgotten. It was a place with bullets flying, people running, tires screeching, and a hell-bound cloud of black smoke filling the air.

He winced, not at the pain he was now experiencing from the wound in his leg, but at the pain he had once caused. Then he pulled a T-shirt from his drawer and wrapped the wound tightly, clenching his jaw while he tried to ignore the pain of the present and the past.

Suddenly, he saw a light penetrate the darkness. He looked down slowly and realized that his iPhone was glowing through his pocket as a text message came through. The light was like an alarm, awakening something that Richard had long since laid to rest. He watched it blink for a few seconds more. Then he pulled the phone from his pocket and saw his memories come to life.

No matter where you go, we'll always find you, the message said. *We're attached, Richard. We're family. Now leave the house and come out through the back door. We'll be waiting.*

There was no number. The text was from a private caller. Not that he needed a number to know who they were. After eight years, they'd found him, just like he'd always known they would.

He slipped the phone back into his pocket and kissed his wife's cold lips. "Goodbye, Corrine."

Richard took off his wedding ring and placed it gently against her breast. Then he rooted under the bed for the 9mm Ruger he'd always kept, waiting for this day to come.

He snapped in a clip and chambered a round, quickly throwing on a T-shirt and sneakers. He took a deep breath and told himself it didn't matter if he made it through the night. By daybreak, his past would be buried, one way or another.

Richard held the gun at his side and crawled down the steps to the kitchen. The dead man who'd crashed through the window was still slumped against the counter. Richard made his way over to him the way he'd been taught, flat against the ground and pulling himself forward with his forearms.

Quickly, he searched the body. In his right pocket, there was nothing. In his left, there was a Glock 9mm with a silencer. Richard took it, then crawled to the stove, extinguished the pilot, and turned the knob.

"Richard!"

The voice calling from outside his house was familiar. It was a sadistic verbal smirk that was at once arrogant and deadly.

Richard didn't answer.

"Come on out, Richard," the man said. "We can talk."

Richard knew that talking was the last thing they would do. He had crossed the line with them. And once you crossed the line with people such as these, there was no turning back, there was no statute of limitations, and there was no reprieve. They could never allow him to live. He knew it, and they knew it. So as the kitchen filled with gas, Richard ripped a piece of cloth from his pant leg and wrapped it around his face. Then he knelt down next to the dead man and hoisted him up from his seat on the floor.

As his wounded leg began to throb, sweat dripped down into his eyes. The rain seemed to tap harder against the broken glass. The wind whipped up angrily. He counted to three. Then he was up, running toward the door and bursting through it as he held the dead body like a shield.

Bullets whistled from muzzles equipped with silencers. A barrage poured in through the kitchen window, sparking a blast that ignited the house and lit the night sky.

Richard dropped the body and leaped to his left, running across 33rd Street and into the park. The rain poured down thicker, and as four men emerged from the gutted school bus at the old tire shop across the street, they lost sight of him for just a second. It was long enough for him to disappear.

"Okay, he's in the park," said the hefty man with the smirk in his voice. "My guess is he went southwest, but I think he's hit, so he couldn't have gotten far. Tyson and Robinson, you two take the right side of Reservoir Drive. Me and Montgomery will search the woods on the left."

"And if we find him before you do?" Tyson asked.

"Try to take him alive."

The men fanned out and melted into the shadows of the blackout while Richard disappeared into the park. He passed by the driving range with its dilapidated caddy shack and ancient golf cart. He moved through the heavy foliage surrounding the Frisbee golf course. He heard sirens from fire engines and police cars blaring in the distance.

As the pain from the bullet wound in the back of his leg intensified, he stopped with his back to a tree, panting and looking over his shoulder at the flames from his burning house. He imagined Corrine, trapped inside without him, her body being consumed by the fire. The thought of it was grisly, but he'd gladly trade places with her now, because the hell of living without her was far more severe than the flames that were cooking her flesh.

He looked away, his bitter tears mingling with the rain. In that instant, the grief she'd spent months helping him to overcome rushed back. A moment later, the grief was gone, and it was replaced with an emotion he knew all too well—anger.

Richard checked his pockets. He still had the phone. He had his Ruger, and he had the Glock with a silencer he'd taken from the dead man in the kitchen.

He looked out from behind the tree once more and saw dome lights whirling outside his house. If he were anyone else, he could've tried to make his way back to the house. He could've told the police that the same people who'd killed his wife had tried to kill him. He could've clarified that he'd acted in self-defense. But Corrine was right. Richard had something to hide, and it all began with the scar on his chest.

Chambering a round in the Glock, Richard stuffed the Ruger into his waistband. A second later, his phone buzzed and his pocket glowed as he received another text message.

For a moment, he considered ignoring the message and leaving the phone behind, but he wanted his pursuers to use the phone to track him. That would bring them closer, and make them that much easier to kill.

Reaching into his pocket, he pulled out the phone, cupped it in his hand, and read the message while the rain pelted the screen.

We know what happened in the mountains at Tora Bora, the text said. *Surrender and you might live.*

A chill went through Richard's body as he reread the message and checked the source. The text had come from a phone number with a 202 area code, which meant they weren't trying to hide their identities anymore. They were CIA, just like the teams he'd fought alongside in Afghanistan.

He'd learned two things about those teams during the war: the only thing that mattered to them was the objective, and they didn't care how they reached it.

Pocketing the phone, he crawled through the slippery, leaf-strewn grass to the edge of Reservoir Drive—the road that snaked through the park from 33rd Street. Then he limped across and climbed a rain-slicked hill until he reached a chain-link fence.

The faded sign on the fence said, *No Trespassing. Property of the Philadelphia Water Department*. He ignored it and scaled the fence, squeezing past the barbed wire that topped it. There was a reservoir on the other side of the fence, and the water inside was rapidly rising.

Richard lay on his stomach on the reservoir's concrete embankment and held onto the fence with both hands. He was flat on his belly and the rain pelting his wounded leg felt almost soothing. Then the fence rattled, and any comfort he felt disappeared.

Sliding into the water, Richard flipped onto his back and allowed himself to float while holding the Glock he'd stolen from the dead body. When the first of two men came sliding along the slippery embankment to see if he was alive, Richard remained still. When the man got closer, Richard opened one eye. When he was almost upon him, Richard sprung into action.

He flipped over in the water, raised the Glock, and fired, hitting the man three times. Before his victim fell into the water, Richard submerged and swam hard to his right. Ten bullets bored into the water around him, but none of them found their target. By the time he surfaced, he was nearly fifty yards away, and the man who'd shot at him was frantically searching for him in the darkness.

Richard climbed the gate and fell on the sloping grass, wincing at the pain in his leg as he rolled to the bottom of the hill. He looked up and saw the man who'd shot at him climbing the gate about forty yards away. Then he heard footsteps running around the bend.

He'd lost the phone and the second gun in the water, but there was no time to lament. Richard got up and hobbled across Reservoir Drive, heading toward the old mansion at Smith Memorial Playground. He crouched as he passed orange construction barriers near the massive house that was buttressed by scaffolding.

Richard's limp was more pronounced than it had been just seconds before, and when he reached the mansion, bullets struck the metal scaffolding. Richard aimed his gun at the lock on the door and fired a shot of his own. A second later, he was inside.

He could see the dim outlines of tricycles and hobby horses strewn about the floor, and the shape of a giant sliding board in the back. The newly painted walls bore pictures that were barely visible in the darkness.

Richard crouched low and ducked into a room thirty yards ahead, knowing that the trail of blood from his wound would lead them to him. But he wanted them to find him now. He wanted it to be over.

The doorknob twisted and three men moved in, spreading out to either side of the room.

"We're here!" said the leader. "Are you?"

Richard recognized the voice now. It was Joe Miller, the same man who'd led the CIA team in the mountains of Tora Bora. Miller was the kind of man others followed. It wasn't because he was especially intelligent or threatening. Nor was it the fact that he'd been a Special Forces major prior to joining the agency. There was just a force about him—a feeling. He had only to speak in that world-weary, cynical growl, and it was enough to make lesser men submit.

Richard was not a lesser man, and he had no intention of submitting. "You know I'm here, Miller," he said as he slid along the wall, his legs even weaker than his voice. "And you know all of us won't be walking out."

Miller used hand signals to point to the area where Richard's voice had come from and his men moved in that direction. "It's hard to know anything when it comes to you, Richard. We thought we knew where you were in the mountains, and we were wrong, weren't we?"

Richard moved toward an opening in the wall that led to another room. "I don't know what you're talking about," he said as his pursuers moved closer.

"I'm talking about Afghanistan, Richard. I'm talking about the reasons you kept going back."

"I wanted to fight," Richard said, sliding down the wall and easing the gun around the corner.

"That's what we all thought at first," the squad leader said as he got down in a prone position and turned on his weapon's laser scope. "And with all the intelligence we gathered and got to you guys in Delta Force, we figured the fight would be easy."

"It should've been," Richard said. "But it's hard to fight a war with the CIA in the way."

"It's even harder when one of your best soldiers is a traitor," he said in an effort to hold Richard's attention. "I have to admit, it took us awhile to figure out how you did it. The simplicity of it was pure genius."

Suddenly, one of the men flew around the wall. Even with his bleeding leg and dimmed senses, Richard was too fast to be caught off guard. He turned and fired one shot from the silenced gun, hitting the agent in the temple. The man was dead before he stopped moving.

Another flew around the wall and was upon Richard, who grabbed his arm and twisted it until it broke. There was a scream and a muffled gunshot, and the agent's last breath came out along with the contents of his bowels.

Richard pushed the body away with a grunt, and when he did so, Miller was standing over him with his gun pointed at Richard's head. His face was just as Richard remembered it—red and pockmarked with a bulbous nose and a mouth that was fixed in a scowl.

"Drop the gun," Miller said, his tone low and angry.

Richard did as he was told. With the blood he'd lost since being shot in his leg, and the energy he'd expended fighting them off, he was too tired and weak to do otherwise.

"I should kill you right now," Miller said.

"Yeah you should. So why don't you?"

"Because I need to hear, from your own mouth, why you helped the enemy in Tora Bora."

Richard was parched. He was finding it difficult to breathe, let alone talk. The house seemed to be getting colder. Still, he wanted to tell him why, because in a perverse way, Richard needed to hear it from his own mouth too.

Richard ripped open his T-shirt, revealing the ugly scar on his chest. "I did it because of this," he said.

Miller looked at him curiously.

"Fighting the battle at Tora Bora was like getting this scar all over again," Richard said wistfully. "It was like reliving ethnic cleansing."

Miller furrowed his brow. He was clearly confused.

"I'm Bosnian. I grew up in a mountain village where you could look out and see minarets from four-hundred-year-old mosques poking through the clouds. It was beautiful. It was peaceful. It was home. Then the war started.

"I was eleven years old when the Serbs came to our village. They stripped the men and paraded them in front of their wives before executing them. Then they raped the women. I was lucky, I guess. They just sliced my chest with a machete and left me to die."

Richard looked up at Miller, who'd been struck dumb by the story. "I saw my mother and sister violated. I saw my father humiliated. I saw all of them murdered. And the only thing I had to remember them by was this scar. Even after I got adopted by a nice American diplomat and his wife, even after they changed my name from Mujo to Richard, even after I learned to love this country, I never forgot what happened to my people. I couldn't, because I had this scar to remind me.

"I never thought when they trained me for Special Forces and put me in Delta Force that I'd end up fighting Muslims in those mountains in Tora Bora. But when I did, something snapped, and it was like I was that frightened, angry little boy back in Bosnia."

"So you sent a radio transmission to make them think you'd been cut off from your unit," Miller said matter-of-factly.

"Then you went over a mountain pass and killed enough Afghan militia to let the mujahideen escape."

The house was silent except for the sound of Richard's increasingly labored breathing.

"Did you realize who you were helping?" Miller asked.

"I realized I was helping Muslims who had the ability to fight back. That was more than my family ever had."

"But you knew that the man commanding those Muslim fighters in Tora Bora was Osama bin Laden. Didn't you?"

Richard closed his eyes and smiled. It was a joyless gesture—one fraught with all the contradictions that had plagued him all his life. "Of course I knew. That's why I kept going back to Afghanistan. I wanted to make up for it by doing my duty for America. But when I couldn't atone for my sins, I wanted to forget I'd ever committed them. That roadside bomb that hit my Humvee was a blessing in disguise. It allowed me to come home and forget Afghanistan. It allowed me to come here and marry Corrine. At least for a little while, I had something beautiful again. But you and your men took that away too."

"Actually, they didn't."

Richard's eyes snapped open at the sound of that voice. It was velvety, feminine, and familiar. It was Corrine. As she walked into the room, Richard tried to make his mouth form the question, but it wouldn't.

Perhaps he'd been struck dumb by the blood loss and the resultant dementia. Or maybe he was already dead, and Corrine was meeting him in paradise.

"You did a good job, Agent Miller," she said to the squad leader who'd captured Richard. "We lost five men, but at least we got our subject, and we got him alive."

"*Our subject*? What are you talking about?" asked Richard.

"The same thing you were talking about a few minutes

ago," Corrine said as she wiped the fake blood from her chest. "Doing my duty for my country."

"But you can't be real," Richard said, laboring to breathe as he began to hyperventilate. "You can't be one of them. You died back at the house. They killed you."

"Funny what a little red paint and a lot of imagination can do, isn't it?" Corrine replied with a wicked grin.

"But you said you loved me," Richard said as his facial expression went from hurt to sadness to outright devastation. "You *married* me."

"And you married me too, even though you knew the CIA could come after you one day for what you did. You valued your happiness more than you valued my safety, and you never trusted me enough to tell me what happened in Tora Bora, no matter how many times I asked you."

"I kept that from you to protect you," he said as a tear rolled down his cheek. "I kept it from you because I loved you. Not that it matters. This was all just another operation for you. The marriage, the house—everything."

"Marrying you was the only way to get close enough to find the truth," she said coldly. "We had to know if you were part of a larger cell or if you acted of your own volition. The fact is, I did it for the same reason you helped bin Laden escape in Tora Bora. I love my people, and I wasn't about to watch you or anyone else hurt them."

Richard leaped forward and grabbed Miller's weapon from his hands, but before he could fire, Corrine pulled a gun from the small of her back and pumped three rounds into his chest.

The gun slipped from his fingers as blood bubbled up in his mouth. He looked at Corrine for the last time before closing his eyes and leaning back against the wall.

At that moment, everything went quiet and Richard was afraid. But it wasn't the numbness in his body or the sensation of blood spilling down his chest that frightened him. It was the silence.

As Richard fought through the depths of unconsciousness to reach back toward life, it was the silence that enveloped him like a shroud, pulling him down into the tomb his life had become.

He was tempted to surrender—to lay his head upon the breast of silence and allow it to rock him to sleep, the way his mother had rocked him as a child. What, after all, did he have to live for? Who would shed tears if death folded him in its arms and held him there forever?

Richard was a scarred man in more ways than one. He wasn't connected to a home, or to a family, or to a wife. Not anymore. He'd been severed from them all, like the silence was severing him from life. Even now he felt it, sliding up through his ears and into the recesses of his mind. He felt it pouring over his body, slow and thick and sweet, like syrup. It was silence, and as his eyes closed for the last time, Richard reached toward it with his very soul, hoping at last for peace.

SECRET POOL

BY ASALI SOLOMON

West Philadelphia

I learned about the University City Swim Club around the same time things started disappearing from my room. First I noticed that I was missing some jewelry, and then the old plaid Swatch I'd been saving for a future *Antiques Roadshow*. I didn't say anything to my mother, because they say it's dangerous to wake a sleepwalker. But then I felt like we were all sleepwalkers when Aja told me about the pool, hiding in plain sight right up on 47th Street in what looked like an alley between Spruce and Pine.

"You don't know about the University City Swim Club?" she said, pretending shock. It was deep August and I sat on the steps of my mother's house. Aja was frankly easier to take during the more temperate months, but since my summer job had ended and there were two and a half more weeks before eleventh grade, I often found myself in her company.

Aja Bell and I had been friends of a sort since first grade, when we'd been the only two black girls in the Mentally Gifted program, though there couldn't have been more than thirty white kids in the whole school. Aja loved MG because there was a group of girls in her regular class who tortured her. Then in sixth grade, I got a scholarship to the Barrett School for Girls and Aja stayed where she was. Now she went to Central High, where she was always chasing these white city kids. It killed her that I went to school in the suburbs with real rich white people, while her French teacher at Central High was a black man from Georgia. Despite the fact that I had no true friends at my school and hated most things about my life, she was in a one-sided social competition with me. As a result, I was subjected to Aja's peacocking around about things like how her friend Jess, who lived in a massive house down on Cedar Avenue, had invited her to go swimming with her family.

"Come off it, Aja. I just said I didn't know about it."

"I just think if you live right here . . . maybe your mom knows about it?"

"Look, is there a story here?"

"Well, it's crazy. There's this wooden gate with a towing sign on it like it's just a parking lot, but behind it is this massive pool and these brand-new lockers and everything. And it was so crowded!"

"Any black people there?"

"Zingha, why you have to make everything about black and white?"

"Maybe because people are starting all-white pools in my neighborhood."

She sighed. "There was a black guy there."

"Janitor?"

"I think he was the security guard."

I snorted.

We watched a black Range Rover crawl down the block. The windows were tinted, and LL Cool J's "The Boomin' System" erupted from the speakers.

"Wow," I said, in mock awe. "That's boomin' from his boomin' system."

"So ghetto," said Aja.

"Um, because this *is* the ghetto," I said, though my mother forbade me to use the word.

"He spoke to me," Aja said suddenly. "The pool security guard. He wasn't that much older than us."

"Was he cute?" I asked without much interest.

"Tell you the truth, he's a little creepy. Like maybe he was on that line between crazy and, um, retarded."

I laughed and then she did too.

"So you been hanging out with Jess a lot this summer?" Jess, a gangly brunette with an upturned nose, was Aja's entry into the clique to which she aspired. But Jess sometimes ignored Aja for weeks at a time, and had repeatedly tried to date guys who Aja liked.

"Well, not a lot. She was at tennis camp earlier," Aja said, glancing away from my face. She could never fully commit to a lie. I imagined my older brother Dahani a couple of nights ago, spinning a casual yarn for my mom about how he'd been at the library after his shift at the video store. He said he was researching colleges that would accept his transfer credits. Dahani had been home for a year, following a spectacular freshman-year flameout at Oberlin. That memory led me to a memory from seventh grade when Dahani said he'd teach me how to lie to my mother so I could go to some unsupervised sleepover back when I cared about those things. I practiced saying, "There *will be* parental supervision," over and over. Dahani laughed because I bit the inside of my cheek when I said my line.

"You mean the pool at the Y?" my mom asked me later that night. We had just finished eating the spaghetti with sausage that she had cooked especially for my brother. She had cracked open her nightly can of Miller Lite.

"Not that sewer," I said.

"Poor Zingha, you hate your fancy school and you hate your community too. Hard being you, isn't it?"

"Sorry," I muttered, rather than hearing again about how I used to be a sweet girl who loved to hug people and cried along with TV characters.

Dahani, who used to have a volatile relationship with our mother, was now silent more often than not. But he said, "I know what you're talking about, Zingha. Up on 47th Street." Then he immediately looked like he wanted to take it back.

"You been there?" I asked.

"Just heard about it," my brother said, tapping out a complicated rhythm on the kitchen table. When he was younger it meant he was about to go to his room. Now it meant he was trying to get out of the house. I wasn't even sure why he insisted on coming home for dinner most nights. Though of course free hot food was probably a factor.

"So what are you up to tonight?" my mother asked him brightly.

"I was gonna catch the new Spike Lee with Jason," he said.

My mother's face dimmed. She always hoped that he'd say, *Staying right here.* But she rallied. "You liked that one, didn't you, Zingha?"

I looked at Dahani. "Sure, watch Wesley Snipes do it with a white woman and stick me with the dishes."

"Oh, I'll take care of the dishes," my mother snapped, managing to make me feel petty. Turning to Dahani she asked, "How *is* Jason?"

"Just fine," Dahani said, in a tight voice. I followed his eyes to the clock above the refrigerator. "Movie starts at seven."

My brother kissed my mom and left, just like he did every night since he'd come home in disgrace. I went upstairs so I wouldn't have to listen to the pitiful sound of her cleaning up the kitchen. After that she would doze in front of the TV for a couple of hours, half waiting for Dahani to come home. She always wound up in bed before that.

I went up into my brother's room. I didn't find my things, but I helped myself to a couple of cigarettes I knew I'd never smoke, and an unsoiled *Hustler* magazine.

It happened after I had done the deed with a couple of contorting blondes who must have made their parents proud. I had washed up for bed and was about to put on my new headphones, which would lull me to sleep.

I realized that my Walkman was gone.

Understand this. I did not care about the mother-of-pearl earrings from my aunt that even my mother admitted were cheap. I did not care about the gold charm bracelet that my mother gave me when I turned sixteen—the other girls in my class had been collecting tennis racket and Star of David charms since they were eight. And of course the future value of nonfunctioning Swatches was just a theory. But Dahani, who had once harangued my mother into buying him seventy-five-dollar stereo headphones, understood what my Walkman meant to me.

Every summer since eighth grade, the nonprofit where my mom worked got me an office job with one of their corporate "partners." I spent July and part of August in freezing cubicles wearing a garish smile, playing the part of Industrious Urban Youth. This summer it had been a downtown bank, where the ignoramus VPs and their ignoramus secretaries crowed over my ability to staple page one to two and guide a fax through the machine. If you think I was lucky I didn't have to handle French fries or the public, you try staying awake for six hours at a desk with nothing to do except arrange rubber bands into a neat pile. It was death.

Most of the money I made every summer went for new

school uniforms and class trips. The only thing I bought that I cared about was the most expensive top-of-the-line Walkman. I had one for each summer I'd worked, and all three were gone. I turned on my lamp, folded my arms, and decided that I could wait up even if my mother couldn't.

The next day I hovered around the living room window waiting for Aja to appear on my block and also hoping that she wouldn't. I needed to tell someone about my brother. But on the other hand, Aja had the potential to be not so understanding. She had two parents: a teacher and an accountant who never drank beer from cans. They went to church and had a Standard Poodle called Subwoofer. It was true that sometimes we were so lonely that we told each other things. I had told her that I liked my brother's dirty magazines and she told me that she didn't like black guys because once her cousin pushed her in a closet and pulled out his dick. But whenever we made confessions like these, the next time we met up it was like those mouthwash commercials where couples wake up next to each other embarrassed by their breath. Besides, I didn't want her to pronounce my crack-smoking brother "ghetto," not even with her eyes.

He lied, he lied, he lied. Dahani, who used to make up raps with me and record them, who comforted me the one time we met our father, who seemed bored and annoyed, and once, back when we were both in public school, beat up a little boy for calling me an African bootyscratcher. *That* brother, said calmly, "I didn't take any of your stuff, Nzingha. What are you thinking?"

"I'm thinking: what the hell is going on? I'm thinking: where are my Walkmans? I'm thinking: where are you all the time?"

"I'm out. You should go there sometimes." He laughed his high-pitched laugh, the one that said how absurd the world is.

"Okay, so you supposedly went to the movies tonight, right? What happens to Gator at the end of *Jungle Fever*?" I asked.

"Ossie Davis shoots him."

"That's right. The crackhead dies. Remember that," I said.

"Crackhead?" Dahani sounded his laugh again. I didn't realize how angry I was until I felt the first hot tear roll down my cheek.

I stomped out, leaving his door open. That was an old maneuver, something we did to piss each other off when we lost a fight. But then I thought of something and went back in there. He wouldn't admit that he'd taken my things. But he agreed that if I didn't say anything to our mother, he'd take me to the pool. He could only take me at night after it closed, and only if I kept my mouth shut about going.

That night, a Friday, we made our mother's day by convincing her we were going to hang out on South Street together. Then, as it was getting dark, Dahani and I walked silently toward 47th Street. A clump of figures looked menacing at the corner until we got close and saw that they couldn't have been more than fifth graders. We slowed down to let a thin, pungent man rush past us. Even though the night air was thick enough to draw sweat, the empty streets reminded me that summer was ending.

"Is anybody else coming?" I asked finally. "Jason?"

"I haven't seen that nigger in months. Ever since he pledged, he turned into a world-class faggot." Jason, my brother's best friend from Friends Select, the only other black boy in his class, had started at Morehouse the same time my brother had gone to Oberlin.

"So it's just going to be us and the security guard?" I had worn a bathing suit under my clothes, but felt weird about stripping down in front of the character Aja described.

"Look," my brother said, "be cool, okay?"

"Cool like you?"

"You know, Nzingha, this is not the best time of my life either."

"But it could be. You could go back to school," I said, teetering on the edge of a place we hadn't been.

"It's not that fucking easy! Do you understand everything Mom's done for me already?"

"Don't talk to me like that."

"Let's just go where we're going."

We passed under a buzzing streetlight that could die at any moment. I had a feeling I knew from nightmares where I boarded the 42 bus in the daytime and got off in the dark. In the dreams I heard my sneakers hit the ground and I thought I would die of loneliness.

We finally reached the tall wooden gate with its warning about getting towed. In a low voice that was forceful without being loud, Dahani called out to someone named Roger. The gate opened and Dahani nearly pushed me into a tall, skinny man with a tan face and eyes that sparkled even in the near dark.

"Hey man, hey man," he kept saying, pulling my brother in for a half-hug.

"What's up, Roger?" said Dahani. "This is my sister."

"Hey, sister," he said and tried to wink, but the one eye took the other with it.

I looked around. It was nicer than the dingy gray tiles

and greenish walls at the Y pool, but to tell the truth, it was nothing special. I'd been going to pool parties at Barrett since sixth grade and I'd seen aqua-tiled models, tropical landscaping, one or two retractable ceilings. This was just a standard rectangle bordered by neat cream-colored asphalt on either side. There were a handful of deck chairs on each side and tall fluorescent lamps. This is what they were keeping us out of?

A bunch of white guys with skater hair and white-boy fades drank 40s and nodded to a boombox playing A Tribe Called Quest at the deep end near the diving board. Then nearby enough to hover but not to crowd, were the girls, who wore berry-colored bikinis. I thought of my prudish navy-blue one-piece. There was a single black girl sitting on the edge of the pool in a yellow bathing suit, dangling her feet in the water.

"Aja?" I called.

"Nzingha?" she replied, sounding disappointed.

Then I recognized Jess, who seemed not to see me until I was practically standing on top of her. Actually, this happened nearly every time we met. "Hey," she said finally. "I thought that was you." She always said something like that.

"What are you doing here?" Aja asked.

"My brother brought me."

"That's your brother?" Jess gestured with her head to Dahani, who stood with his hands in his pockets while Roger pantomimed wildly.

"You know him?" I asked.

"He's down with my boys," she said. I tried not to wince. "Speaking of which, hey, Adam! Can you bring Nzingha something to drink?"

We looked toward the end of the pool with the boys and the boombox. One of them, with a sharp-looking nose and a mop of wet blond hair sweeping over his eyes, yelled back: "Get it for her yourself!"

Jess's face erupted in pink splotches. "He's an incredible asshole," she said.

"And this is news?" said one of the other girls. She had huge breasts, a smashed-in face, and a flat voice. Suddenly I remembered the name Adam. Aja had a flaming crush on him for nearly a year, and then Jess had started going out with him on and off. Last I heard they were off, but now Aja liked to pretend she'd never mentioned liking him.

"I don't want anything to drink anyway," I said.

Aja asked if I was going to swim and I don't remember what I said because I was watching my brother walk down to the end of the pool where the boys were, trading pounds with wet hands. He reached into a red cooler and pulled out a 40. Roger stayed at the tall wooden gate.

"They think they're gangsters," Jess said, rolling her eyes in their general direction. "They call themselves the Gutter Boys. All they do is come here and smoke weed."

"That's not all," the girl with the smashed-in face said with a smirk.

"Is my brother here a lot?" I asked.

"I've only seen him once. But this is only the third time I've been here, you know, after hours."

My brother didn't seem interested in swimming. I didn't even know if he was wearing trunks. Instead he walked with a stocky swaggering boy toward the darkness of the locker room. *Don't go back there*, I wanted to scream. But all I did was stand there in my street clothes at the water's edge.

Adam cried out, "Chickenfight!"

"Not again," said smashed-in face. "I'm way too fucked up."

Adam swam over to us. "Look, Tanya, you'll do it again if you wanna get high later."

Tanya's friend murmured something to her quietly. Tanya laughed and said, "Hey, Adam, what about this?" Then she and her friend began kissing. At first just their lips seemed to brush lightly, and then the quiet girl pulled her in fiercely. I stepped back, feeling an unpleasant arousal. The boys became a cursing, splashing creature moving toward us. "Day-ummm!" called Roger, who began running over.

"Keep your eye on the gate, dude!" yelled one of the boys.

"Okay, you big lesbians get a pass," said Adam when they finally broke apart. Then he turned to Jess. "What can you girls do for me?"

"I think we're going to stick with the chickenfight," said Aja, giggling. She still liked him. I could not relate.

While they sorted out who would carry whom, my brother emerged from the locker room. I waited until he and the stocky boy had parted ways before I began walking over.

"Dahani," I called in a sharp voice.

"You ready to go?" he asked. I examined him. He didn't seem jittery and he wasn't sweating. This was what I knew of smoking crack from the movies.

"What are you looking at?" he asked.

I glanced back at the pool, where Adam, laughing, held Jess under the water. Aja sat forlornly on the shoulders of a round boy with flame-colored hair waiting for the fight to start. "I'm ready to go," I said.

When Roger closed the gate the pool disappeared, and though "Looking at the Front Door" sounded raucous bouncing off the water, I couldn't hear anything at all.

"Are you smoking crack?" I blurted.

Dahani came to a full stop and looked at me. "This is the last time I think I'm going to answer that dumb-ass question. No."

"Are you selling it?"

He sighed in annoyance. "Nzingha. No."

"But something isn't right."

"No, nothing is right," Dahani said. "But this is where I get off." We had reached my mother's house. He kept walking up the dark street.

It wasn't until a couple of nights later that Dahani didn't show up for dinner. My mother, who barely touched the pizza I ordered, kept walking to the front window and peering out.

When it began getting dark, I slapped my forehead. "Oh my God!" I said.

My mother looked at me with wild round eyes. "What?"

Without biting the inside of my cheek, I said, "I totally forgot. He said to tell you he wouldn't be home until really late."

"Where is he?"

"Don't know."

My mother folded her arms. "Thanks for almost letting me have a heart attack."

"Mom, he's a grown man."

"Nzingha," she said, "what is this thing with you and your brother?"

I didn't answer.

"You don't seem to realize that he's having a really hard time. I mean I'm the one stuck with loans from his year at college. I'm the one supporting his grown-ass now and I'm the one who's going to have to take out more loans to send him back. So what's *your* issue?"

"Nothing," I said. "Can I go upstairs?"

"You really need to change your attitude. And not just about this."

"Can I go upstairs?" I said again.

My mother and I sometimes had strained conversations. It was she and Dahani who had fireworks. But now she looked so angry she almost shook. "Go ahead and get the hell out of my sight!" And I did, hating this.

That night I wasn't sure if I was sleeping or not. I kept imagining the nightmare bright scene at the pool, those girls kissing, my brother disappearing into the back. Night logic urged me that I had to go back there. After my mother was in bed with her TV timer on, I climbed out of bed and dressed. Then excruciatingly, silently, I closed the front door. I plunged into darkness and walked the three blocks as fast as I could.

"Roger," I called at the gate, trying to imitate my brother's masculine whisper. I tapped the wood. There was a pause and then the tall gate wrenched open.

"Where's Dahani?" Roger said, waving me inside. His clothes were soaked and he was in stocking feet. "Oh God. You didn't bring Dahani?"

I felt my legs buckle, and only because Roger's sweaty hand clamped over my mouth was I able to swallow a scream. I had seen only one dead body in real life, at my great-grandmother's wake. Though with her papery skin and tiny doll's limbs, she'd never seemed quite alive. I'd never seen a dead body floating in water, but I knew what I was seeing when I saw Jess's naked corpse bob up and down peacefully. I ran to the water's edge near the diving board. There was a wet spot of something on the edge of the pool that looked black in the light.

Roger began pacing a tiny circle, moaning.

"Did you call 911?" I asked him.

"It was an accident. They're gonna think—"

"What if she's alive?" I said.

Roger suddenly loomed in front of me with clenched fists. "No cops! And she's not alive! Why didn't you bring Dahani?"

In the same way I knew things in dreams, I knew he hadn't done it. Not even in a Lenny in *Of Mice and Men* way. But I needed to get away from his panic. I spoke slowly. "It's okay. I'll go get him."

"You'll bring him here?"

Before I let myself out through the tall gate, I watched Roger slump to the side of the pool and sit Indian style with his head in his hands. I took one last look at Jess. Later I wished that I hadn't.

I found myself at Aja's house. It was after midnight, but I rang the bell, hoping somehow that she might answer the door instead of her parents. I heard the dog barking and clicking his long nails excitedly on the floor.

Aja's dad, a short yellow man with a mustache and no beard, answered the door. "Zingha? Now you know it's too late. Does your mom know—"

"Mr. Bell, I really need to see Aja."

"Are you serious, girl?" Then he started pushing the door shut. The dog was going crazy.

"Aja!" I screamed.

Her mother appeared. She grabbed Subwoofer's collar with one hand and pulled him up short. He whimpered and I felt bad for him. All I'd ever known him to attack with was his huge floppy tongue.

"Shut up and get in here," she said.

Aja's father moved off to the side but he wasn't happy about it. "What the hell do you think you're doing?" he asked her.

"Quiet, you!" she responded. She was nearly a head taller than he was, with eggplant-colored lips and very arched eyebrows.

"Look, Nzingha," she said, "Aja's not here. We don't know where she is."

I shook my head frantically. "We have to find her! You don't know what's going on. There's a—"

"Stop talking and listen," she said, getting louder. "If anyone comes around asking where my daughter is, tell them the truth. That she has disappeared and that we are very worried. Mr. Bell will walk you home."

Mr. Bell fumed as he escorted me. "I guess there's no point in any more stupid fucking shit happening," he muttered. I didn't answer; he wasn't talking to me.

I let myself in as quietly as I had left, shocked by the thick silence of the house. I tried not to imagine Jess's closed eyes, her blood on the asphalt. I had to remind myself that she was dead, so she couldn't be as cold as she looked. I tried to tell myself that her floating body, Dahani, and Aja were in another world.

But the next morning I learned that my mother hadn't been home. She'd been down at the precinct with my brother.

By the time the police had arrived at the pool, Roger was nearly dead. He had tried to drown himself. He couldn't answer questions about Jess from his coma, but the police knew he hadn't done it.

It seemed to me, from what I managed to read before my mother started hiding the papers, that Jess's death had been an accident. But her dad was a lawyer and Aja was dragged back from an aunt's house in Maryland to do eighteen months in the Youth Detention Center. I went to visit her once that winter, in the dim, echoing room that reminded me of the cafeteria at our elementary school. I didn't tell my mother where I was going. She hadn't let me go to the trial.

Aja and I made painful small talk about how the food was destroying her stomach and about her first encounter with a bed bug. She said *fuck* more than usual and her skin looked gray.

Then she blurted, "I didn't do it."

"I know," I said.

"Things just got crazy." She told me about that night. Everyone had been drinking, including her, and Adam called for another chickenfight.

"First I fought that girl Tanya and I beat her easy. Then it was me and Jess. But I had won the time before, the night you came, you remember?"

I nodded, though I hadn't seen her victory.

"So she was really getting rough. And then she fucking—"

"We don't have to talk about this anymore," I said, trying to be the sweet girl my mother remembered.

"She pulled my top down. I kept telling them I wanted to stop. But they were yelling so loud. And Adam was cheering me on. It was so—" Aja's voice seemed to swell with tears, but her eyes remained empty.

"It doesn't matter," I said, and we were quiet for a moment. The din of the visiting room filled the space between us.

"But Jess was my best friend," she said. I had come to be good to her, yet I wanted to shake her by the shoulders until her teeth chattered.

My brother was able to convince the police that he hadn't done it. But he not only needed an alibi, he also had to rat out the Gutter Boys, with whom he'd apparently tried to go into business. Tried, I say, because he was such a crummy drug dealer that he had to steal to make up for what he couldn't sell. Dahani told the police what he knew about the small operation, and after that, a couple of Jeeps slowed down when he crossed the street, but he didn't turn up in the Schuylkill or anything. He got his old job at the video store back, but he got fired after a couple of months, and then our VCR disappeared. After two weeks in a row when he didn't come home, and my mom had called the police about sixteen times, she changed the locks and got an alarm system.

Sometime after that she looked at me over a new tradition—a second nightly beer—and said, "Nzingha, I know we should have talked about this as soon as I knew what was going on with your brother. But I didn't want to say anything because I know that you love him."

The scandal didn't break the pool. They held a floating memorial service for Jess and hired a real security company. The scandal did, however, break the news of the pool to the neighborhood. But at $1,400 a year, none of the black folks we knew could afford to join it anyway.

DEVIL'S POCKET

BY KEITH GILMAN

Grays Ferry

S ince Charlie died, I'd been spending a lot of time at Johnny Izzard's. I'd walk through the front door of his tailor shop and that bell he still had hanging over the door would ring and Johnny would look up from behind the counter and smile out of the corner of his mouth. I'd told him more than once to keep the door locked at night. Point Breeze alone seemed to be averaging a couple murders a week. But he didn't listen.

He'd be fiddling with a pair of trousers on a wooden hanger, running his hands gently down one leg at a time, the soft cool fabric sliding between his bony fingers as he adjusted the hem with a few straight pins between his lips and his glasses sliding down his nose. I'd lean on the counter and watch him work and when he was done, he'd pull out a bottle and a few glasses and start to pour. We'd pick up where we left off, the conversation always turning to our old friend Charlie Melvyn and the barber shop he had on Tasker Avenue and the way he died and whether he was better off dead than alive.

The barber shop had been boarded up like many of the storefronts in that neighborhood. Since then, I'd been getting my hair cut at the Gallery Mall by a twenty-something girl with breast implants, a tattoo of a snake on her neck, and a man's haircut of her own, parted on the side and trimmed neatly around the piercings in her ears.

Johnny's tailor shop was a little farther up on 25th and tonight we were celebrating his eightieth birthday. Johnny's son had been trying to get him into one of those assisted living places out in Delaware County, get him a nice clean room with a view of the Lexus dealership across the street and a rotating shift of nurses and aides to take his pulse and do his laundry and wipe his ass. I think he was actually considering it.

"Look what the cat dragged in. My, my . . . another Irish cop with a bad attitude. You come to roust me, officer, or just steal my liquor?"

"Ex-cop, Mr. Izzard. With a capital X. I'm not playing that game anymore."

"It was fun while it lasted, though. Wasn't it?"

"It had its moments."

"You smell nice. You got a date?"

"Meeting an old friend."

"A woman?"

"She asked me to do her a favor. That's it. It's not what you think."

"It never is." Johnny's eyes lit up, a greenish tint coming through the clouded glasses like dusty emeralds. He unplugged a hot iron that sat on an ironing board behind him. Next to that was an old sewing machine that rested on black iron legs with a heavy square pedal the size of a sewer grate and a black spinning wheel and a sewing needle secured to a silver arm like a glistening metal spike. Johnny ran his hand over his bald, chocolate-brown head, wiping away a layer of cold sweat. The wrinkles around his eyes smoothed out as his smile softened.

"He was like a father to you, huh?"

"Yeah, he was."

"Still ain't over it?"

"Are you?"

"We lookin' at the same thing, right? But we don't see it the same."

"How do you see it?"

"After Chawlie died, I was angry. We both were. But I'm trying to think what Chawlie would want us to do?"

"Charlie didn't die, Johnny. He was murdered."

"And you think I don't know that. But if he's looking down on us right now, what's he thinking?"

"He knows I'd like to catch the guy that shot him."

"And do what with him? Lock him up? And for how long? What good will it do?"

"Maybe I'll save the taxpayers of Philadelphia the expense of a trial."

"You don't mean that, son."

"I'm starting to think I do, Johnny."

"And what if it turns out to be some sixteen-year-old kid?"

"So be it."

"You changed that much? You really that hard? What, Chawlie Melvyn gets killed and suddenly there's no hope left in the world? You know, son, when I'm talkin' 'bout carryin' out the wishes of the deceased, I mean more than just buryin' him next to his mother or crematin' him and dumpin' his ashes into the Delaware River or puttin' a tombstone on his grave the size of the goddamn Washington Monument."

"I heard George Washington had over two hundred slaves. Did you know that?"

"Don't change the subject, son."

"It's the truth."

"Only two hundred?"

"Maybe more."

"What I'm sayin' is that Chawlie didn't die in vain. He didn't believe that and neither should you. That's the truth."

"If you saw his blood on the sidewalk, Johnny. It was there for days, like a black stain."

"Chawlie was fightin' a war, Seamus. Like a lot of us are. Like you are. Otherwise, we'd pick up and go. It's a war of attrition, son. Chawlie was just hangin' on and then he saw the chance to do somethin' real. He died savin' a bunch of kids who'd never have learned what Chawlie Melvyn was all about. He put himself in the line of fire. It wasn't an accident, what he did. He saw a gun and chose to shield those kids. He was willin' to die saving someone else. That means somethin'."

"You mean he's a martyr?"

"Yeah, maybe."

"Well, the cemetery is full of them, Johnny."

We sat there in silence for a few minutes, not looking at each other but aware that we were both thinking the same thing. Charlie's barber shop had instilled itself in our common memory, a dream of a better time when the old men sat around that place telling stories about how great Philadelphia used to be, about South Street in the summer, about the fish market and the Phillies and the old singers that stopped coming around and the prostitutes on Lombard and how many more dead cops there were with each passing year and that if they didn't get out of Grays Ferry soon, they'd end up dying there, and how nothing would ever be the same unless someone did something about it.

I raised the glass of whiskey and held it up in front of me. Johnny did the same. We nodded and drank. I wished him a happy birthday and went out the door with the bell ringing in my head.

* * *

I took 27th Street through the heart of Point Breeze and onto Grays Ferry Avenue and then onto 30th, where I pulled into the lot at St. Gabe's. There was a church, a monastery, and a school, all made of redbrick and jagged gray stone, the three buildings surrounding a parking lot and a deserted playground. At night, the shadows from the old church spread across the lot and the nuns would creep to their second-story windows and peer out at the sun sliding behind the gray skyline, and in the darkness it wasn't unusual to see a car pull in and park at the far end of the lot. St. Gabriel's seemed to be looking down on the entire city of Philadelphia with a weary eye.

Millie Price had asked me to meet her there at ten. I was early.

I looked across the lot at the flimsy wooden backboard and the rusty rim clinging to it. The metal pole swayed in the cold wind. The concrete that held it in the ground had long since turned to dust and been blown away. A wall of chain link made the whole place look like an old prison, where inmates might have come out into the cold air once a day and stared at the broken basket and laughed like crows at a rankled scarecrow. And the crooked weather vane sitting at the top of the arched steeple of St. Gabe's would point down at them and laugh back.

The diocese had planted trees along a narrow strip of lawn bordering the playground. Thin dogwoods that bloomed in spring, the delicate white flowers emerging shyly for the first few years and then going into a kind of permanent hibernation, the dried bark peeling away and exposing the speckled, wind-blown skin beneath. They stood like that year after year, leafless and gray, their thin, petrified branches frozen in place.

I'd pulled my ten-year-old Jeep Cherokee into the lot. It was navy-blue, with an exhaust system that made it sound like a tank. The front wheels grinded as I circled toward the back. It had been making that same noise for two months. I'd taken it to Eddie's garage earlier that day and he'd told me it needed bearings on both sides. It was a three-hundred-dollar job, the same amount of money Millie Price had offered me to take an old boyfriend off her hands.

"He just won't take no for an answer," she'd said.

"He'll scare easily," she'd said.

I turned the key and the Jeep went suddenly quiet. It was a sound that made me nervous. It made most cops nervous, and though I wasn't a cop anymore, there was nothing like a quiet night to start me thinking. I'd put my time in with the Philadelphia Police Department, most of it spent right here in the 17th Precinct. I'd paid my dues and all I had to show for it was the Jeep and a pension that qualified me for food stamps and Section 8 housing. I lit a cigarette and rolled down the window. I imagined Father Kane up there in the rectory sipping a hot toddy and thinking maybe he should call the cops about the guy in the lot, sitting in his car and chain-smoking.

My father had grown up in the same parish and he'd told me there had been a shallow pond in the small courtyard between the monastery and the old cathedral. The priests had kept swans there. On Sunday afternoons the parishioners would stand around the pond as solemnly as if they were still in church and watch the swans glide effortlessly over the clear water. Some of the women would bring stale bread from home to feed to the hungry birds. They'd keep it wrapped in a napkin in their purses until after mass when they'd tear it into small pieces the size of a host and watch as the long curved necks of the swans bent for the soggy bread, their heavy-lidded black eyes almost haughty as they fought for every scrap.

It'd been like that for years, my father had said, since before he'd joined the force, young mothers pushing their babies in strollers along the narrow path, the babies pointing with their chubby little fingers at the swans floating across the glassy pond. The kids would all be wearing red baseball caps, as if everybody expected their child to be the next great third-baseman for the Phillies. Even the old folks came out to see the swans, congregating around the pond when it was warm and sunny and the glare from the sun off the water brought them to tears.

But it wasn't very long before the *Inquirer* ran the story of the dead swans. Some people in the neighborhood were calling it murder, as if killing a swan was the same thing as killing a person. To some it was worse. I guess it depended on who was doing the killing and who was getting killed.

Someone had come in the middle of the night with a crossbow and killed the swans, every last one of them, leaving their blood-stained bodies, impaled with arrows, for the children and young mothers and old folks from the neighborhood to find the next morning. Their white feathers were the color of rust, their wide staring eyes like glass.

My father had been the first responding officer and he'd called the detectives in as if it were an actual homicide. They never caught the guys and for a lot of people in Grays Ferry, including my old man, it was the last straw, time to get out. They could have dealt with the beer cans in the park and the dog shit and the garbage lining the streets and an occasional strong-arm robbery and the sirens at all hours of the night, but they couldn't deal with butchered swans, not even in Grays Ferry.

That was the first time I'd heard my father refer to our

square patch of neighborhood in Grays Ferry as Devil's Pocket. I wasn't sure what it meant back then. I am now.

A week later he was killed responding to a domestic dispute on Christian just off 25th and I knew we weren't going anywhere. Devil's Pocket would always be my home. They drained the pond and filled it in with gravel and turned it into a rock garden with a small fountain and a statue of St. Francis with the pigeons flocking to his outstretched arm and the water rolling gently off his back.

I went through four or five more cigarettes when I began to think that maybe Millie wasn't going to show. It shouldn't have surprised me. From what I remembered, she never was known for her punctuality. She wasn't usually too hard to find though. There were only a couple places to look. I decided to hang in there a little longer, nurse one more cigarette and then take off. Millie had my cell number and could have called if she was going to be late. But Millie was never known for her consideration either. She'd been working behind the bar at the Arramingo Club for a long time. She lived only a few blocks away on Catherine. That's where I was headed.

I parked in front of a vacant lot on 24th and walked the rest of the way. I'd grabbed a fresh pack of cigarettes from the glove compartment and tapped it against my palm and peeled it open and lit up a cigarette as I walked down the dark street. I passed a couple of black-haired Asian girls leaning against a brand-new red Camaro. Their short skirts and high heels and red lipstick matched the car perfectly. They were a little out of their territory, I thought, and I wanted to say something to them. I wanted to tell them what could happen to a girl in a miniskirt and high-heel shoes and naked legs leaning against a red-hot Camaro. I wanted to tell them all that I'd seen but

I knew it was no use. I'd never really been able to speak their language, and even if I said something, they wouldn't listen.

Millie Price lived in one of those buildings where you ring the doorbell and they buzz you in. The problem was there were rarely any names under the mailboxes in the vestibule, and even if there were, it was often too dark to see. I struck a match and noticed that someone had wedged a crushed beer can into the door jamb. I pushed through and into the dark hallway and started up the stairs. I remembered Millie lived on the second floor but I wasn't sure which apartment was hers. The door on the left had a peace sign spray-painted on it in a fluorescent yellow. The door on the right hung open a few inches.

I was starting to get a bad feeling. It was the kind of feeling cops get just before something bad happens, an intuition you develop after a few long years on the street. Some guys are just born with it. Either way, if you don't develop it sooner or later, you might just find yourself dead.

And that's how I found Millie Price, in a heap on the floor just inside her front door. She was wearing a thin leather jacket and jeans as if she was just about to go out. She probably heard the knock and opened the door and the gun was the only thing she saw. She was lying on her back with two bullet holes in the Snoopy shirt she was wearing under the jacket and a dark bloodstain spreading over two well-formed breasts. She was still as beautiful as I remembered.

I looked down at her, at the blood on her chin where it had spilled from her mouth and the blood pooling on the floor beneath her, and I felt a little ache in my own chest. I was thinking I should have felt something more, and maybe I would have if things had been different between Millie and me all those years ago. Now, she was just another corpse in an apartment on the border of Grays Ferry and Point Breeze, where stray corpses were becoming more and more common.

I phoned it in and Detective William Trask showed up in record time, only about an hour after the first uniformed officer arrived and handcuffed me in the backseat of his cruiser. I showed him my retired Philly Police badge but it didn't seem to change his mind. It was for his protection and mine, he said. I didn't think I had anything to fear from the police, so he must have been protecting me from myself.

While the steel bracelets were cutting into my wrists and my fingers were going numb, I thought about Millie, up there growing cold on her living room rug. She'd be going rigid by now. They could probably stand her up and lean her against the wall and fit her with the perfect size body bag and walk her down the stairs. I wiggled my fingers and fidgeted on the hard plastic seat, thinking now of all the prisoners I'd had in my backseat and how many times I'd told them to shut up and sit still and how many times they'd puked and pissed themselves along the way.

Just then, the door opened and Detective Trask yanked me out of the car, spun me around, and unhooked my wrists. He didn't look happy, but as I remembered, William Trask never looked happy.

"What the hell, Seamus! How are you involved in all this?"

"Her name's Millie Price. She's an old friend."

"Sure. How about the rest of it?"

"There's nothing else to tell, Bill. You saw what I saw."

"So you were paying a surprise visit to an old girlfriend and when you get here, she just happens to be dead. Shot to death with two large-caliber slugs at close range."

"There's a little more to it than that."

"I'm listening."

"She was supposed to meet me earlier tonight outside St. Gabe's. She'd called me this afternoon, asked me to do her a favor, said an old boyfriend was hassling her. She wanted me to scare him off. Said it wouldn't be a problem that he'd scare easy. She was going to pay me three hundred dollars."

Trask pulled out a pack of cigarettes and offered me one. He lit one for himself and then mine with the same match.

"I think she got her money's worth."

Two techs from the medical examiner's office carried Millie down the stairs in a gray body bag. They swung her onto a flimsy metal stretcher and wheeled her to the back of a dark-blue van with tinted windows and a municipal license plate. One of the techs opened the door while the other rammed the stretcher into place. I thought I glimpsed the shadows of other black bags neatly packed inside the van. At least Millie would have company.

"Any idea who the boyfriend was?"

"None."

"You wouldn't be holding out on me now, Seamus Kilpatrick? You know better than that."

"What reason would I have not to tell the truth?"

"That all depends on the nature of your relationship with Miss Price."

"I haven't seen her in ten years."

"And before that?"

"We were friends. I knew her from the neighborhood."

"For God's sake, Kilpatrick, she was a stripper. What do you expect me to believe? You were members of the same book club. You met at the library every Tuesday afternoon."

"She's been out of that business for a long time."

"She used to be married to Billy Haggerty? I suppose you knew that."

I drew hard on the cigarette, letting the smoke drift and blow away like a bad dream.

"Of course I knew. That was over a long time ago too."

"We'll see."

A young cop in a brand-new pinstripe suit came out and handed Trask a collection of crime scene photos. He thumbed through them as if they were a deck of playing cards, his face expressionless as he stared down at the lifeless body of Millie Price. He slid them into a manila envelope and pointed its sharp corner into my chest.

"You and I never had a problem, Kilpatrick, not when you were with the force and not since you left. I'd like to keep it that way."

"Am I free to go?"

"If you find something out, I'll want to hear about it."

I took one last drag on the cigarette and threw it past them into the street. I could feel the eyes of the detectives on my back as I walked away.

The Aramingo Club didn't look like much from the outside. It was on the corner of 30th and Tasker, with a front door painted a dingy white and a lot of burned-out neon over blacked-out windows. It was the end of the line for aging strippers with a few good teeth left and maybe a set of implants they'd conned off some old horny gangster who didn't want his wife to know he could still get it up. It was getting late and there wasn't anybody collecting at the door and not many drinkers hanging around for last call.

I dropped a twenty-dollar bill on the bar, slid the pack of cigarettes in behind it, and waited for the bartender to notice me. She was a petite blonde in '80s spandex, black and tight from her neck to her ankles. She was stubbing out a cigarette in a glass ashtray, doing her best to ignore me as her fingers moved the dead cigarette around in the bed of gray ash. When she was satisfied the cigarette had stopped smoldering, she took the long walk down to my end of the bar.

I ordered a beer and she put the glass down on a clean white napkin and I slid the twenty in her direction and told her to keep the change. She still wasn't smiling but her eyes had grown a bit larger as if some of the meanness had been squeezed out of them.

"Big spender."

"In exchange for some conversation."

"What do you want to talk about?"

"Millie Price."

I took a sip of my drink and looked at her through the glass. She had the body of a twenty-year-old and the face of a woman in her fifties, a woman who'd walked some hard miles. She looked like she could stand up to just about anything.

"She's not your type."

"Says who, Billy Haggerty?"

"What are you? A cop?"

"Not anymore. Millie asked me to meet her tonight. She never showed. I'd like to know what happened to her."

"What makes you think something happened to her?"

"She's dead. Shot twice. I found her in her apartment. The cops are there now and I don't doubt they'll soon be on their way here."

She started crying. Not hysterical crying, no moans or loud sobs, just tears escaping from her reddened eyes and rolling down her face. Her mascara ran in a spiderweb of black lines under her eyes and she dabbed at it with a napkin from the bar. I offered her a cigarette from the pack and she took one with a trembling hand. She held it to her lips and I lit it for her and the smoke seemed to calm her nerves.

"What about the baby?"

"What baby?"

"Millie had a baby, a little boy about two years old."

"I never knew. Where's Billy Haggerty?"

"He's not the father."

"Then who is?"

"A guy named Nathaniel. He lives down in Point Breeze."

"Millie's boyfriend is from Point Breeze?"

"Yeah. Billy was furious when he found out. He's still furious. It's one thing when you find out your wife's been running around with another guy. It's another thing when you find out he's black. I thought something like this was going to happen."

"Where does this Nathaniel live?"

"Twenty-second and Moore over the laundromat."

"Do you know where Billy is?"

"Haven't seen him all night. If he's not here, he's at the Golden Rose."

"Thanks."

The tears began to flow again and she reached out and took a long drink from my glass. The cigarette had gone out and she drew on it, frantically trying to bring it back to life, and when she couldn't, she threw it down on the floor.

"You know, I talked to Millie last night. She said she talked to a guy she used to know a long time ago. She said he was real nice and that they might have had something together once and maybe they could get it back. She said that when she spoke to him she heard something sweet in his voice like maybe he was hoping for the same thing. She wanted to get away from this place, away from the Arramingo Club, away from Grays Ferry, away from Billy Haggerty, away from this whole life. She was hoping he could help her. She said he used to be a cop."

She turned her back to me and lifted her eyes just high enough to see my face in the mirror behind the bar. "Now would you please get the hell out of here."

I parked behind Lanier Playground and hurried across the crumbling asphalt. As I ran across it, I couldn't help but think that this had become a wasteland, a memory of a long abandoned dream for so many kids that would take a miracle to resurrect. It was dark, the spotlights broken by those same kids—they used them for target practice, throwing pieces of broken pavement like stones from a slingshot until the area was in total darkness.

I got halfway across when I heard them, five or six figures silhouetted against the concrete ledge, the light from the Golden Rose casting distorted shadows over the sidewalk. Haggerty was there, strutting back and forth like an alpha male while his pack of wolves sat before him, tuned to his every word, his every move. He saw me too and a snicker of recognition snaked across his lips as I emerged from the darkness.

"Seamus Kilpatrick. What the fuck are you doing here? Did someone call a cop?"

His gang laughed in unison, up on their feet now, the rusty chain-link fence like an iron curtain between us.

"Did you have to kill her, Billy? Was it because she went out and got herself a boyfriend? Was it the kid, Billy? Or was it because she came to me for help?"

"You think I killed her? Jaysus, Kilpatrick. You are a piece of work. You think I give a shite about that whore, Millie

Price? She could have taken that kid of hers and gone down into the gutter to live. That's where she belonged."

"Where's the kid, Billy?"

"How the hell should I know? You got it all wrong, as usual, Kilpatrick. You'll never learn. Trying so hard to be something you're not."

"And what's that?"

"A fucking martyr. A pathetic fucking martyr. But even a dumb shite like me knows there's no such thing as a live martyr."

I came around the fence and Haggerty's gang circled us. I recognized most of them. Jimmy Connors and Chris Dougherty looked inseparable, as if they were still sixteen and just snuck out of the house with their father's quarts in their pants. Denis McNulty was the biggest of the crew, leaning against the fence with the fingers of one meaty paw hooked onto the chain link.

"I don't presume to judge you, Billy Haggerty. But don't expect me to agree with your way of thinking."

"You always pick the wrong side. Don't you. Deny your people, your family. This is your fucking home, Kilpatrick, and you won't lift a finger to save it. Just don't get in our way. We'll show you no mercy."

"You can't build a wall down the middle of this neighborhood, Billy."

"Watch me." His finger was pointed at my chest as if it were a loaded gun. "And one more thing you'd want to know before you leave. I have from a reliable source that not only has this rooster Nathaniel Jeffers been banging my ex-wife, word is he's the trigger man what put down your old friend, Charlie Melvyn. Now ain't that a kicker, boyo?"

Chris Dougherty crossed himself and they all laughed and

my fists went white at my sides. I looked at Billy Haggerty and our eyes locked and at that moment it was like no one else in Grays Ferry mattered, like it was just the two of us and we were telling the whole world to go fuck themselves. Not knowing where else to look, I turned my gaze to the Philadelphia skyline in the distance, the dark sky behind it like a black veil.

"One more for the road, boys?"

They all shuffled back inside the Golden Rose and left me alone on the deserted sidewalk.

I walked a few aimless blocks until I found myself in front of the twenty-four-hour laundromat with its fluorescent lights shining through the glass and the dryers whirring inside and a fat old black lady thumbing the pages of a worn newspaper on the bench. The stairwell to the second floor smelled like piss but it didn't matter. I reached around to the small of my back and pulled out the Glock that had been gathering dust in a drawer since the day I left the Philadelphia Police Department. I took a deep breath and kicked in the door.

I was face-to-face with Nathaniel Jeffers. He didn't move. He was younger than I thought he'd be but not childlike in his appearance. He had short cropped hair over a broad forehead and a thin mustache and the body of an athlete. I pointed the gun at his chest, holding it with two hands, my arms thrust out in front of me, my grip beginning to tremble. The look in his eyes seemed to say that he knew why I was there, that he knew it wasn't because of Millie Price or their son or Billy Haggerty or all the bullshit that defined him as black and me as white. It was because of Charlie Melvin, and Nathaniel Jeffers knew it.

"Did you kill Charlie Melvyn?"

"Who?"

"The old man in front of the barber shop."

His lips were sealed firmly across his face but I had my answer in the way he stood, shifting his weight from one foot to the other, and the way he shrugged his shoulders and ground his teeth. He was a typical Philly liar, I thought. The truth made him squirm.

My fingers curled around the trigger and the hammer slowly lifted from its seat, and in my mind I heard the voice of Johnny Izzard telling me how once I pulled the trigger, everything would change, my legacy with the Philadelphia Police Department, the reasons I became a cop, and the reasons I left. But it was too late to think about regrets. I owed this to Charlie Melvyn.

I adjusted my aim and fired. The blast stung my ears and Nathaniel Jeffers jumped back onto a dingy yellow couch. The sound of that single gunshot was so loud I thought it would wake the entire neighborhood. A door opened in the hall and out stepped the boy as if the sound of gunfire was a sound he'd become accustomed to. He had waves of curly black hair and sleepy eyes and caramel-colored skin. He ran to his father and dropped into his arms.

I'd fired wide and the bullet had lodged in the wall, a crack in the plaster spreading from floor to ceiling like a fault line. I heard the sirens already, wailing in the distance, coming closer with that sense of urgency like they knew what they'd find when they got there.

"You better take the boy and get out of here. Billy Haggerty is coming for you."

"This is my territory, my house. He know better than to come down here."

"No, I don't think he does."

I turned and went out the door and down the steps and

onto the street, the gun still in my hand. Billy Haggerty and his boys were on the corner. They were drunk and Denis Mc-Nulty had a large rock in his hand. He wound up like a Major League pitcher, took a couple of steps, and hurled it through Nathaniel Jeffers's second-floor window. The sound of breaking glass on the street accompanied the crescendo of blaring sirens. Three squad cars converged from different angles and the officers jumped out with guns drawn. A crowd was forming on both sides of the block.

I was pointing with my free hand at Billy Haggerty and his thugs, trying to tell the cops what was happening, but they wouldn't listen. They were screaming at me to drop the gun and then I felt the first bullet crease my shoulder, the initial burn, my collar bone shattering like a broken twig. The next bullet caught me just above my left hip and spun me around and knocked me to the ground.

I lay on my back, staring up at the clear night sky and the flashing red and blue lights from the police cars, and suddenly, there was Johnny Izzard. He'd heard the sirens and was now emerging from the crowd on the corner, ignoring commands from the police to get back. My legs were numb and I tried to lift my head and I felt Johnny take my hand. I heard him call my name and his voice seemed to come from a long way off, as if I was dreaming and couldn't shake myself awake. And in the dream I saw myself in the early days with the department and even before that, at the vigil over my father's casket at St. Gabe's and the baseball games he'd taken me to at the Vet, climbing all those stairs up into the nosebleed seats. "Just us and the pigeons," he'd say. And then I saw the blood-soaked body of Millie Price and the sleepy eyes of her son and I felt like I was floating and I felt a sudden shudder of cold.

I opened my eyes and Johnny was still there, his bony grip

harder on my hand; he was saying my name but I couldn't hear him. I saw his lips moving and I tried to smile, that awkward, boyish, embarrassed smile I had, and Johnny was shaking his head and saying, "Seamus. Seamus. Seamus."

PART II

CITY OF OTHERLY LOVE

ABOVE THE IMPERIAL

BY DENNIS TAFOYA

East Falls

J immy Kelly started making lists of the things he stole. He came out of the Staples on Germantown Avenue with one of the composition books like the kind he'd used at St. Bridget's and a box of plastic Bics, so when he got back to his apartment he smoked a joint and tried to remember everything he'd boosted. He sat in the old split-open chair that had been there when he moved in, ropes of batting spilled like blue gut around his feet.

He drew spirals to start the cheap pen, then wrote, *8/22, two books, borders chestnut hill*, and, *8/24, crackers, p-nut butter, acme.* After he'd filled a page he started over, made columns first and went back to June, when he'd walked away from the Youth Study Center on Henry Avenue. He took his time, clicked the pen against his teeth. Listed headphones he'd taken from a stereo store downtown, six DVDs from a bin at a video store way out Ridge Avenue somewhere.

It became his project. He'd fill his coat, stuff things into his pants, then scurry back to the apartment over the Imperial Gardens and add to the list. He never got caught. If things looked too dicey, he'd move on because there was always more to steal. He kept it out of the neighborhood, mostly, and took what was easy rather than what he wanted. He took gum and a Mounds bar from a CVS, a yellow sweater with a golf club over the heart from a thrift store in Germantown. Walmarts and Kmarts were too risky, big chains with too many cameras. Once in the Plymouth Meeting Mall he'd dumped everything in the bathroom and walked out with a guy in a red blazer right behind him. But he never got tagged.

One September night he burned a couple of joints and went downstairs, two bottles of blue nail polish that he'd lifted from a bin at the Rite Aid in his pockets. He dropped down the narrow stairs, his feet bouncing, the muscles in his legs quivering. His friend Jesús had a black Epiphone bass that was called a Nikki Sixx Blackbird, and sometimes Jimmy would put his hands on it while Jesús plucked the wound metal strings. When he was high the feeling in the wires and cords in his legs was like that, a resonant buzzing and snapping that made him smile and put pictures in his head of running through alien landscapes populated by shiny, sexed-up female robots.

In front of the Imperial people came and went with their orders or guys would walk out picking their teeth and patting their bellies, like it wasn't enough to be full, you had to put on a play about it for your friends. He wanted to ask them why they did it, but half of life seemed like that to Jimmy, like people didn't want things as much as they liked to dance and sing about how much they wanted them. Jimmy's theory was that was why people liked movies and videos, because everyone was starring in their own movie all the time. When he'd first escaped from the Youth Study Center up on Henry, he'd spent three days hiding at the movie house at the end of Main Street in Manayunk just going from theater to theater and there was always some scene where a guy is about to take on the bad guys, or just lost his wife, or his best friend, or his dog or something, and the music that's supposed to make you cry is going and the guy's just barely holding it together. People loved that moment, Jimmy thought, and they wanted it in real life too.

The real reason to come down from the apartment was because sometimes Grace Lei would step out and take her break, smoke a cigarette and stare out at the traffic. Jimmy liked to watch her, try to catch her eye, try to make her laugh.

"So what's the difference between sesame chicken and General Tso's?" he asked her, wishing she'd turn and look at him.

"The seeds." Grace Lei watched the street. She was tall, and he stood straighter. Her hair hung down to her shoulders. He pictured running his finger along the ends of her hair and wondered if it would be soft, or maybe stiff, like bristles. Nothing would surprise him. He wanted to take the nail polish out and pass it to her, and watched her hands move as she smoked, trying to see if there was color at the tips of her fingers.

"The seeds, huh. That's it? They should call it General Tso Plus Seeds."

Jimmy watched through the glass as a Latino kid came out of the back of the restaurant and dropped a plastic bag on the table nearest the door.

Grace turned to Jimmy. "Where do you live? You're always here."

"Upstairs."

A car pulled up, an old Chevy he'd seen before. A kid got out, an Asian kid with a red ball cap on backward and baggy jeans. Gold chains on his wrists and around his neck. He said something to Grace, but she just looked at the street, or at the firemen washing the trucks, or at nothing at all. The kid went into the Imperial and came back out again holding his order up to his face and miming hunger for his friends in the car.

She said to Jimmy, "Yeah, what's it like up there?"

He turned to Grace, who he thought had never really looked at him before. He kept his body angled away and stole glances at her, as if she was something he was going to put in his pocket. He kicked at a yogurt cup crushed at the curb, its spilled contents a lurid, clotted pink.

"It's okay. You can see the river, which you can't really from down here. Sometimes you can." He was aware that he was high, that he smelled like weed, and took a step farther away along the curb. He didn't know how she'd feel about that, him being high. She might be cool, but the black-and-white work uniform and the way she held herself made her look somebody who was strict. You never knew about girls.

The kid with the bag got in the car and the guy behind the wheel stomped on the accelerator, almost clipping a van making the turn from Midvale. The Chevy was an old convertible with green metallic paint that glittered, a comet disappearing down Ridge toward Manayunk in a ribbon of green. Jimmy smiled, suddenly conscious of the neighborhood coiled on the hills above them, getting that way you could get under a head full of dope. Everything seemed connected; dark forces were at work moving cars and people around like pieces on a game board.

He turned back to Grace, but she was walking back inside, throwing away a cigarette. Her fingernails looked the same pale color as her fingers, some color that wasn't yellow and wasn't brown. There was a thin red stain on the white shirt at her hip. She wore tight black jeans and he let himself picture her stepping into them, her long legs that pale cream shade that he didn't know what to call. He was suddenly too lonely to head back upstairs and walked around the corner to Buckets for a drink.

* * *

He stood at a window at Buckets, trying to see inside, to see who was behind the bar. A few weeks before he had swiped some change from off the counter and thought the girl bartender might have seen him do it, so now he only went in when she wasn't there. While he was standing there, squinting through the dark glass, he saw Evan walking up toward the front door and stop. Evan waited for a short girl with hair dyed white-blond except for hard black roots and dark eye makeup. She was standing between two parked cars, rooting in her purse. He nodded at Jimmy, who smiled, his tongue out, and raised a hand.

"Hey, man. You getting a drink?"

"Oh, hey." Evan looked at the bar, then doubtfully at Jimmy. "Ah, yeah. Well, no. Just getting something to eat." The girl came over and hooked her arm around his. "Well, see you."

"Man, you ever see Jesús and them?"

"Nah." The blond girl moved a step toward the door, pulling Evan. "I got a job. At the Rite Aid."

"Stacking boxes and shit?"

"Ah, I'm the manager. At night. You know." Evan looked apologetic. "Anyway, Jesús went in the army."

"No shit. Remember that time we took that grader and ran it in the creek? That was fucking retarded."

"Yeah. Well." He nodded his head. "I gotta go."

Jimmy fished in his pockets and held out a bottle of blue nail polish to the girl. There was a long pause, then the girl fluttered her fingers to show him the rose tips.

"Sorry, not my color." She turned to the door, her arm still hooked to Evan's like they were chained together.

Evan lifted his shoulders, as if he wanted to stay and

bullshit but he had to go. "Hey," he said, looking at the bottle in Jimmy's hand. "We carry that stuff."

Jimmy got up the next afternoon and went to see his aunt to get more money. He walked up Stanton along the back of St. Bridget's, feeling the heat coming up through his sneakers. The kids were in school, and he thought it was funny you could tell without seeing any sign of them, like the building gave off a kind of hum when it was full of people. He had dated a girl, Cheryll, who said he had a shaman aura, some kind of power to tell about things, a sense other people didn't have. She had a tattoo of a tree and an owl and a pyramid with an eye in it. When he got pinched and sent to the Youth Study Center, he had been trying to steal a huge wheel of wire from the cable TV place where her brother worked. Jimmy thought she was in love with him. She was always saying what a dick her brother was, but she still wouldn't talk to Jimmy after that, would hang up on him when he called from the center, the kids lined up behind him and tapping him on the shoulder so he'd give up the phone. So maybe she was wrong about his aura.

His aunt wasn't really his aunt, she was his great aunt or his mother's aunt or something. She lived near the tracks that ran in the gulley in front of Cresson, in a house so narrow he could almost reach out and touch both walls in the front room. He'd go over there once every couple of weeks and listen to her talk and leave with a couple hundred bucks. It paid for his rent, and he sold enough of the stuff he stole to stay in weed and the orange Drake's cupcakes he liked.

The house was full of little green animals. Ceramic donkeys and horses and birds in a million different styles, but all of them green. There were also pictures cut out of the newspaper and put in crooked frames, including one that his aunt said was Princess Grace at a wedding at St. Bridget's. Once when he came over his aunt was sitting in the dark watching movies of some kind of procession of kids dressed up in matching outfits, the colors faded into a muddled blue. The girls all had on the same uniform dress and veils, and he said, "Is this Muslims?" before he realized it was little kids at St. Bridget's getting first Holy Communion. His aunt didn't seem to hear him, shaking her head and saying something like, "There's your uncle Pete," or, "Oh, look at Mary, how young she is," but he didn't know any of the faces.

She made him drink blue skim milk and gave him cookies from a tin. He thought if he could get her to give him some extra money sometime, he could invest in a quarter-pound of weed. He told her he wanted to go into business.

"Doing what? You should be in school."

"I don't know. Selling things."

"You're a dreamer. You get that from your father." She walked him to the door, stopping to look at the framed clippings. "I used to tell people we were related, me and Grace. Because of the Kelly name. I just wanted it to be true."

Jimmy looked at a picture of Princess Grace in a green dress, her hair swept back and her body arched, like a bow.

His aunt held out a small wad of cash. "But we're not the princess kind of Kelly, are we? We're just the other kind."

The next afternoon he wrote, 9/06, *silver bullet lighter, AM/PM market*, in the composition book, and went downstairs, his pockets full. He had glass bottles of makeup, lipsticks in two shades. He came through the door in time to see the Latino kid handing the bag to the guy from the Chevy and saying something, his head close to the guy's ear.

Something was going on. Jimmy watched the Chevy drive

off and the kid in the doorway watching them go and then turning to look at Jimmy. The kid was big, with a shaved head and tattoos on his neck. His eyes were dark, with heavy lids that made him look sleepy, and when he looked into Jimmy's face it was like there was a tunnel in the air between them so that Jimmy couldn't turn away. But it meant something, the kid hitting him with an attitude.

Grace Lei came out then and said something to the kid so that he sneered at her, showing her the back of his hand. Jimmy couldn't dope out the gesture, but he got that it was something disrespectful, and when the kid turned to go inside Grace gave his back the finger. There was shouting from inside and then she came all the way out and got a cigarette from a pack in her purse.

Jimmy stumbled a little getting across the sidewalk to offer her the lighter. She lit her cigarette and held the lighter out, but he waved her off.

"Keep it."

She stuck it in her pocket without looking at it and turned back to the street.

He said, "That guy giving you a hard time?"

"Ah, never mind about him. That's Luis. He thinks he's a big deal because he's friends with Tiger." She pointed to the street.

"Tiger?"

"That Chinese boy who comes here every day." She looked over her shoulder, lowered her voice. "He's in a gang. They sell drugs. They're idiots."

Jimmy wanted to do something to the kid, but he couldn't think of anything. He lifted his palms and looked at them, the fingers of his left hand smeared with ink from the pen. He noticed for the first time a stripe of maroon in Grace's black hair. Was it new, or had he just never noticed?

"I like your hair."

She shook her head and threw away her cigarette. "It's just hair."

"If you could go anywhere, where would you go?" He figured he had about a second before she went inside.

"Go? I can't go anywhere."

"I see you watching the cars. Do you wish you could get away somewhere?"

She looked at him again, and her eyes were tired. "I'm not going anywhere."

The next two days he didn't leave to steal anything. He sat around the apartment smoking weed and waiting on the end of the day so he could go downstairs and watch. At about six the first night he went down the stairs quietly with his notebook and crossed the street. He sat with his back to a tree in the tiny park next to the fire station across the street and watched the front of the restaurant. The tree was one of those with the leaves that he thought looked tropical, like a fern or something, and it was as if he was on an island, only the island was between Ridge Avenue and Kelly Drive and instead of circling sharks there were cars running up and down the river.

He had on three cheap watches he'd stolen, two of them with the same time. When the big kid, Luis, walked out of the back with the bag and put it on the table, he wrote down the time from each of the three watches and then waited. He could see Grace inside, but she was at the counter and didn't come out. After six minutes by the top watch (a girl's watch with a lavender band and fake gemstones around the face), the Chevy pulled up and the Asian kid with the cap and the chains got out and grabbed the bag. He said something to

Grace that made her face go tight and then walked out again and the car pulled away.

Jimmy wrote down the time again and then got up and walked the long way around the block.

No money. That was how Jimmy knew there was something going on. Luis came out and dropped the plastic bag, and not on the counter where all the other bags went, but on a table near the door. It looked like any other bag, full of food, but it wasn't. The Asian kid came in and took it, and didn't pay anybody. Didn't talk to anyone except Luis, and sometimes Grace, who wouldn't talk back, but kept her eyes down.

The next afternoon Porter came over to buy more of the stuff Jimmy had piled up around the apartment. Jimmy liked Porter because he was older, a grown-up, and still out of control, and because he had red hair that stood up on his head. Most of the adults he ran across seemed like someone had let the air out of them or something, or like they were all nearsighted and not being able to see anything made them cautious and slow. Porter charged in and threw shit around the room, did lines of coke he never thought to offer anyone else, would spend fifteen minutes beating Jimmy's price down only to hand him more money than he'd promised. Jimmy asked Porter's opinion about the Imperial Garden.

"Oh, that's a fucked life, kid. They bring a hundred people at a time sealed in containers, then they owe so much money they gotta work shit jobs for years to pay off."

"Containers?" Jimmy picturing Grace Lei in a giant shrink-wrapped plastic package, like the headphones from Best Buy he could never get open and had to saw at with a steak knife.

Most of the stuff piled up in the apartment was worthless crap. Porter never got tired of pointing this out to Jimmy, but he also went through everything meticulously; holding up and identifying each baseball, coffee mug, book, candlestick, decorative plate, and teapot Jimmy had stacked up around the apartment, and then guessing what it was worth.

"What the fuck is this?" he'd say, holding up a collectible action figure from a comic book store. "A doll?"

"It's Wolverine. From the comic book. It's worth like a hundred and fifty bucks."

"To little kids. Or retards, maybe. I'll give you ten. This?"

"It's a fork. I think."

"You got no eye, kid. Honest to Christ. A fork. Did you at least get the spoon?"

"Fuck you."

"You need to start boosting jewelry."

"That shit's all locked up."

"You need to put together a crew. When I was your age, I stole with five, six other guys. A girl with a cute ass. She bats her eyes, the clerk opens the case."

"I don't want to get put away again."

"At your age? What'd you get, like three months? In kiddy jail. That's nothing. That's the cost of doing business."

"It sucks. It's boring. The big kids fuck with you and steal your shit. I couldn't wait to get out of there."

"How old are you? Jesus Christ, you're in the prime of life. You should be boosting everything you can get your hands on. Steal every fucking thing and run like a jackrabbit."

"Why don't you?"

Porter's eyes got big. "I'd go to real jail, kid, and that's no fucking joke. Not like Henry Avenue."

"You think I want to go? Back to jail?"

Porter looked around, his eyes going back and forth. "Kid,

I got to tell you. Living like this? In this rathole? It's not that different than prison."

The night he stole the bag from the Imperial he didn't smoke, but sipped at a bottle of peach brandy that had been in the apartment when he moved in. He stood in the window a long time, looking down at the cars and the river and working himself up to it. The brandy tasted weird, and he wondered if that was how peaches tasted. He ate a cupcake he'd gotten at Major Wing Lee's, the little store on the corner. He leaned on the window frame and looked up and down Ridge. The road was busy, and it was getting a little dark, which he liked.

He pictured how it would go, flitting through the shadows, the bag sliding across the table to him like a magic trick. Him and Grace Lei together, dumping out the money onto his mattress, maybe five or ten thousand bucks, and him seeing her smile for the first time, maybe the first time since she came to America. He cupped his hands in front of himself, mentally calculating how much might fit in the bag.

Coming out onto the street he could hear a rising scream, the siren from one of the trucks starting up across the street, and he pressed himself flat against the door like a bug caught in the light. He moved sideways, looking left and right, his back flat against the storefront of the hair place next to the restaurant. He had his watches on and looked at his wrist. Three minutes more, give or take. He stood at the edge of the window and looked in.

Grace was standing at the counter, her back to the street. He looked east up the street for the Chevy but there was a line of cars stretching away toward Philly and he couldn't tell if it was coming. At the same moment that he saw the bright grillwork of the old Chevy, Luis came out of the back, swinging the bag. The Chevy approached, a few cars back from the light at Midvale. Jimmy's eyes went back and forth, back and forth, while the car inched along and Luis took his fucking time getting to the front table.

Jimmy crabwalked along the front of the Gardens, his head on a swivel. Luis seemed to be looking out the front door, and Jimmy was ready to drop to his shaking knees if Luis swung his head around. The Chevy was there, three cars back from the intersection, and Luis was still standing at the door. Jimmy could see the Asian kid in the front seat, his cap bright red. Jimmy was breathing hard and mumbling under his breath, *Come on, come on.* There was a gap open in front of the Chevy and Luis still hadn't dropped the goddamn bag.

The light changed, going yellow and then red, and the Chevy stopped hard. Luis opened his hand and dropped the bag, turning to the counter. Jimmy took two steps, three and stuck his head in the door. Luis was close, his back turned. There was a line of sweat baked through his massive white T-shirt and he smelled like starch and fried food. Jimmy put his hand out and touched the bag, his hand formed into a hard L shape that scooped it off the table. Luis said, "Hey," and Jimmy looked up to see who he was talking to and it was Grace, who cocked her head as Jimmy stepped backward out the door, the bag up at his chest, and they looked at each other and she saw Jimmy plain with the bag, and her eyebrows went up but he was gone.

He walked past the bar next door and Major Wing Lee's at the corner looking straight ahead. The Chevy must have gone by but he didn't see it. He felt naked and cold walking down the street, the plastic bag feeling like it was melting his hands, something inside folded up the size of maybe a sandwich. The money, or the dope. He wanted to look, but he just made the turn up Midvale and then took a clumsy skip step that became an uneven lope and then he was jogging past Buckets and the little storefronts until he hit Frederick, cut left, and ran hard.

He made his way uphill to Stanton, out of breath after thirty yards. Where the road turned to the left, he jumped the low wall and tumbled down the incline to the tracks, ran half a block to the base of a high-tension tower. He dropped down onto the gravel by the tracks, spit up some peach brandy, and sat wheezing, his heart going, wiping at the sweat leeching out of his hair. He wanted to look in the bag, but instead he stuck it in his jacket and forced himself up again.

For some reason he expected sirens, though he knew that was stupid. He ran a few steps, then slowed to a jog, then walked, one hand pressed against his chest like an old man. He kept moving east, sticking to the tracks, watching cars move on the nearby streets, looking for the green Chevy. When he had a gone a few more blocks, he threw himself over a fence into some weeds and lay down, overwhelmed for a minute by the luxuriant smell of leaves and long grass. The sun was going down, and lights snapped on at the familiar-looking highrise he could see over the tops of the trees ahead. After a minute, he realized he was back on the grounds of the Youth Study Center. He bolted up, threw himself over the fence, and ran back west, laughing.

He walked slower and slower the closer he got to Ridge, dropping down the narrow, canted streets, stopping to glance back up the hill behind him and keeping his head down. There were people out on the stoops, kids coming out after dinner to play until they couldn't see anymore. He remembered that, stubbornly standing in the street in the dark with a hockey mask on, chasing up and down until it got so black they'd lose the puck.

It was full on dark when he stopped at the last driveway on Eveline and made his way behind the stores and restaurants that fronted Ridge. The first two buildings were unoccupied, and he could see through the empty first floors to the street in front of the Imperial. There was an ambulance in the driveway of the firehouse, its strobe lights flashing crazily and turning the street red and blue and white. There were cops in uniform stringing that yellow tape they always show on TV and guys in suits with badges hanging from their pockets. Everyone was pointing, making notes on clipboards, or talking into radios. Stunned by the sight of it, Jimmy forgot for a minute why he was there and wondered what had happened, figuring there must have been an accident.

When one of the cops shined a flashlight into the store, he dropped like he'd been shot and scuttled along the gravel to the end of the building, then ducked into the alley that led to his fire escape and pulled it down, wincing at every metallic groan and breathing through his mouth, his face hot, his hands slick with sweat.

Upstairs, he dropped onto his bed, breathless, and watched the lights from the cop cars and ambulances flash onto his ceiling. He got up slowly, keeping his head down, slid along the floor to the bathroom, and closed the door before turning on the light. He splashed water on his streaked face. He looked in the mirror, angling to see his T-shirt, now gray with dust. Inventoried his scrapes and bruises, the open cut over one knuckle, and his torn jeans. He patted at his face and hands with a dirty towel, shut the light off, and stepped out into the dark room. Strange, plasma-like shapes floated in his eyes and seemed to climb the walls. A moment later he saw someone near the bed. Grace Lei.

She was standing over the bed, motionless. The lights from the street played over her white shirt and pale face and the bag. She looked like the robots in his dope dreams, catching the pulsing light, breasts swelling as she breathed. She peered at him, and then the bag, and then him again.

"I'm sorry," she said. "The door was open."

"It's okay." He pointed toward the street. "What happened?"

"Luis got stabbed. Tiger stabbed him."

"Jesus, because . . . ?" He pointed at the bag.

"Maybe. Who knows what it was about? There was so much blood." She put her hands over her face. "Tiger came in and said something to Luis, and Luis said something back. And then he pushed Tiger, and Tiger just stuck him. It was fast. I never even saw him get the knife out, he just . . ." She made a motion with her hand, the knife going in and out, in and out. "Boys like Luis? Tiger? They're so angry all the time, who knows? You can't talk to them."

Jimmy walked over to the bed and they looked down at the bag.

"He said something stupid," Grace continued, "and Tiger just stuck him. So Luis took off running into the street and Tiger went after him, and this pickup came zooming through and just, you know." She swallowed. "Just *wham*. I never saw nothing like that. The truck went right over Luis. I got sick. Tiger's friends just took off. Two firemen from across the street ran him down, Tiger. They held him until the cops came and took him away. They had all these questions, and I didn't know, so I just came up here."

"Did you say anything? About, you know, me? And the bag?"

"No, I didn't even think about it, really. Until I was in the room just now." She looked at him, or seemed to. It was tough to tell in the dark. "I knew you'd be all right to talk to. That you aren't like Tiger, or Luis."

They both stood, not saying anything for a while. The bag was dotted with grit from the gravel bed and smeared with Jimmy's fingerprints. They could hear the police talking to each other in the street, doors slamming.

Finally, Grace squared her shoulders and reached for the bag. Jimmy smiled and she stopped and stared at him, her body taut, arched like the picture he had seen at his aunt's house, and he thought, yeah, he was the wrong kind of Kelly, but maybe she was the right kind of Grace.

Her slender fingers closed on the bag and he smiled wider, so she said, "What?"

He said, "What if it's sesame chicken?"

She smiled back, and for the first time he saw her teeth, white and even. "Then," she said, "we'll eat."

A CUT ABOVE

BY LAURA SPAGNOLI

Rittenhouse Square

Beth pinched the skin between her thumb and index finger almost hard enough to draw blood. She took every step to the beat of a mantra—*Don't cry, don't cry*—and every step placed more distance between her and Tinto, a tapas bar where she'd left Kyle, who was the latest man to think she was *a great girl* (a girl? at thirty-four?) but who wasn't ready for *a relationship. It's not you, it's me.*

What an actor. Literally. And Beth had to see him again to rehearse their final scene. She'd signed up for an acting class at the suggestion of therapists and friends alike, who urged her to find an artistic outlet for her emotions. And they were right. She had a knack for acting. It was just bad luck she and Kyle were doing a piece from *The Glass Menagerie* in which, ironically, she'd be pitied for lacking gentlemen callers.

Now she needed to focus on another scene: Walnut Street on a lovely August night, with her in a lovely white dress. It was eleven o'clock. Anyone who saw her might think she was heading out to canoodle with someone at a sidewalk café and not that her evening was a failure. She concentrated on an *actable objective*: to be in a rush to meet a date. Glancing at her watch for emphasis, she began to believe it. She walked east on Walnut confidently, passing packs of college girls in skimpy dresses and college boys in untucked button-down shirts headed toward the Irish Pub.

Some boys followed her with their eyes as she passed. It was working.

She continued alongside shuttered boutiques and the oddly empty dirt lot north of Rittenhouse Square, where neighbors rejected development ideas as tacky or liable to attract an unwanted element. She sailed through the north entrance of the square when, suddenly, she slipped and fell. It was the heel of her right shoe, purchased last month at the Payless on Chestnut Street, now jutting out at a sixty-degree angle from the rest of the sole.

This latest twist plunged Beth into despair. She couldn't focus on counting to ten or any of the calming self-talk she'd been taught. The lights in the square blurred and came back into focus when she blinked, then blurred again, but somehow she stood up. Carrying her shoes, she continued along a paved path. She nearly jumped when nearby automatic sprinklers surged on, then nearly jumped again when a woman screamed. The woman screamed a second time, but it was followed by laughter.

"It's too late now," a man said.

Beth stopped. A young woman stood on the path ahead. She wore a wet dress, once white but now semitransparent, that clung to her body. She leaned to the side and wrung water out of her long hair, looking in the mist-filled air like a modern water nymph.

"Thanks for the warning," she said sarcastically to the man next to her. "I'm sliding everywhere." She leaned one hand on his shoulder for support and with the other removed a pair of strappy sandals.

The man, in a light gray suit without a tie, was far less wet and kept joking. "Can you make it home barefoot, my little blossom? My bitter teacup?"

"Be quiet," she said.

"Want me to take off my shoes so we match?"

"No, darling. I want you to carry me." She held onto his lapels as if to draw him in for a kiss, and they remained in this pose like intertwining statues against the lush background of haloed park lights. Beth was moving past them, awkward in the shadow of their glamour, when she felt a tap on her shoulder.

"Miss," the man said. He was close enough for her to see droplets of water on his dark blond waves of hair. "Excuse me—"

His companion giggled, arms crossed over her chest. They looked young, maybe just out of college.

"Yes?" Beth asked, a bit too energetically.

"In your opinion," the man began, "is it worth it to take a cab just two blocks away? We're damp and my friend here finds it impossible to wear her shoes without slipping." The man's voice was higher than she expected and somehow sweet, with a slight British accent.

"Of course it's worth it," Beth answered, waving her shoes in front of her. "I was thinking of hailing a cab myself," she lied.

"A good answer," the man said, catching her eyes and holding on to them with his. "We're at the Belgravia. Any chance you're headed in that direction?"

"I'm actually on Pine Street—"

"Why don't you join us," he offered.

The woman flashed him an indecipherable look, then smiled. She ran her hands through her wet hair and spoke with an accent similar to the man's. "Company might be fun."

The man rocked slightly on his heels. "We'll toast to a fine evening, all's well ending well or ending drenched or something."

"Okay," Beth said. *I am open to invitations*, she told herself. *I am trying new things*.

When they rolled up to the Belgravia, they stepped into what seemed to Beth like another universe—one that would make returning to her walk-up studio harder.

"Alex, Chloe," the doorman waved them into the marble-lined corridor strung with bright chandeliers.

"Welcome home!" Alex announced when they reached a door at the end of a hall on the sixth floor. It opened into a stuffy living room, cluttered with suitcases and clothing. A mahogany coffee table was covered with papers. More papers spilled out of accordion folders on a stained Persian rug below it, competing for space with numerous keys, empty glasses, and takeout food containers.

"Cleaning," Chloe remarked in a stage whisper, "is not our highest priority." She walked into another room.

"We've been traveling," Alex added. "I want to share something we picked up. Do you like port?"

"I love it." Beth didn't know if this was true. *I am trying new things*.

Alex rummaged through a suitcase in the corner. He was slender but broad-shouldered and she noticed he wore no socks under his loafers. The wall next to him was covered with masks she assumed were African, and the other walls had paintings—abstract, with a gray, white, and red palette, one of them hanging cockeyed as if posted hastily and never fixed.

"Aha!" He turned around, wielding a dark brown bottle. "You'll like this. It's supposed to have," he squinted at the label, "*notes of honey*." He handed her a glass and their eyes met again. Beth couldn't decide if they were blue, gray, or green.

Chloe reappeared in a red dress and high-heeled black shoes. Her hair was drying to a lighter blond.

"That's a good dress," Alex said when Chloe spun in a catwalk turn. Beth saw it was backless and still had a price tag on it.

"A toast to our new friend," he indicated Beth. "Our friend . . ."

"Beth," she said.

"To Beth, a fellow underwater traveler."

The drink was sweet and went down easily.

"Beth," Chloe suddenly said. "What's your shoe size?"

"Seven. Why?"

Chloe left the room and came back carrying a shoe box. "I got these last summer."

Beth pulled out a pair of white high-heeled Manolo Blahniks and gasped.

"They're yours," Chloe said. "No worries."

"I couldn't," Beth objected.

"Obviously I never wear them, so they're of more use to you."

Elegantly shod, Beth felt ready to dance but opted to lounge, given the steady refills Alex provided. After the port he dug into the rest of his collection, presenting a Calvados from Normandy, a Scotch from Scotland, and more. Beth envied the jet-setting pair. She loved traveling but hadn't taken any trips lately. She had little time off from her desk job at a plastic surgeon's office near the square, and besides, she was saving money. There were debts to pay from years ago, the upshot of ill-advised exotic vacations with boyfriends and splurges on clothing. She knew she hadn't been herself during these periods of excess, bursts of exuberance followed closely by profound regret or worse, but credit card companies didn't want excuses. They wanted their money back, with interest.

But she didn't worry about debt or anything else just then. Hours blurred into each other and the three of them got silly. They played several rounds of "Would you rather . . ." with Alex supplying the most unappealing choices: Would you rather clean a monkey cage or a chicken cage? Go blind and lose the use of both arms or just lose the use of your legs? Shoplift from a store or steal from a very wealthy friend who'd never miss the item in question?

Finally, he asked a straight question when Chloe left the room. Eyeing Beth and crawling over the Persian rug, he kneeled in front of her, placing both hands on her knees and lowering his voice to a whisper: "Would you rather kiss me now or kiss me later?"

"Now," she whispered back, not certain whether Alex's discretion was merely that or part of a deception, and amazed either way by what happened. The kiss was brief, but warmer and more promising than any she'd had in a long time.

It was almost six a.m. when Alex accompanied Beth outside to wait for a cab. Bands of pink light appeared in the sky in the east. Beth shivered.

"Here," he said, placing his jacket over her shoulders. It felt warm and smelled like Earl Grey tea. She closed her eyes and inhaled. They kissed.

"Let me get your number," he said, reaching around her waist to get to the phone in the inner pocket of his jacket.

A cab finally appeared.

"Have a nice morning, beautiful," Alex said. "I'll be in touch."

But he wasn't, not later that week or in September, and Beth felt too awkward to call again after leaving two messages. She slogged through the humid days, working and taking lunch breaks in Rittenhouse Square, often sitting on a bench near the little bronze statue of a goat with her old friend Leah, who reminded her there were plenty of guys out there when Beth whined about Alex.

"And these guys don't have girlfriends," Leah added.

"Who knows if she's really his girlfriend?" Beth replied.

"After all the trouble you've had, all you've gone through . . ." Leah continued, as if to say, *Enough said.*

Meanwhile, Beth started another acting class and dyed her hair jet-black, much to her mother's dismay.

"That color only works with certain skin tones. Change it, at least for your sister's wedding."

But *strong choices* was the theme of Beth's class and she ran with it. Sure, she was playing another aging, tragic Tennessee Williams character, but she was shining in the part. Rehearsals kept her spirits up. She even went on a few dates with someone Leah deemed *a nice, normal guy*—a forty-something divorcé named Todd who worked in computers. He never made her laugh but he was attentive.

When she received a text one October night while watching *Law & Order* reruns at home, she assumed it was Todd until she read it: *Please rescue me.* She didn't recognize the number and it had been a long day. An elderly patient in for the routine removal of a skin lesion had suffered a heart attack and was transferred to the hospital but died a few hours later. This meant paperwork, and the next day the widow would be coming to the office to pick up her husband's belongings that hadn't made it onto the ambulance.

Then another text appeared: *Thinking of you, Beth. Sorry to disturb.*

Beth texted back asking for clarification and her phone rang.

"Hello, beautiful," Alex said.

She felt awake again.

Half an hour later in Rittenhouse Square, she sat on a bench and waited for him, peering into the damp fall air until he materialized on a lamp-lit path. He smiled. His hair was slightly unkempt, making him appear boyish despite his suit. He carried a briefcase, and when he reached Beth, he dropped it to the ground before dropping to his knees.

"I kept thinking about you," he said. "I had to travel, unexpectedly, and now I can't go home, it seems."

"What do you mean?"

He sighed, resting his hands on her knees. "The arrangements I made for rent fell through while I was abroad. A ridiculous misunderstanding."

"Isn't Chloe there?"

"She's in France," he said.

"You broke up?"

A smile spread across Alex's face, emphasizing a slight cleft in his chin. "She's in France visiting our uncle."

"Your uncle?"

"With our parents gone, he's our closest relative."

"She's your sister?" Beth asked.

"Yes, we just get on well and share a place sometimes. I thought you knew that."

"No," she said, smiling too.

"No?" Alex asked, standing up, helping Beth up, then kissing her. He ran his hands through her hair. "It's a shame I missed the end of summer with you . . . So much family business. But the good news is we're here now."

"Just in time for the rain," Beth said, holding out her hand.

"I don't suppose you have an umbrella?" he asked.

"I know where we can find one."

It was a quick dash to the blush-colored suites of Drs. Morris, Kent, and Fleischer on 19th Street.

"We'll borrow one of these," Beth said, indicating the umbrellas stored behind the reception desk. They were pink, large enough to shelter a picnic table, and said, *Beautiful dreams come true*, in bold black letters.

Alex eyed them skeptically. "I guess masculine pride will take a hit tonight." He surveyed the office. "Very pink, but swank. Is this your desk?"

Beth nodded.

"Who forgot his clothes?" Alex asked, pointing to the pile of things on Beth's chair.

"They belong to a man who died, actually," Beth said, at which point Alex laughed. "I'm not making it up," she protested. "The man had a coronary!"

"Not funny at all," Alex said, with such seriousness he meant it was. Then his face lit up. "I may have no roof over my head, but I'd like to take you for a drink. Have you ever gone to Nineteen?"

Ten minutes later, the gilt-framed mirrors of the Bellevue Hotel elevators sent Beth and Alex's reflection back to them from multiple angles, all bathed in golden light. When they sat down in a love seat next to the fireplace in Nineteen, Beth already felt tipsy. More alive than she had in years.

They drank until almost two a.m., when Alex made an announcement.

"Surprise."

He pulled out a platinum American Express card bearing the name *Gerald F. Mitchell*. Beth's heart began to race. It was the dead patient's card.

"How did you get this?"

Alex looked at her. "You're not worried, are you?"

She knew Leah would walk out. Call the police. But Leah wouldn't be in this bar with Alex in the middle of the night in the first place, and Beth felt a strange, giddy sense of trust in him. If he'd pulled out a gun and said they were going to ditch the check by shooting their way out, she would have been game. *Strong choices*, she thought, not sure it applied but feeling too elated to question it. With the fire behind him, Alex seemed to possess a kind of glow, and Beth was enveloped in it.

Alex continued: "I'm sure the widow hasn't canceled his cards yet. With everything going on, she probably won't notice extra charges."

Beth watched him hand over the stolen card, the waiter bring it back, and Alex devise his best Gerald F. Mitchell signature.

"By the way," Alex said to the waiter, "we'd like a room. Can we book one without going down to the lobby?"

"Of course."

They spent the next eighteen hours in a suite, sleeping little, moving from the bedroom, with its red drapes, king-size bed, and countless pillows, to an airy off-white living room where light streamed in from the south and west the following afternoon. Beth had called in sick and now gazed out the window.

"We're in heaven," she smiled, polishing off what remained of a room service cheese plate.

"We'll have to die more often," he said. Then his phone rang. He stared at it and made a face.

"What's wrong?"

"Chloe. About the apartment debacle, I'd guess."

"I thought she was in France."

"Must have just flown in. She can sort out the problem—I just hate to deal with that now."

His phone stopped, then rang again.

"I should get this. Do you mind? Chloe can get hysterical."

"Of course," Beth said. "I'll try the hot tub."

When she emerged a half hour later, Alex was beaming.

"I can go home! Not that this hasn't been a wonderful adventure. Let's do it again."

"When?"

"When another patient dies and forgets his wallet," he winked.

Beth had forgotten they were enjoying this luxury suite on a dead man's dime and the reminder left her chilled. Alex began gathering papers into his briefcase.

"Do you have a job?" she asked.

"In my family's business, as a matter of fact. My uncle— the one Chloe just saw overseas—he's well off and wants me to manage his investments one day. Right now I'm managing other people's money."

"Do you have family in England?"

"Some there, some in France. We're a bit spread over the map." He motioned for Beth to sit next to him and put his arm around her. "I do legitimate business. I just thought we'd have some fun on Mitchell because even if his widow catches on, she won't have to pay for it. You can't object to nipping a bit out of the credit card companies, can you?"

Beth shook her head. "They're kind of douchebags."

Alex squeezed her tighter. "You're not just a pretty face. You're a potty mouth."

When Leah called her that night, Beth recounted her activities of the last twenty-four hours, minus the stolen credit card, in a torrent of enthusiasm.

"What about Todd?" Leah asked.

"He's too boring for me."

That night she should have been exhausted but felt too energized to sleep. She couldn't stop making plans. She wanted to prove to Alex that she could contribute her share to the relationship. He'd shown her a magical night. The least she could do was take him to dinner. With someone else's money.

The next day she went to work with a target in mind: Valerie. Her cranky coworker frequently left her purse under her desk. It wasn't the best spot—if Valerie came back, she'd be caught—but Beth had issued herself a dare and had to go through with it. She found it surprisingly easy to rifle through the bag, fish out a Visa card, and put everything else back in its place so the theft would remain unnoticed.

Contacting Alex proved more difficult. She called and left a message, saying she had a surprise, but didn't hear back that evening or the next day or night. The waiting stoked her restlessness. She paced inside her apartment for an hour the third night before putting on sweatpants and going for a run. She took her usual route up 18th Street from Pine, around the square, then west on Locust Street until she reached the Schuylkill River path. She ran for miles. It was nine o'clock when she got home and showered, but she felt stir-crazy again, her mind brimming with ideas. Her phone rang around nine forty-five. It was Todd. She didn't answer. Then it rang again at ten.

"Hello, my long lost," Alex said, as if he were the one who'd been trying to reach her.

They picked up where they'd left off, meeting in the square and heading to Parc, a French brasserie, where they enjoyed a bottle of champagne and some food.

"Surprise," Beth announced when the check arrived.

Alex's eyes went wide with admiration. "Tsk, tsk." He

took the credit card and examined it. "You're a naughty girl, *Valerie*."

He leaned against the high-backed banquette and studied her. "Is this something you enjoy?"

She spent the rest of the month snagging credit cards—often the numbers alone. Alex used some for online transactions, while Beth got her nails manicured, enjoyed massages at Body Restoration, hired a personal trainer, had a makeover at MAC, and bought more dresses and shoes than her closets could hold, even after she discarded old, cheap stuff. She went to Knit Wit, Cole Haan, Anthropologie, and Barneys, and she still had plenty of income to pay down her own credit card debts.

Her new look attracted attention.

"Are you getting in over your head again with debt?" Leah asked. She was sitting across from Alex and Beth at a table at Twenty Manning, where they'd invited her for dinner.

Alex answered, "With me, she has nothing to worry about."

Beth smiled and cut another piece of steak. Leah stared at them as if studying exotic zoo animals, then took a sip of wine and turned away.

Some time before Thanksgiving, Alex started talking about Christmas plans. He was expected at his uncle's place outside Paris and might stay as long as three weeks.

"It's part business," he said when Beth looked sad. "I have to show him what I'm doing for my clients so he'll want me to help him some day."

The thought of three weeks without Alex was unbearable. As it was, she had to attend her sister's wedding alone right after Thanksgiving because Alex had a meeting in New York.

But Beth made it through. Her relatives typically asked her questions with caution, always afraid things might be going badly, but her new appearance emboldened them. She exuded energy. She looked beautiful. She felt electric. And she told everyone she'd be going with her boyfriend to Paris.

Though her mother seemed stunned, her grandmother was thrilled. "It's wonderful how things have turned around for you."

Alex was less enthusiastic.

"I want nothing more than to have a romantic vacation with you, but this is a family thing—"

Beth put her finger on his lips. She hadn't felt this certain about anything in her life. If they loved each other, they could work it out. Especially if they didn't have to pay for it.

She told Leah about her plans one Saturday at Miel, a quaint patisserie with bumblebee-shaped door handles. Beth bought two hot chocolates and Napoleons in honor of her announcement: "Alex and I are going to Paris!"

Leah reacted as if Beth were talking about the moon.

"How can you object to Paris?" Beth asked. "And how can you be so unsupportive when I finally find a great guy?"

"Is he great?" Leah asked. She studied her plate. "I don't know how to say this, and I don't want to provoke a bad reaction. I mean, you're handling life really well now. But the thing is, I saw Alex with another woman."

"I don't think so." Beth tapped her manicured nails on the wrought-iron table.

"I'm sure of it. He was with a blond woman coming out of the Bellevue."

"It's probably his sister."

Leah shook her head. "They were kissing. On the lips."

Beth tightened her grip around her empty china cup,

stood up from the table, and smashed it on the floor. A girl in an apron rushed out from behind the counter, but Beth dug into her purse and thrust a twenty-dollar bill into her hand.

She turned to Leah, who appeared stricken, and hissed, "You're so jealous, you can't stand to see me happy. You're *toxic*."

Beth didn't mention the ridiculous accusation to Alex. They'd spent the evening in bed in her cramped apartment, and now she straddled him, teasing him, bringing him closer and closer to climax and suddenly stopping. She pushed his hands down with her hands.

"I want to go to Paris."

"Let's talk later," he said, breathless.

"I. Want. To. Go." With each syllable she pushed his hands down harder.

Alex shook his head no, shutting his eyes tight and scrunching his face, but finally opened them.

"You can be independent?"

She nodded.

"You can see the most romantic city in the world on your own some of the time?"

She nodded.

"You can spend some nights alone if need be?"

She took her hands out of his to slam her fists down on the mattress in protest, but then nodded with a pout.

Alex shook his head as if unable to believe the words coming out of his mouth: "Come to Paris with me."

Beth shrieked and threw her arms around him again.

"Come to Paris, Beth." They kissed, and between kisses Alex spoke with some desperation. "Please, just don't stop what you were doing before."

Beth smiled. "No?"

"No."

"No?" She started rocking back and forth on top of him.

"Never," Alex said. "Never."

They made a plan not to spend their own money for Paris.

"We'd do best hitting someone who can take a substantial cash advance," Alex advised.

This involved knowing someone's PIN, however, and there was only one person whose code either of them knew: Leah. She'd mentioned to Beth once that she used the last four digits of her childhood phone number, which Beth remembered. So Beth gave an Oscar-worthy performance—*actable objective*: to make up with a friend. Then she took Leah's card and scored a $5,000 advance.

Alex was impressed. "With friends like you, who needs thieves," he said one night over dinner, contemplating Beth with what seemed like wistfulness. "You really are amazing. A quick study, I might add. A cut above the rest."

Alex was handling the tickets, taking some of the cash to New York when he went on business and going through an old friend, a trusted travel agent. He'd get back on the 22nd or 23rd and they'd leave December 24th.

Beth had never been happier. She bought gifts for family and friends, including Leah, who was dealing with the headache of identity theft, and gifts for herself. More dresses, more shoes, even a cute fox-trimmed jacket from Jacques Ferber.

"Wow. Are you moonlighting to buy all these clothes?" Valerie joked on their last day at work before the holiday.

"Trunk sale," Beth answered without looking up from her computer screen. But then she got scared. Police showed up at Morris, Kent, and Fleischer around noon and Beth had no idea what they were investigating. Valerie's card? Gerald Mitchell's? Someone else's? At one point the cops questioned

Beth and Valerie together. A young blue-eyed officer with a mustache leaned toward them with an air of confidentiality.

"Notice anyone around the office who's been acting different lately? Dressing different?"

Beth's chest tightened.

"Nothing out of the ordinary," Valerie said, then looked intently at Beth.

The officer looked at Beth too, waiting for her to speak.

"Nothing unusual," she confirmed, adding, "I'm famished. Could I go to lunch now?"

The cops left, but the bad news didn't stop.

"I'm stuck in New York another day," Alex said when he called. "Possibly two."

"But we leave in two days!"

"There's nothing I can do. Family stuff. I'll explain later. In Paris, *mon amour*."

That night Beth stole the show with her performance as Princess Kosmonopolis, in a state of nervous collapse when Chance threatened to leave her for his true love, the younger Heavenly. The acting teacher loved it. Everyone had drinks at Good Dog after and talked about local auditions Beth might consider come spring.

She couldn't wait to tell Alex, but he wasn't answering his phone then or the next day. It was December 23 and she walked around the neighborhood aimlessly, past the beautiful red doors of St. Mark's Church on Locust Street, then up 17th Street past Little Pete's, the Plaza-Warwick, and Sofitel. She strolled along Chestnut Street and looked at the windows of discount shoe and clothing stores, glad she never went there anymore.

That night she managed just a few hours of sleep, and the next morning saw she'd missed a text from Alex. He was still in New York but had both their tickets. He'd go directly to the Philadelphia International Airport from there and meet her by the counter at six-fifteen for the eight o'clock flight. Thrilled, Beth sprang into action. She started packing but her suitcases looked shabby, so she headed to Robinson Luggage on Broad. It was a cold day under a bright sun, and the streets were crowded with last-minute shoppers. When she finally arrived at the store, she heard a familiar voice and spotted a woman with blond hair.

"I'll call as soon as I land," the woman said into her cell phone. "Nothing more depressing than an airport Christmas morning."

It was Chloe. Beth hadn't seen her since their first meeting in August because Chloe was always out of town or wanted the apartment to herself. But Chloe was practically her sister-in-law. Shouldn't they get to know each other?

Beth approached her. "Hi. It's Beth. Remember, from the night with the sprinklers?"

"Of course," she smiled warmly. "How are you?"

"Great. I'm going to Paris so I can't complain, right?"

"Paris? I'm traveling there myself."

"Really?"

They stood there a moment before Chloe continued: "My flight's tonight and I have so much to do, I should be on my way."

"I guess Alex and I might be on your flight."

Chloe sucked in her breath. She looked at the ceiling, then seemed to cave in to the inevitability of doing something she didn't want to do.

"That's unlikely. Alex is already in Paris."

Beth leaned for support on a glass case filled with wallets and passport holders. "But he's got my ticket. He texted me to meet him at six-fifteen."

"Let's talk," Chloe said.

They crossed the street and sat in the lobby of the Ritz-Carlton Hotel near a fragrant gingerbread house display. Children ran around while weary grown-ups sat surrounded by shopping bags. Beth's head was spinning.

"Alex is a sweetheart," Chloe explained. "So sweet he has trouble saying no. He's charming too, so he's always got admirers. I'm used to it. It's been this way ever since we declared our feelings for each other—"

Beth flinched. "How can you contemplate such a thing?"

"How do you mean?" Chloe asked, surprised.

"With your brother?"

"Stepbrother," Chloe corrected. Now Beth was surprised. "You have to understand," Chloe said. "Alex gets involved easily with people, but he always comes back to me. Always."

Beth heard the blood whoosh through her veins, melding with the general din as Chloe kept talking.

"My uncle—our uncle—would like nothing more than to see us marry. It's odd, but he's very protective of me since my father died, and he knows I love Alex. This would be good for Alex, of course. He didn't make it into our parents' will, and his mother had so little . . ."

Chloe, her eyes downcast and her hair falling in perfect waves just below her shoulders, looked like an angel delivering the truth. Nausea washed over Beth.

"Thank you," Beth whispered. "I should have known. It seemed complicated. Even getting the tickets—"

"The money," Chloe interrupted. "I know how he is, how unfair he is. How much did you give him for tickets?"

Beth tried to recall what each one cost. Eight hundred dollars? Nine hundred? It was Leah's money, but Chloe clearly pegged Beth as someone Alex had duped. Perhaps he had.

"Let me write you a check," Chloe said. "My uncle's generous with me, as is Alex, though I worry about things he does. Whatever the case, it's terrible for you to be out any money. Do you have five minutes? We'll run back to the apartment now. No worries."

Nothing had changed about the Belgravia except the bright wreaths now festooning the front doors.

"Chloe," the doorman said, then nodded at Beth.

Passing through the marble lobby and under the chandeliers, Beth tried to imagine herself back into the first time she came here, but couldn't.

They entered the apartment and Chloe began looking for her checks.

"They must be in the bedroom."

Beth felt pressure build behind her eyes. She imagined telling everyone the trip to Paris had been canceled. She imagined Leah and her mother looking at her, thinking she'd screwed things up or gotten too emotional. Again. She imagined her grandmother telling her she shouldn't waste time feeling sorry for herself if she wanted to meet another nice young man.

Her head throbbed and her mouth was dry. She noticed an Air France ticket on the coffee table for the flight she was supposed to have taken. The ticket had Chloe's name on it and a receipt confirmed its purchase by Alex two days prior. How could he? But Beth had trouble blaming Alex. Perhaps he was trapped—all the "family stuff" he mentioned. And here she was, sitting in his apartment, allowing his stepsister to send her away with a check. What would Alex think when he found out she'd accepted a paltry sum—nothing compared with the fortune the two of them could make—instead of opting for a life of love and adventure with him? Her mind reeled. It made no sense to let Alex down. She loved him too much. He loved her.

There, on the table, a silver letter opener with a filigreed handle caught her eye. It wasn't sharp, but it might do. She stepped on the Oriental runner in the hallway to avoid making noise as she came up behind Chloe, who was searching a drawer beneath the bed. Before Chloe could turn around, Beth plunged the letter opener into her neck. Chloe gasped and collapsed over the drawer.

But something was wrong. The weapon wouldn't go deeper and Chloe was still alive, trying to move. Beth withdrew the makeshift knife, causing Chloe to scream and blood to gush out of the wound onto her white cashmere sweater. Beth forced the weapon into a new spot in Chloe's neck. More blood, more gasping, but Chloe still breathed. Her eyes were open and her mouth twisted with pain. *Focus*, Beth told herself when she started to tremble. Find an *actable objective*: to kill Chloe in order to live a life of happiness with Alex. She scrambled to the closet and found a plastic bag, then lifted up Chloe's head by the hair and fastened the bag tightly around her neck, squeezing with her hands to speed things up. Tremors wracked Chloe's body, her arms and then legs. Then nothing.

Beth stood up, sweating and weak. She didn't have much time. She found Chloe's passport first. They both had brown eyes but Beth's hair was dark. To play a convincing Chloe and make it to the airport by six-fifteen, she'd need to leave the Belgravia, visit a hair salon, and return to pack. She didn't want to take any chances and decided to leave and come back as Chloe in case the doorman was paying attention. Finding scissors, she slit open the bag around Chloe's head, then cut off all the blond hair not covered in blood. She tied up her own hair, then used clips to fasten Chloe's to the edges, hiding the jagged line between the two with a winter hat. It looked amazingly natural. She hustled into Chloe's coat, grabbed her purse, and ran out.

The afternoon became a series of tasks: she was Chloe, rushing to finish errands; she was Beth, discarding hair in the restroom at Liberty Place and washing flecks of blood off her wrists; she was whichever one's credit card she used, stopping by Liquid Salon, explaining she was about to go to France to meet her fiancé and wanted to surprise him by going blond. Could a colorist do that in the next two hours?

She was Beth, but with honey-colored hair, anxious to get things from her apartment, then suddenly aware of a police cruiser parked on Pine and 19th, so she was Chloe again, walking past Beth's apartment, no turning back, and heading home.

"Chloe," the doorman nodded.

She packed as if she might stay in France a long time and got ready to leave. It was a shame about the body—how odd it looked with hacked-off hair. She turned off the heat and opened the bedroom windows. The corpse might not smell for weeks if it stayed cold.

She was Beth, anticipating a romantic getaway with her boyfriend. She was Chloe, anticipating holidays with family. She was *trying new things, making strong choices*. She was her own mind, racing a thousand miles a second, already in Paris.

Soon, love, she texted Alex from Beth's phone.

Soon, love, she texted Alex from Chloe's phone.

Soon, mon amour, he replied to each.

SWIMMING

BY HALIMAH MARCUS

Narberth

Tom and Jackie Middleton's swimming pool is the jewel of Narbrook Circle. The cool aqua rectangle is nestled on the western side of the Middletons' house, which sits atop a hill and presides over the neighborhood. Standing on the porch of that home, one can easily survey the luscious green neighborhood, the houses that border it, and the stream that divides it in two. Narberth, their town, is a self-conscious time capsule of small-town America, always preserving old traditions alongside new ones: the Memorial Day parade, relay races at the playground, fireworks on the Fourth of July. Although the outskirts of Philadelphia begin only a few miles away, Narbrook Circle is the isolated within the isolated, a suboasis of the suburban oasis, a place as calm and beautiful as any place you could hope to be.

Tom, a psychiatrist, sees clients in the finished side of their basement. There is a separate back entrance to a room containing an armchair and a comfortable couch adorned with too many pillows. There's a side table with a box of tissues, a Venetian screen hiding an exercise bike, and nothing on the walls. One of Tom's clients is a seventeen-year-old boy by the name of Seth Lever. Seth attends a private Quaker school on City Avenue, where Jackie happens to be the guidance counselor. Seth is tall for his age and good looking, although he doesn't seem to know it. He dresses the same way he probably has since middle school: old T-shirts, jeans, and sneakers. In recent months Seth has become noticeably withdrawn and begun to fail his classes. While she did her best to help him, Jackie felt that Seth needed more frequent, longer sessions—beyond what she has time for—and that he might benefit from the positive male influence of her husband.

During their first session together, Seth plops down on the couch and says, "First off, you should know that I don't want to be here, and that I think therapy's bullshit."

After that, Seth says very little. He reveals only the most basic of information: his parents are divorced; he is bored by high school and thinks maybe he'll go to college to study music, if he goes at all. When Tom presses for more information, Seth mentions that he is also in the chess club at school and reads chess strategy books.

"I play a little chess myself," says Tom.

"Oh yeah?" Seth brightens.

"Sure, not so much now, but I was crazy about it in college. Used to reenact Bobby's games and whatnot. Fischer, I mean. We could play sometime."

"No thanks," says Seth, but Tom can see that he's tempted.

For Seth's next session, Tom brings the chess set down to the basement, just in case. He's read about therapists doing this—playing games with their clients to put them at ease. Seth is fairly nervous and it would be good for him to be able to relate to Tom over something he already understands.

The thing is, Seth isn't a shy kid. Tom can see that by the way he sits on the couch, leaning back, taking up lots of space. When he does speak he speaks confidently, knowing exactly how much he will reveal before he opens his mouth, unlike many people who negotiate with themselves halfway through a sentence.

At first, Tom doesn't mention the chess set, and Seth doesn't bring it up either. Tom begins as he normally would, by asking Seth what his goals are for therapy.

"I haven't set any goals," says Seth. "I already told you, it wasn't exactly my idea to come here."

"Whose idea was it?" asks Tom.

"My mom's, I guess."

"And why do you think she wants you to go to therapy?"

"I don't know, you'll have to ask her," answers Seth.

There is a touch of defiance in his voice, but it's nothing Tom hasn't seen before. Tom lets the room stay silent, giving Seth the space to say more, if he wants. Part of being a psychiatrist is learning to endure these awkward moments.

"I see you brought the board down," Seth says, after a while.

"I thought we might play a little, if you're up for it."

"I'm up for it."

As it turns out, Tom and Seth are pretty evenly matched. Tom lets the game run out the clock, and when he says, "Time's up," Seth doesn't conceal his disappointment.

That night, before going to sleep, Jackie asks Tom about Seth.

Tom thinks for a moment. "He's doing all right, I guess. He's a funny kid."

"You know, he's not popular. As far as I can tell, he doesn't belong to any groups at all. There aren't many students like that at Friends' Central. If they're not popular, they're into drama or something," says Jackie.

"He's into chess," says Tom.

"Oh really? I didn't know that."

"We played today. He's good. Really good."

"Hey, you know what you should do?" says Jackie.

"What?" he asks unenthusiastically.

"Switch sides. Turn the board around. Then you'll have to think like him and he'll have to think like you." Pleased with herself, Jackie kisses Tom and turns off the light.

The next time Seth comes in, Tom has the board set up between them on an old card table. The pieces are ready and waiting. They play five moves and then Tom turns the board around. Seth looks at him skeptically but doesn't ask for an explanation, and Tom doesn't offer one.

Viewing the board from Seth's perspective, Tom sees a complex web of attacks and defenses he only half understood from the other side. Seth's strategy is impressive, and as the board turns back and forth neither gains nor loses much ground.

It isn't until the third session of this game that Seth begins to open up on his own. Over the next several weeks, he tells Tom, in pieces at first, of an older woman he works for named Marianne. Several months ago, he saw a job posted on the Whole Foods community board for a gardener/general yard worker for a house in the neighborhood, and when he went to ask about it, Marianne hired him on the spot.

Seth even describes the house—a big, gray Victorian with azaleas out front. "She had me paint the columns on the porch pink and green," he tells Tom.

Immediately, Tom knows the house. There aren't many Victorian-style houses around, and he can picture that porch. At first he can't place it, but then he remembers; it's just around the corner on Windsor Avenue.

It doesn't take long for Tom to realize that Seth and Marianne are having an affair. Seth is smart and deliberately drops little hints. Initially, it's just the general way he talks about her, saying things like, "Marianne likes me to come over straight from school," or Marianne wants this and says that, etc. The more Seth lays it out for him, the more dubious Tom becomes. It's possible, isn't it, that Seth's leading him on, just to stay entertained? Of course, if Seth really is having this affair, the worst thing Tom could do is not believe him, so he puts his doubts aside, confident that the truth will out itself.

From what Tom can gather, the affair is surprisingly sexually mature, and other than the considerable age difference, there is no outward manipulation. But when Seth answers Tom's questions, he's using someone else's words. This is what worries Tom the most—Seth has no perspective. He doesn't know which way is up and which is down.

Tom thinks very carefully about how to proceed. He considers it to the point of agony, but doesn't discuss it with Jackie, sure that she'll overreact. Ultimately he decides that since Seth is almost eighteen, he should keep the information confidential. The circus that it could create would be far more damaging to Seth than if they managed it together, through therapy.

So, in their next appointment, Tom decides to address the topic more frankly, and ask questions that encourage Seth to speak freely about the relationship. What do you talk about? Not very much. What do you do? Have sex, mostly. Are there any other girls who you are interested in? No, not exactly.

Eventually Tom asks, "Do you love her?"

"No," Seth laughs, as if to say, *Come on, we're all adults here,* which of course they aren't.

The following weekend, Tom finds himself driving by the gray Victorian. The car in front of him has one of those bumper stickers that Tom hates: *I drive under 25 m.p.h. in Narberth, PA,* a pledge the driver observes with due diligence. As Tom creeps along well under the speed limit, he gets a good look at the house. He can see that Seth and Marianne haven't only been fucking; Seth's been working too. The yard looks immaculate.

The next day, passing by, he sees her. She is leaning against her doorframe, staring into nothing as if she is remembering something. Tom takes off his sunglasses to get a better look. He can't believe it, but it's her: Amelia Watson. She's lost some weight and she's dressing differently, maybe even dyed her hair too, but it is most definitely, unmistakably her, Amelia goddamn Watson. From the dark of the hallway, Seth emerges. She leans forward like she is going to kiss him goodbye, right there in the open. But before she gets too close, she catches herself and touches his shoulder instead. Tom slumps in the seat as Seth walks away, and Amelia retreats into the house.

At home, Tom unlocks his filing cabinet and thumbs through the manila folders until he finds it. *Watson, Amelia.* The first page of the file is the form that he requires all patients to fill out: a brief medical history and a confidentiality agreement. At the top of the page, in her tight handwriting, it reads, *Watson, Amelia Marianne.* Shaking, Tom closes the file.

It'd gone on for several months, and Jackie never knew. They'd kept up their weekly appointments for appearance, and they'd even done it on the couch in this very office. Once they started fucking it became impossible to talk, and the fifty-minute sessions were painfully slow. He'd ended it eventually, and Amelia had agreed it was best for her to move in with her sister in Rhinebeck, New York, where things are quieter and there are more open spaces. Tom even gave her the name of a therapist up there, a woman who'd come highly recommended.

That night, Tom takes Jackie out to dinner. Almost every Saturday they go into the city to try the latest restaurant written up in the *Main Line Times*, and tonight cannot be any different. They eat overpriced Mexican tapas, and on the way home, when Tom is careening down Schuylkill Expressway, Jackie reaches over and gently squeezes his crotch. Tom is stiff and guilty but he tells himself nothing's wrong. It is a warm summer night and Jackie turns off the air-conditioning and opens the windows.

At home, Jackie suggests they to go for a night swim, something she likes to do when her belly is full and her mood is high. They change into their bathing suits, wrap themselves in towels, and go out onto the deck. Jackie walks down the steps to the poolside, and Tom crosses the deck to switch on the underwater light. As soon as he flips it on, Jackie screams. In their neighborhood, which some say was designed to be an outdoor amphitheater, whispers carry like they do in the valleys of mountains. Hers is not a scream that Narbrook Circle has heard before, and to be sure, all of Narbrook Circle hears her scream.

Tom is at the railing. He sees what she sees, a body of a man—a boy—floating facedown in the pool. He doesn't have to look any closer to know that it's Seth Lever.

The police arrive, Jackie is crying, and the whole neighborhood is out, trying to get a look. Tom wishes, more than anything, that he were wearing something besides a bathing suit. The yard is roped off, there are police swarming the property, red lights shining on the pine trees. Everyone whispers that it's suicide. By the time they get Seth out of the pool, it's after midnight. They ask Tom to put on some clothes and drive down to the station, which he does. They don't make him bring Jackie with him. He tells them everything he can, but he doesn't mention Amelia Marianne.

When Tom gets home, Jackie is waiting up for him. She's

upset and wants to talk. Tom sits down next to her in the bed, and holds her while she cries into his armpit.

"How could this have happened?" she asks.

"Seth was a very disturbed person," says Tom.

"I know, I know. But it's just . . . Was he? Really? And in our pool? Why in our pool?" she moans.

Tom pulls his arm away and swings his legs off his side of the bed.

Jackie kneels behind him and rubs his back. "Oh, honey, I'm so sorry. It's not your fault."

Tom recoils. "I know it's not my fault!" he snaps, and goes to brush his teeth.

Several days pass and Tom is deteriorating. He can't sleep and on the rare occasions when he does drift off, Amelia is there, whispering something to him that he can't decipher, coming to him in dreams and nightmares both.

And so, when he can no longer bear it, he knocks on the door of the Victorian. She is wearing a tight skirt, a silk blouse, and high heels—all of them black. Her straw-blond hair is tied up in the style of an earlier decade, and her eye makeup is heavy and dark. Dangling from her ears are two large turquoise-and-silver earrings. The weight of the jewelry stretches her pierced ears, making the holes look like tiny twin urethras.

"Tom?" she asks, without smiling. She is only vaguely surprised, as if she'd known he would come, but hadn't expected him before noon.

"Hello, Amelia."

"Come in," she says, almost as an order, and pushes back the door.

She leads him into the parlor. There's a Persian rug, a baroque sofa with matching armchairs, a sculpture of Buddha,

Flemish-looking paintings, and African pottery. The coffee table appears to be covered in Turkish tiles.

"I see you've been doing some traveling," Tom observes.

"Here and there." Amelia gestures to one of the chairs. Tom sits, and she perches nervously on the center cushion of the sofa across from him. Couch and armchair, just like the old days.

Tom tries to find his practiced voice of authority—empathetic, but stern. "Amelia," he begins.

She winces at the sound of her own name. "Marianne, please. I'm going by my middle name these days. I never did like *Amelia*, it sounds like the name of a rock."

"All right, then. Marianne," Tom continues, as if he's talking to a child who insists on being treated like a grown-up. "I am not going to pretend that I'm not here for a reason."

"I assumed as much," she says. She takes out a cigarette.

"You smoke?" asks Tom accusingly.

As an answer, she lights her cigarette. "Look," she says, "I knew Seth was seeing a therapist, but I didn't know it was you, okay? I had to read it in the paper."

It occurs to Tom that now that she's gotten this out of the way, she expects him to console her with his professional opinion, *You couldn't have saved him, none of us could have,* and all the rest. To her, he is still her doctor.

So he asks questions. He makes her comfortable and earns her trust as he would with any patient. This doesn't take long. It seems that the minute he walked in the door her trust for him was renewed, on principle alone. He indicates that Seth told him about the nature of their relationship and invites her to talk about it. She is immediately forthcoming. So forthcoming, in fact, that Tom is taken aback. She tells him how it began, about the first time they had sex, about many times after that. She goes into great detail. She tells him how Seth was a virgin and how she made him into the lover she wanted.

With every detail she gives, Tom swallows his jealousy like a sword, one after another. He doesn't know quite how to respond; it was her reckless honesty that had attracted him to her in the first place—her titillating descriptions of her sexual encounters, and her eventual shameless acknowledgment of the tension between them. *It's okay*, she had said. *I want it too.*

Completely disarmed, Tom falls back on an old therapist standby. "Did you have reason to believe that Seth wanted to hurt himself?"

"No," she answers unequivocally. "I'm still in shock. I know he was depressed and was seeing someone, but we talked about it and it seemed within the range of reason for a seventeen-year-old boy."

"So you were comfortable with Seth being seventeen?"

"Yes, of course. I never asked him to be anything he wasn't," she says.

Tom is quiet, watching her. The old therapy trick, only she says nothing further. Unlike his patients, she is not bound to him for a full fifty minutes.

At this point, Amelia stands. She looks at Tom and waits for him to stand as well. "Look, Tom—"

"It's okay," he cuts her off. Whatever it is, he doesn't want to hear it.

"You are just the picture of professionalism. That's all," says Amelia.

Tom doesn't take this as a compliment. "I should go."

Amelia nods, and sees him to the door.

"I am sorry for your loss," Tom offers awkwardly.

"And I for yours," says Amelia.

Tom asks if he can come back sometime, to continue the conversation.

Amelia hesitates. "As a friend maybe. I don't need a therapist. Anymore." She smiles gamely. He's seen this look before. Tom wants to say something, but can't. She closes the door.

Tom stands on her porch and surveys the neighborhood. Children are coming to and from the playground, running ahead of their mothers and babysitters who call out for them to wait when they near a corner.

Reluctantly, he starts down the steps. A young man is mowing the lawn next door. He stops and waves to Tom, but Tom pretends not to see.

Rather than walking by the playground, Tom turns right and takes a shortcut down what the kids of Narbrook Circle call the "secret path" but what is really a short, wood-chipped foot trail between yards that isn't a secret at all.

From across the stream, Tom can see a black town car parked in front of his house. He hesitates, and contemplates turning around. But where would he go?

Tom crosses the little cement footbridge and starts up the hill to his house. As he draws near, he sees Jackie standing on the front porch. She has the same terrified look on her face she's worn since she found Seth. All she wants to do is close the pool; drain it, cover it, and forget it all ever happened. The detective on the case won't let her; he says that for now, it's still a crime scene. For as long as she looks out the windows of their house and sees the clear blue water collecting leaves and pine needles, as long as the caution tape stays strung around the fence line, she will continue to turn that terrified look on Tom. What pains him most about the look isn't that she's afraid he's capable of doing something awful, she's afraid he's incapable of doing something good.

"Hello, sweetheart," he says when she's within earshot.

"Did you enjoy your walk?" she asks, softening a little.

"Yes, although I probably should've driven out to Wissahickon and gotten some real exercise."

"Well, anyway," says Jackie, "it's good you didn't. Detective Hendricks is here to see you. He's waiting inside."

Jackie sets them up in the living room, each with a cup of coffee.

"Dr. Middleton," begins the detective. He pauses, presumably waiting for Tom to say, *No, call me Tom*, but Tom keeps quiet. The detective continues, "I apologize if I am repeating myself, but were you prescribing Seth any medication?"

"No," answers Tom, "you have his file."

"Yes, it's true, we do have his file. It's been very helpful, thank you. But what I'm wondering, Dr. Middleton," the detective leans forward on the floral couch cushions, "is if there is any information that didn't make it into Seth's file."

Tom repeats the spiel he gave at the station. "I don't take notes while I talk to patients. It unnerves them. After they leave, I write down all the important aspects of our conversation. It is not a transcript. They're meeting minutes, more like. We even recorded our moves when we played chess, sometimes. You can have those too, if you want."

"No, that won't be necessary," says the detective. "See, the autopsy results have come back, and there was a large amount of Xanax in his system. Did Seth suffer from anxiety?"

"Sure, but not enough for me to give him anything for it, in my professional opinion."

"Any idea where he might have gotten it?"

"My first guess would be from his mother. I'd be willing to bet she's had a prescription at some point. Having a depressed son causes a lot of anxiety. If not from her, a friend's parent, maybe."

"Thank you, Dr. Middleton," says the detective.

"Of course," says Tom, "if there is anything else I can do . . ." He stands up.

"Actually, there is one other thing," says Detective Hendricks. He waits for Tom to sit back down. "Now, this is sensitive information, and I'd appreciate it if you kept it confidential."

Tom agrees.

"You see, in the autopsy, there was no water found in Seth's lungs."

"Excuse me?"

"Yes. There's a thing called 'dry drowning' when a victim doesn't inhale any water and eventually dies of cardiac arrest. One sees this in a very small percent of drowning victims. But normally, even if someone wants to die, there is panic before it actually happens, and they open their mouth and, well, you know the rest. So in the case of a suicide, if someone were to 'dry drown,' so to speak, they would have to be, excuse me for saying this, very determined." Detective Hendricks looks Tom in the eyes, but only to prove a point. He doesn't invite Tom to respond. "Now, in your notes, there is almost nothing about Seth being suicidal, am I right?"

"That is correct, detective," Tom answers. "I didn't perceive it to be a concern. However, Seth was extremely intelligent. And if he was truly determined to end his own life, then he would have deliberately kept that from me."

"I suppose so," says Detective Hendricks. This time, the detective stands up first.

Tom puts out his hand, and the man holds on for too long.

As soon as the detective's car is out of sight, Tom goes

down to the unfinished side of the basement. He reaches his hand behind a shelf and pulls out several sheets of white paper. He kept his notes on "Marianne" separate from all else he and Seth talked about. The moral ambiguity of his decision to keep it confidential, and the unique nature of the affair—well, that's what he'd done anyway. It's no crime to keep something on a separate sheet of paper.

The night that Seth died, before the police arrived, he'd gone downstairs and removed those pages. He did it almost without thinking—it was a reflex of self-preservation—and now, here they were, stuffed behind a dirty tool shelf.

Tom stands there, reads through every word, and then burns them in the utility sink with a kitchen match.

The answer he gave Detective Hendricks is technically sound. If Seth had taken a lot of Xanax it might have helped him to stay calm through the experience, more so if he'd also been drinking. He might have even passed out and fallen in. Tom should've said that.

It's a decent theory, but he doesn't want it to be true. As soon as he admits that to himself, the dam breaks, his instincts rush in, and suddenly he is swimming in them. He must see Amelia.

Tom leaves the house out the back door, the one reserved for his patients, and walks directly to Amelia's house. He resists the urge to run so as not to attract attention.

When Amelia answers the door she is crying. She has changed into a sleeveless red dress that grazes the tops of her knees, paired with the same turquoise earrings, as if she had planned to go out.

Tom touches her face, sensitively, to see if she'll accept his comfort. She doesn't pull away.

He steps inside, draws her to him, and they are kissing.

He's surprised by how much he wants her; his desire has its own inertia, like a feverish fit or a drunken tirade. Amelia wants it too, he can tell, but in her own way.

"Don't stop," she says.

He holds her tighter. She doesn't want him to be anything he isn't, he reminds himself.

After, Tom is getting dressed. There is no postcoital relief. Neither wants to hold the other. Tom goes into the bathroom to wash up and checks her medicine cabinet. Xanax.

In that bazaar of a living room, Amelia is lying on the couch in her bra and panties, smoking a cigarette. Tom looks down at her.

"Did you do it?" asks Tom.

"Do what?" she says.

"Kill him. Fuck him then kill him."

"No I didn't kill him. What the hell's wrong with you?" Amelia stands up and starts collecting her clothes. She touches one ear, feels her earring, and then touches the other and finds a bare lobe.

"Wrong with me?" Tom yells, "Nothing's wrong with me! How am I supposed to know what you're capable of?"

"Listen to me," Amelia says in a tone that indicates that actually, she is capable of a lot. "Seth killed *himself*. He went to you for help and you didn't help him. Why the hell else do you think he ended up in your pool, of all places? He wanted you to know you failed him." Amelia sits down on the sofa, looking at her dress crumpled in her lap. "You know," she turns to look at Tom, "people always say that this sort of thing isn't anyone's fault. But you and I both know the truth. It's always someone's fault. Every single time." At this, Amelia straightens. "Get out of my house."

Tom is standing over her. He looks at her face, expecting

to find either vengeance or guilt, but she is expressionless. He has never known her to lie.

He turns to leave, and in the foyer by the door he sees Amelia's other turquoise earring lodged in the carpet. He picks it up, slips it in his pocket, and slams the door behind him.

The following day, Detective Hendricks tells the Middletons they're going to drain the pool. Detective Hendricks comes to supervise a crew of crime scene investigators dressed in navy-blue jumpsuits and latex gloves. It takes half a day for the water to drain, siphoned out onto the street and running down the hill into the gutter. Tom and Jackie watch from the deck as the men sweep the cement and unclog the filter. The last remnants of summer combed together with the early signs of fall give the yard the look of an unvisited cemetery, the diving board marking the head of its only grave. Tom squeezes Jackie's hand, knowing that after today he will have to deny almost everything, and knowing, too, that she will believe him. Satisfied, Tom watches a young man, not much older than Seth, reach his hand into the drain at the bottom of the pool and pull out a piece of jewelry that catches the light, ever so slightly, through its scummy exterior.

PART III

The Faker City

PART III

FISHTOWN ODYSSEY

BY MEREDITH ANTHONY

Fishtown

Megan stepped out of her fashionable red door in the trendiest part of Fishtown, drinking in the cold, clear afternoon air. She stood on the stoop, locked the door behind her, and turned, putting her keys in her handbag, juggling her Kenneth Cole overnight bag. She walked down the first of the three steps that led to the sidewalk and stepped on a woman's hand.

Megan shrieked. The woman shrieked. Megan stumbled and, for a moment, thought she might fall.

"I'm so sorry. So sorry," she said, apologizing reflexively as she righted herself. Luckily, she was wearing snow boots instead of her strappy high heels or she would certainly have fallen. And why she should apologize she didn't know, since the woman, old and dirty, had no business lounging on Megan's well-kept steps. She shrugged to settle the Michael Kors cashmere coat on her shoulders, pulling it together against the cold.

"That dress is too young for you. You're not that young," snarled the old woman malevolently, rubbing her injured hand, having caught a glimpse beneath the coat of the bronze metallic sheath that Megan had bought for an extravagant price the week before.

"Excuse me," Meg muttered, losing all sympathy with the old crone. "I'm in a hurry." She went down the rest of the steps, giving the woman a wide berth.

"You won't be the prettiest one there. Or the youngest," the old woman called after her.

"Jesus," Meg breathed. "What a bitch." But she shook off her irritation. Nothing was going to spoil her mood. Today was the high point of her year.

The Daggers' New Year's Eve extravaganza was, for Megan, the party to end all parties. First, it was a truly great, well-planned gathering. Drinks at seven, buffet dinner at nine, desserts and coffee at eleven for a little jolt of caffeine and sugar, watch the ball drop at midnight, karaoke and drunken dancing after that. The party ended with a hot breakfast the next morning, where bedraggled women avoided meeting the eyes of the friends whose husbands they had made out with in dark corners of the enormous suburban house. Second, it was a social coup to be invited to the best New Year's eve party on the Main Line. Most important, for Megan, it was a taste of the life she wanted, the life she was working toward, the life she was destined for.

Megan had prepared like an athlete, sleeping in this morning, eating a big lunch, laying down a base. When she jumped on the subway at Girard Avenue and Front Street bound for 30th Street Station and then the Paoli local to Bryn Mawr, she was ready. It was only a one-hour trip but it was a journey to another world.

Megan had inherited her family's home in Fishtown, a former blue-collar ghetto that was being steadily gentrified. She was renovating it, bit by bit, to improve its value, watching the real-estate market for the right time to sell. Many young professionals would love to live in increasingly fashionable Fishtown, but Megan dreamed only of an address on the Main Line.

Megan was one of Bess Dagger's best friends. Bess, having

spent the day in Bryn Mawr helping her sister Anise prepare, picked Megan up at the Bryn Mawr train station. As they drove through the lovely town to Anise's large, comfortable house, Bess chattered away about the guest list. Both Anise's daughters were home. Glamourous Carrie had brought home a girl, a classmate from Yale, while her slightly mousy sister Celia had brought home a boyfriend from law school. Anise wasn't sure which of her girls she was more worried about. Celia's boyfriend from Georgetown Law was tall and good looking. Her sister Carrie had already wondered aloud why Celia could get such a prize and she couldn't. Of course, Celia wasn't unattractive. She was a Dagger, after all. Beauty was an acknowledged family trait among the Daggers. Beauty and loyalty, Meg mused, really defined them.

Among the older set, Anise's neighbor and best friend Paula and her faithless husband, the cute French bond trader Henri, had split up. Again. Paula was coming, naturally, but everyone wondered if Henri might just turn up too, since he had always been invited before. They were trying to decide what to do about it if he did. The ugly next-door neighbors were already there, of course. They didn't have a life of their own, with their ramshackle house and ghastly, troubled children—they virtually lived through Anise and Thom.

As they drove from the station, Bess went on and on, pausing only to admire Megan's low-cut gleaming dress and her newly botoxed forehead that matched Bess's own. Megan listened, looking out the car window, drinking in the snowy town. Bess, who had grown up in nearby Ardmore, was non-chalant, but it still took Megan's breath away. Philly's best address. One of the East Coast's most exclusive moneyed enclaves. The fabled Main Line.

Bess and Megan were both a little over forty, although

each admitted only to thirty. Bess was lovely, blond like all the Daggers, smooth-skinned, perfectly made up, dressed in vintage Versace. Megan herself was still quite attractive, no matter what the old hag had said, with her gym-toned body, her chic auburn shag, her bronze sheath, her Judith Lieber lioness minaudiere.

Bess worked in corporate marketing, Megan in Philadelphia's top ad agency. They both made good money, lived well, took care of themselves. They didn't really date anymore—there were no straight, single, solvent men between forty and sixty-five left in Philly, as everyone very well knew—but they went out with each other or various friends and colleagues several nights a week, and frequently drank a bit too much.

At New Year's, though, Megan knew how to pace herself. She had a system. You start slow, have plenty of hors d'oeuvres, enough dinner to count, and only drink champagne. Her first flute was handed to her by Anise, who greeted them at the door. "My other sister," she declared as she always did, hugging Meg warmly. "You look gorgeous, darling."

It was a greeting that never failed to delight Megan, herself an only child of cold, judgmental parents, sparing in their love and praise. As Meg was trading her boots for high-heeled sling-backs, Michelle, the third blond Dagger sister, swept her up in yet another bear hug. Laughing, Meg held her champagne aloft with difficulty to avoid a spill. She fairly purred with pleasure.

"Sisters," Meg murmured. "The divine Dagger sisters."

Thom also hugged her and took her overnight bag up to a guest room he called "your room," which made her laugh even more. If only it were true.

As the party kicked in, she got buzzed enough to enjoy herself. She remained gracious in the presence of the unendurable ugly neighbors, listening to the sad story of their surly daughter's latest drug-fueled escapade.

Meg exchanged air kisses with Paula and tolerated her whining about her faithless French husband, the delicious Henri. And then there he was. Henri. He did indeed show up—how dare he?

There was a breathless pause as every conversation stopped. Then Anise strolled over and, after the briefest moment, standing before him—would she kiss him or slap him—kissed him on both cheeks. "Henri."

"*Chère* Anise," Henri murmured, holding her hand to his lips. He was darkly handsome with his perfect stubble, kissable mouth, and single diamond earring. The Dagger sisters couldn't resist him. He enhanced their blond beauty with his own dark European charm. He took a flute of champagne and prowled around the party, providing titillation and frissons of mock horror wherever he circulated. He looked every bit the dissipated Eurotrash he was, lured back, no doubt, by the realization that all the money was from Paula's family and was still in Paula's name.

Megan gave a warm hug to Anise's lackluster daughter Celia and shook hands with her tall, damp-palmed boyfriend. Then she made a point of bonding with the more beautiful daughter Carrie and her college friend Lulu, a blond look-alike from Boston. Meg prided herself on remaining hip—dropping pop culture references and pertinent song lyrics from the latest Grammy winners and catchphrases from hip TV shows like *Gossip Girl*.

Carrie, tall and glamourous, was particularly striking tonight in a low-cut, short, creamy silk Grecian tunic, which showed off her considerable cleavage and long, tan legs. With her father's lanky grace and the Dagger blond beauty, Carrie was a remarkable girl and she had always loved Megan. Her friend Lulu, every bit her match, wore a white angora mini-dress, which had to have been planned to coordinate with her friend.

The college kids were amused by Megan and stayed with her for some time, laughing and making sly comments about the other guests before trailing down to the large family room to warm up the karaoke machine for later. Megan smiled with satisfaction. The Daggers were a large, close-knit WASP clan so unlike Meg's own small, disaffected, heathen brood. She adored them all and would do anything for them, anything at all.

Meg got some more champagne from the jeroboam of Moët that Michelle Dagger's brash alcoholic husband insisted on bringing every year. He never tired of hearing the women coo and squeal about how big it was. Meg never tired of drinking good champagne so she endured his usual size-really-matters jokes with aplomb.

Then came the scream. Because Meg observed her stringent party regimen, she was sober, or sober enough, to respond quickly when she heard it. She was the first to arrive in the doorway of the darkened den off the living room, lit only by Christmas lights and candles and typically functioning as a sin bin for guests' brief, illicit, champagne-fueled encounters.

Meg stopped abruptly in the doorway, causing other party guests to pile up behind her. Anise Dagger was sitting in the center of a velvet-upholstered sofa, her tall, gorgeous daughter Carrie sprawled, on her back, over Anise's lap, head dangling like a broken doll. Carrie's long bare arms and legs hung on either side of her mother. Anise held her and looked up at Meg with an expression of pure anguish.

It took a minute to register the tableau, as still and composed as any Renaissance sculpture. Then Meg realized that the scream, more of a howl, really, had been Carrie's and that the girl was limp but breathing, weeping extravagantly in her mother's arms.

"The Bryn Mawr *Pietà*," Meg whispered involuntarily, and guests behind her took up the phrase and repeated it in low tones. Bess pushed past Meg and crouched before her sister and her stricken niece.

Anise's husband Thom shouldered his way into the room and scooped up Carrie, who hung on him, upright but limp, still weeping into his starched white shirt. He shot Anise a look and she returned it with a shrug. Bess was still crouching beside Anise, holding her hand.

Carrie started mumbling and slurring about how life was hell and she couldn't bear it, couldn't bear it, it was so difficult, so hard, she couldn't, no, no, no, she just couldn't. Thom, full of concern a moment ago, stiffened and held her out from him, her head still wobbling on her long neck, her expensively layered hair tousled, eyes red and rolling.

"Carrie, you're drunk," he announced sternly in a loud and serious baritone.

"Life is hell, just pure hell, and I can't." His daughter paused to hiccup. "I can't, can't, can't bear it. I can't."

"Carrie." Thom shook her slightly, this tall, gorgeous creature, limp and sodden but still beautiful in her lavish distress. "You are going to your room. Right now."

Megan suppressed a smile. Would the drunken, nearly adult Amazon-like Carrie go to her room like a disobedient child? Poor Thom was clueless. He shook her again until she straightened up enough to walk and nudged her to the door to send her upstairs. She broke loose and turned back to her mother with another bone-chilling wail.

Anise opened her arms and Carrie flung herself back on her mother's lap, burrowing her face in Anise's shoulder and blubbering into her neck. Anise shrugged again at Thom and wrapped her arms protectively around her large, distraught daughter, rocking her in her arms. Bess reached up and tenderly rubbed Carrie's back, exposed in the backless silk tunic. Michelle, the third Dagger sister, squeezed by Megan and rushed to help console her niece.

Poor Thom. He opened his mouth to protest again, but evidently realized he could never prevail against the massed determination of the Dagger sisters when they closed ranks. He stood for a moment, helpless, until Megan took his arm. He let her lead him from the room, the other guests scattering in front of them, muttering and giggling. Megan heard the phrase "Bryn Mawr *Pietà*" repeated a number of times. She wished she'd never said it.

Thom rallied then, and called out, "Let's have more champagne, shall we? It's almost midnight." And that, Meg thought, was that.

The party rolled on inexorably. The ball dropped. Kisses were exchanged. Anise circulated again, her composure restored, laughing charmingly about young women and their angst. Even Carrie reappeared, her face freshly scrubbed, tossing her blond hair and looking only slightly embarrassed.

Henri and Paula were evidently having a rapprochement in the butler's pantry, breathing heavily, startled like deer when Megan discovered them. They were kissing in a dark alcove beside the Sub-Zero, his hand inside her sweater, her pale face reddened where his stubbled chin had rubbed it, his leg between hers, her skirt hiked up around the tops of her thighs. Paula gasped and he laughed darkly when Meg, in search of some ice water, walked in.

Meg, who had herself spent some time in Henri's arms an hour earlier, her own face still smarting from his fashionable stubble, her own thighs aching where his leg had thrust between them, smiled benignly and closed the refrigerator door, darkening the tiny pantry again. Her smile disappeared as she returned to the dining room, reflecting on the faithless, feckless ways of men, particularly the French.

The college kids emerged from the family room downstairs to announce that the karaoke machine was ready for action. Pulsing rock music beckoned, drowning out the Christmas carols on the iPod upstairs. Most of the revelers who were still standing trooped unsteadily down the steps, ready to continue drinking and watch each other strutting and mugging and stumbling over complicated lyrics sung alarmingly off-key.

With very little prodding, Carrie gave her patented rendition of Cher's "Believe" in her perfect, sexy, adenoidal alto, complete with reverb on the chorus, "*After love, after love, after love, after love.*" It was a tough act to follow.

Carrie's college friend Lulu took up the challenge with an overheated version of Beyonce's "If I Were a Boy." Meg thought she saw something smug and proprietary in Henri's dark admiring look as he watched the young woman shimmy up and down the structural pole that pierced the makeshift dance floor like a ship's mast.

Meg followed, jumping in with a Gwen Stefani number that allowed her to wiggle her well-toned ass while soothing her overheated thighs by clamping them around the pole. "*I know I've been a real bad girl,*" she cooed as suggestively as Gwen ever did. She gave a nod of sympathy to Paula, who was disheveled after her clinch with her husband, but who nevertheless looked pleased with herself.

Henri had eyes only for his wife as he vamped to a Kanye

West number, almost making Meg believe he had reformed. Then he disappeared, no doubt upstairs kissing someone else's wife and congratulating himself on his renewed conquest of his own poor spouse. Paula, the pathetic victim of his many indiscretions, was now passed out in a chair in the corner.

An hour later, Meg was moving from pleasantly buzzed into the more dangerous territory of completely torched. Her patented system, she had to admit, was failing. She was on a sofa in the family room trapped between the ugly neighbors. She listened halfheartedly to the ugly wife whine about her dissolute teenagers; on her other side, the ugly husband surreptitiously trailed his pinky along Meg's thigh. Did he really think that was sexy? she thought irritably. Did the ugly wife really think that dressing for a New Year's Eve party meant a pilled Fair Isle sweater? Meg raised her glass only to find it empty.

Bess was wrapping her supple leg around the pole, growling like an improbable Justin Timberlake that she was going to bring sexy back. *"I'm bringing sexy back. Just like a heart attack."*

Meg was pretty sure those weren't the actual lyrics. She got up abruptly, interrupting the ugly wife in mid-whine and the ugly husband in mid-whatever. Ignoring their surprised expressions, she headed up the stairs.

Walking fairly steadily, Meg made a fairly complete circuit of the house, from the karaoke-singing sirens downstairs to the trash-strewn buffet table where men like Michelle's dissolute husband had turned into pigs. Congealed meatballs dribbled from his mouth as he leered at her lasciviously. Another porcine guest saluted her with a chicken wing dripping sauce in one hand, a scum of dip across his sweatered chest.

Hearing a groan as she passed a powder room, dark as a cave, she nudged open the door to discover the ugly neighbor, one hand clamped to his eye, mumbling that someone had hit him and knocked out a contact lens or maybe knocked it in and scratched a cornea. He beckoned her in to help him. But Meg shook her head and kept moving.

She watched as various mini-dramas played out. On the sunporch, the beautiful daughter Carrie, evidently almost sober, talked intently to someone on her cell phone. Upstairs, the mousy daughter Celia sat weeping hopelessly outside a closed bedroom door, crooning her boyfriend's name.

In the living room, she saw Michelle's husband again—was he everywhere?—drunk as a monkey, suddenly smile wolfishly and lean in to lick the face of the startled ugly neighbor. The ugly man pushed him, and Michelle's husband fell against the mantle, laughing manically. He laughed even louder when the ugly husband roughly pushed his own ugly wife, as she tried to wipe the spittle off her husband with her sweater sleeve.

Megan stepped neatly between the two men, the Scylla and Charybdis of the party, both dangerously drunk, staggering, both reaching for her with sticky, amorous hands. The grotesquely ugly man, groping toward Megan, was deaf to the angry scolding of his monstrous, homely wife. Meg left the sorry spectacle behind her and kept going.

Anise in the kitchen talking seriously with her sister Michelle. Lulu laughing huskily as she tottered down the stairs in impossibly high heels, wiping her mouth on the back of her manicured hand. Upstairs, Henri furtively leaving a darkened bedroom in which Megan glimpsed someone—Carrie?—on the bed. Henri sidled past Megan, tucking in his shirt, favoring her with his handsome, slightly sneering Gallic smile. Downstairs, Bess stalking angrily out of the den, her botoxed forehead unwrinkled but her eyes flashing her displeasure. Thom almost surreptitiously collecting glasses and ferrying them to the kitchen to be tucked into the capacious dishwasher.

Meg kept circulating, watching, stopping only occasionally, like some restless voyager searching for home.

It must have been four a.m. when a scream again rent the air, parting the haze of candle smoke, potpourri, and the mild fug of sweating, tired revelers. Again, Meg reacted, galvanized, as though she had somehow known it was coming.

Again, she drew up short at the doorway to the dimly lit den, adrenaline making her feel suddenly sober. Anise was sitting as before in the center of the velvet sofa, surrounded by candles and Christmas lights, her anguish evident on her lovely face. Again, the tall, gorgeous young woman was draped across her lap, head dangling, blond hair streaming across her face, arms and legs hanging limply.

Meg stepped into the room. It was the same as before, but also completely different. She knew that this time it was Anise who had screamed, not her daughter. Anise howled again, more animal moan than scream.

This time the doll was really broken. A thread of red blood trailed from the corner of her mouth. Anise shifted her grip, almost as if to offer the girl to Megan. The girl's head lolled grotesquely and her hair spilled to one side.

Megan gasped, realizing that it was not Carrie who Anise held, but Carrie's college friend Lulu. And Lulu was quite, quite dead.

Anise's face, pale and ravaged by a terrible grief, told Megan, even without a word, that Anise thought the girl across her lap was her beloved daughter.

"Oh no, Anise. It's not Carrie. See?" Meg knelt beside her, her impulse to curb Anise's dreadful suffering blotting out everything, even the awfulness of Lulu's death. "See?" She touched the girl's head, sickeningly wobbly on her neck, brushing aside the razor-cut blond shag. Anise, evidently in shock and not far from fainting, slowly, slowly looked down. She slowly, slowly focused her gaze of bottomless pity and terror on the dead girl's ghastly, waxen face.

Anise stood up abruptly, unceremoniously dumping Lulu's corpse onto Megan. Meg toppled backward, panicked, scrambling to right herself and get out from under the dead girl, a primitive fear kicking in.

Strong hands helped Meg. Bess pulled her up and steadied her. Thom picked up the girl's body and laid it tenderly on the sofa where Anise had been sitting. He took a minute to straighten the clothes, pulling down the short angora dress, putting the arms straight at her sides, tilting the head, lolling on the broken neck, so that the thread of blood did not mar the upholstery.

Thom then turned to Anise, but she was already moving, staggering out of the room, shouldering aside anyone in her way, looking for her daughter. Bess followed close behind her.

Meg registered all these details as pandemonium broke out around her. Guests, summoned by Anise's howls but slowed by alcohol, appeared in the doorway, reacting to the tragedy. Megan heard weeping, at least one person vomiting, someone calling 911. She turned to Thom.

"Help me, Meg," he said quietly. "We've got to get everyone out of this room."

She nodded and together they started herding out the curious, nudging, even pushing, until the dimly lit room was empty of the living. They stood together, shoulder to shoulder, looking in at the lovely room. Chintz sofas, comfy chairs, warm Aubusson carpet, silk shaded brass lamps, the traditionally decorated Christmas tree in one corner, the dead college girl on the couch.

It seemed like only moments until a rush of cold air from the foyer and gruff men's voices heralded the arrival of the Lower Merion police.

The investigation was a blur, managing to be intrusive, hyper-real, boring, unfocused, and intense, all at once. Most of the time Meg felt as though she were underwater. Technicians took over the living room. The immediate family was sequestered downstairs in the family room. Guests were asked to wait in the dining room, guarded by two uniformed officers who coped with a barrage of requests to use forbidden cell phones, to go to the bathroom, to leave and come back in the morning.

One by one, they were each brought to the kitchen for an interview with the two detectives, who put their questions quietly and took notes. A steady stream of uniformed officers and technicians came and went, each leaning down to whisper information or request instructions from the seated detectives. Someone had made coffee.

Among the last to be interviewed, Meg told the detectives what she could. It was a party like many others, confused, eventful, inconsequential. Soon forgotten, except, of course, for the murder.

She was leaving the kitchen, gratefully clutching her mug of coffee, when an officer brought Henri in for his interview, his head down, disheveled, looking even more broodingly handsome than ever. Meg glanced at him, passing, then stopped. Henri had already begun to speak in his charmingly accented voice, roughened by alcohol and a hint of something else. Megan stood stunned to hear Henri confess.

"I did it, you know? I murdered that poor girl. I didn't mean to, you know? But I did it. I'm sorry. *Désolé.*"

His anguish was genuine. Tears streamed from beneath his

long lashes. He ran a hand through his tousled hair, then over his stubbled, cleft chin. "I'm sorry. You know? I didn't mean it. It just happened, you know?"

Meg gaped at him. He was almost as broken as Lulu had been, a monster, a chimera assembled from parts of his former self. His life was over too, and he knew it.

"I wanted her, you know? Sex, it's what the party is all about, no? Sex. She wanted it too, but then she changed her mind, pushed me away." A trace of a smile crossed his face, a remnant of his old roguish charm. "Me. She pushed me away. I knew she wanted it, you know? I took her shoulders and shook her, hard, to make her see reason, you know? But she passed out. I was sure it was only that." He drew himself up a little. "I make love to a lot of women, you know? But never when they are passed out. So I left the bedroom, my beautiful little *chérie* untouched on the bed. But I must have killed her. Shook her too hard. Her neck must have snapped, you know? I am . . . I am *désolé*."

His voice broke, his shoulders shook, he dropped his head into his arms on the counter and wept. Meg's mind reeled. She watched until, at a signal from a detective, an officer put his hand on her arm and led her out of the kitchen.

As she left the room, Meg heard the detective ask Henri how the body had ended up in the den. She knew without looking that Henri only shrugged.

After a long while, the guests were released, shocked, tired, bedraggled, and grief stricken, to make their way home. No one met anyone else's eyes. An officer asked Meg if she wanted to return to Philadelphia at once, but Thom told them she had planned to stay overnight and was considered family. Meg smiled at him gratefully. She would stay.

Brought back through the living room, Meg stood at the

entrance to the den and saw the body was gone. Most of the family was now gathered there, sitting on the sofa where the dead girl had lain. Carrie was hunched over, hugging herself, crying. Anise was sitting beside her daughter, looking stunned, reaching out to stroke her arm occasionally, reassuring herself that she was still there. Celia and her boyfriend, their spat evidently forgotten, cuddled in a large chair, her eyes puffy and red, his hand unsteady as he stroked her head.

Bess stood by the fireplace, a glass of champagne, incredibly, in her hand. She smiled at Meg and raised her glass a fraction of an inch, a vestigial toast between friends. In her look there was a trace of something more, a hint of a question, a challenge. Meg, her eyes clear, calmly nodded back. Friends. More. Sisters.

Michelle and her drunken husband had evidently gone home. Most of the police were gone as well. Henri, shattered, had been led out in handcuffs, his leather coat draped raffishly over his shoulders. Henri's wife Paula, distraught and incoherent, had been bundled out by a female officer before Henri was led away.

Poor Paula. Poor Henri. Megan knew that Henri had not killed this girl. Henri, guilty of many unsavory things, had killed no one.

Oh, he believed he had. His confession had been genuine and it would be accepted as fact. He would receive his punishment, his marriage over, his life, and Paula's, in ruins. But actually he hadn't done it, Meg knew. Meg didn't care. She knew it was callous of her, but she just didn't.

Her heart was with her friends, the Daggers. The Daggers of Bryn Mawr. The beautiful blond Dagger sisters and their families. Her sisters. Her friends. Bess. Dear Bess, standing by the fireplace, drinking champagne, looking so *soignée*.

Meg had known it wasn't Henri from the moment she heard his touching, sad, rambling, French-accented confession—"So I left the bedroom, my beautiful little *chérie* untouched on the bed. But I must have killed her. Shook her too hard. Her neck must have snapped, you know?"

But it hadn't been Lulu on the bed. He had left his beautiful little Carrie there. Not *chérie*, Carrie. Passed out, or just pretending, teasing him. He shook her, yes, but when Meg had glanced in she was sure she had seen the girl stirring. And while Henri might have been drunk enough to confuse the two beautiful college girls, Meg wasn't. It was Carrie on the bed, alive and well. And although the police had probably asked Henri repeatedly how the body ended up in the den, Henri would only demur, shrugging, maintaining that he didn't know. Had no idea. It didn't matter. They had a confession.

Meg knew that Henri hadn't done it. But who had?

Standing there watching the family, Meg carefully replayed the evening in her head. It passed before her eyes like stills from a movie. Celia outside a bedroom sobbing, calling her boyfriend's name. Why? Someone had surely lured the hapless college boy into a dark bedroom. Lulu, smug and tipsy, wiping her mouth, heading downstairs. Had Celia killed her in a drunken, jealous rage? She stared at Celia, mousy and red-eyed. Hard to believe.

She thought of Bess coming out of the darkened den, angry at something or someone. The den. Lulu was killed in the den right where she was found. She had fallen to the floor beside the sofa and lay there until Anise found her and scooped her onto her lap, in a mother's anguish for her lovely daughter. She had indeed been shaken by someone quite angry. Shaken until her neck snapped.

Meg looked at Bess. She could see how it had happened.

Bess, protective of her nieces, furious that Lulu had come on to poor Celia's handsome, spineless boyfriend, had confronted the drunken college girl in the den. Angry that a gorgeous little interloper would come in to the fabulous Dagger family and hurt even the least of its members, the weakest sister, poor little Celia.

No one spoke for a long time. Finally, Thom roused himself. "I'll make breakfast," he announced flatly.

And so, life goes on, Meg thought, reaching up to brush her hair away from her eyes. She wished she could brush away what she knew, which seemed to be pressing, almost physically, on her skull.

Bess threw back her head and downed the champagne, then headed after Thom, slipping her arm through Megan's on the way, pulling her gently along past the law students cuddling, almost cowering in their armchair.

"We'll help," she said brightly, irrelevantly, since Anise and Carrie were still lost in their cocoon of grief, guilt, relief—a girl was dead but it wasn't Carrie. Gorgeous, glamourous Carrie, full of life and hope, momentarily shattered by the proximity of death, but soon to rally. She was too full of gusto to mourn too long. *Joie de vivre.* That's what Carrie had, Megan thought. *Joie de vivre.* Funny that the perfect phrase to describe her should be French.

Megan squeezed her friend's arm as they followed Thom to the kitchen. The last silent policeman was leaving with an armload of notebooks and evidence bags. A good start to his new year. Justice had triumphed on New Year's Day.

Of course, Meg knew that justice had not triumphed. Justice had not triumphed at all.

Bess stopped in the doorway to the kitchen. Thom had already pulled on his chef's apron and they could see him rummaging in the refrigerator for the casserole of eggs and cheese and ham that had been resting overnight and just needed to be slipped into the oven. Bess touched Megan's face and met her eyes.

"It's okay," she told Meg quietly. "I'll keep your secret."

"My secret?" Meg was startled.

Bess looked closely at her. "It wasn't you?"

Meg shook her head. "I thought it was you."

Bess stared at her and shook her head.

"Then who?" Meg asked.

Megan and Bess stood and stared at each other as they both silently thought through the suspects. Thom. Anise. Carrie, herself. Michelle, even. Any of the Daggers. Meg was suddenly, strangely proud to have been suspected.

"But I saw you coming out of the den," Meg blurted out. "You looked so angry."

Bess just stared at her.

"You looked like you could kill someone. I thought you must have confronted Lulu over poor Celia's boyfriend."

"Confronted her?" Bess laughed mordantly. "I wish. No, she wasn't there. I was angry with her. Very angry. I was talking to Anise. I told Anise."

"Anise?"

Bess and Megan were standing there outside the kitchen, staring at each other, and they both jumped a little when Anise came up behind them.

"Anise," Bess murmured.

"Anise," Meg echoed. And for a moment, Meg flashed back to the old hag on her steps, telling her she wouldn't be the youngest one. Nor the prettiest. True, but she was one of them, the Daggers. That's what counted.

Anise hugged them both. Anise, who could never have

mistaken another girl for her beloved daughter. Anise, who could never have mistaken the feel of an angora dress for a silk one as she held the dead girl in her arms. The mythology was all wrong. It wasn't the *Pietà* at all. It was Penelope among the dead, unwelcome suitors, her knitting all unravelled.

"My sisters," Anise whispered, hugging them hard, then breaking free to look from one to the other.

"Sisters," Bess said.

"Sisters," Meg said firmly.

Anise released them and they entered the kitchen.

"Tell you what, let's empty the dishwasher and fill it up again. Give Thom some room to work."

"I'll do the glasses by hand," Meg offered.

Thom shot them a smile.

Anise kissed Megan lightly on the cheek. Then she pulled an apron down from the hooks near the door and tied it on, and passed another to Bess, laughing as Bess rummaged through an army of bottles, all empty.

"I'll open more champagne," Bess declared, heading for the refrigerator. "We can't work without champagne."

They bent to their tasks. Meg looked forward to breakfast on a sunny New Year's Day morning in a sparkling clean kitchen on Philadelphia's Main Line. She belonged here. She had arrived. She was home.

YOUR BROTHER, WHO LOVES YOU

BY JIM ZERVANOS

Fairmount

Friday night, and Nicky Krios is getting dolled up for Nostradamus of all places. These biker boots are made for ass-kicking, he thinks, and tries the eyeliner he borrowed from Janet the bartender's purse. He hams it up in the mirror, imagining the two of them in another lazy romp, picking up where they left off after work the other night, before passing out on his couch. The darkened eyes bring out the family face—his brother's, his father's. He smirks. A veritable *Night of the Living Dead*.

Nicky spends most of his days wishing he were anywhere *but* Nostradamus, or at least *doing* anything else. Three years experience, and he's still a busboy, despite his pleas to Victor Gold, who treats him like a fucking retard. Still, Nostradamus is the hottest place in Philly, so where else is he going to go on his night off? Plus, he and his workmates have made a game out of sneaking drinks to spite Victor, who parks his yellow Maserati right outside and cocks around, convinced he's got the world licked.

Such is life for Nicky at twenty-four, living rent-free, at least for now, in a nearby brownstone, thanks to his older brother Chris Krios, the lawyer, whose face is everywhere in this city—in the subways, on the sides of busses. No recovery, no fee. This week Chris said it's time for Nicky to pony up, be his own man—this in spite of busboy tips he knows don't even cover living expenses. "You don't want to end up like Dad," Chris let slip. "Hopeless, I mean." Not dead, which goes without saying. "A man needs to move forward in life." Tough love. You should be happy, Chris always tells him, working at any one of Victor Gold's restaurants—it's a great company, he says, as if Nicky's poised for some rags-to-riches story of his own. We're *brothers*, Chris says, to remind Nicky that they share the same DNA; that if the one son can make it, so can the other; that he's not a chip off the old block. People's lives can change for the better, Chris insists, just as quickly as they can change for the worse.

Nicky doesn't want to get too high, so he takes one last hit, pinches the tip with moistened fingers, and tucks the half-joint, the last of his dwindled stash, back into *Moby Dick*, which he swore he was going to finish this summer. He flips up the collar of his black silk shirt and fakes a roundhouse kick at the mirror, his eyes looking badass.

Chris got Nicky in the door with Victor Gold. The rest is up to you, Chris always says. I can't ask him to make you a bartender. You create your own luck. Chris and Victor were college roommates, and they both have the Midas touch. Chris bought the brownstone for peanuts, now uses the rent he collects from three downstairs units to pay the mortgage on the condo he just picked up on Spring Garden. Victor's a whole other story. He must have opened Nostradamus on a dare, Nicky jokes, to prove once and for all to the city, or just to his own world-class ego, that he could create another gastronomical goldmine out of the least appetizing concept—this time serving up Gothic fare in a renovated church a block south of Eastern State Penitentiary.

Night after night, unimaginably lovely creatures, local celebrities, sports stars, and wannabe hipsters in their thirties and forties, and maybe even fifties for all Nicky can tell, find this veritable morgue hiding in residential Fairmount; many of them have the requisite wit, donning sexy vampiric getups—tight leather, flared collars, ruffled shirts, spiked jewelry—downing drinks with names like Edgar Allan Poetini and Exorcism on the Beach. Ordinarily Nicky lies low, winding invisibly through the crowd, carrying plates soiled with remnants of blackened this or deviled that, head down, in the standard black-T-shirt-and-jeans busboy uniform, but tonight he's playing along, monster shades and all, at least until the sun goes down.

"I saw you snake my fucking eyeliner yesterday," pale-eyed Janet says the second Nicky snags the corner spot at the half-full bar, best view in the house, where Victor usually sidles up late-night. "I thought you were just playing around, but you snaked it."

"Shit." Nicky hops off the stool and pats down the pockets of his slim-fitting cargo pants. He pulls out his cell phone and sets it on the bar. When he proceeds to check the lower pockets puffing at his knees, Janet rolls her eyes.

"Maybe it's in your sock," she says. "Bullshitter."

"Come over to my place later and get it," he says, and straddles the stool, grinning.

"Yeah."

"We had fun," he reminds her.

He can see she's already shaking up his Inquisition Fizz. Drink to excess before Victor gets here, is their strategy, bartenders included. The extra Fizz goes into a shot glass, which Janet clinks, cheers, with Nicky, and throws back in a fluid move, turning toward the cash register, as if she's going to ring him up.

"You look good with no makeup," Nicky calls out.

Janet flashes him a smile, then slinks up to him, elbows on the bar. "I'm wearing makeup, sweetie. Lose the shades and see for yourself." She hooks the frames with a finger and sets them down next to his cell phone. "I just don't look like a raccoon for once, unlike you."

He forgot about the shades, and squints now, adjusts his vision. Waning sunlight illuminates the tabletops by the windows. Throughout the shadowy room, dim candles flicker in wrought-iron candelabra.

And then he spots his favorite patron, famously sexy anchorwoman Stacy Fredericks, whose sliver of a profile he recognizes despite the lineup of beer taps and the distance from here to there, not to mention her uncharacteristic Black Widow getup and the familiar swarm of blunderers already stuck in her web. Apparently, like Nicky, Stacy decided to get into the spirit of Nostradamus tonight, to lose the anchorwoman skirt suit and play along, in the fashion, neo-medieval style. By her side, and forever unable to extricate himself, is her network sidekick, Lester Dent, who evidently doesn't see his own combover in the mirror when he leaves his house, or doesn't yet appreciate the fact that his thin orangey coif is just one of the reasons that Stacy always maintains a polite distance—his nearly senior-citizen status, baggie pastel suits, and wife and kids rounding out the list of other reasons.

Nicky drains his drink, and Janet is there with a fresh shaker of Fizz.

She follows Nicky's gaze. "Well, that didn't take you long."

Lester Dent lets out an awful laugh as he wraps an arm around Stacy.

"They are *so* fucking," Janet says.

"No way," Nicky says.

"Never underestimate a woman's love for power and money."

Nicky lets his jaw drop in mock astonishment. "Not Stacy Fredericks." Janet sneaks her shot, and Nicky follows suit with a good slug, secretly eager to get the scoop, egging her on: "She already has power and money."

"*Especially* the ones with power and money, honey," she says.

"I guess I'm out of luck," Nicky says.

"Hardly, sweetie. You're cute. Cute trumps everything."

She fills his glass, and his heart swells. Still, his eyes return to Stacy Fredericks, who in one splendid motion twists at the waist, finishes her drink, and sets her martini glass on the bar. Before she turns back to the dull network crew, Nicky can swear she locks eyes with him, but his mind is playing tricks, of course. He feels as if he knows her, ever since last year when she spilled her guts at the end of that broadcast, tearing up, still battling a broken heart, she said, grateful for the city's welcoming embrace. Welcoming embrace, his ass. Still, Nicky fell for the whole bit, hook, line, and sinker. Two divorces. A woman in a man's business. From the South, no less. He remembered what it was like to be new in the city. He defended her against the cynics who thought the performance a ploy, a false confession, meant to dupe hard-hearted Philadelphians who'd dubbed her Ice Queen.

After that, Nicky started TiVo-ing the news, fast-forwarding through the Lester Dent parts. He studied her expressions. He imagined her at home with her dogs, kept his eyes out for her on Spring Garden, caught a glimpse of her a few times on the sidewalk, heading from the network building to the parking garage, always appearing sad and alone, despite her buoyant gait, that gleaming smile as she clapped her cell phone shut, the white Land Rover sailing out from the shadows in a kind of triumph over her broken heart—it was all a mask.

A month ago, when she went national, gushing with Oprah about her abusive deadbeat exes, commiserating about the dearth of men capable of loving a strong woman, it was as if she were appealing directly to him, confessing her shyness, her hope that some such man would emerge from some unlikely place, as Nicky went on hiding in the shadows, his encounters limited to flybys as he hauled a bus tub to the kitchen. And yet, he has always maintained the belief that she could go for a low-life like him—or a nice guy with a shit job and no prospects. After all, her two husbands had been a hack disc jockey and some strapping clod stuck in the minors—not exactly high-class millionaires. In those brushes in the barroom, he swears he sensed a subtle leaning, a longing to shake these studio geeks and let loose.

"I see you all the time," she says, the familiar voice electroshock silky in his ear. "I mean, where have I *seen* you?"

The majestic swoop of hair falls into view, elbow lands, a finger floats, and now she might as well be slipping into Nicky's Inquisition Fizz.

"Yeah," he says, dizzy, but not stupid-drunk enough to look up and give away his low-class identity too soon. Milk this moment to the end of heaven, he thinks. There's a part of him—beyond his own shame—that wants to spare the girl her own embarrassing moment when she realizes he's the busboy on his night off. Still, Stacy Fredericks walked over here on her own, Nicky reminds himself, just as Lester Dent barks, "We're outta here, Stace," hovering nearby. "You comin'?"

Nicky utters, "I see you all the time too," and in a flash he can hear her glossy grin, smell the metallic glint of her silver-skull earrings, taste the waxy scent of this whole leather masquerade—just as he feels Lester Dent huffing and fleeing into the altered night.

"1-800-INJURED!" she blurts, and now it's too late—he's looking right at her, giving her the full view. "You are *everywhere*. Oh my God, every SEPTA bus—the billboard on 17th, near the studio." She smiles, awaiting some confirmation, which Nicky is too stunned to offer. "Stacy Fredericks," she introduces herself.

Nicky shakes her hand.

"You seem surprised. Don't worry. I'm not going to ask you for free legal advice," she says, beaming. "You must get that all the time."

Nicky nods. "I'm not sure I'm the kind of lawyer you need."

Her smile sinks.

"Sorry," he says. "It was a compliment—a ridiculous one. I just mean you don't appear to be injured." There isn't the slightest thing wrong with her physically. "You're even more beautiful in person."

He's hit a soft spot, apparently—to think, a blushing anchorwoman. She seems genuinely moved, her hand fluttering at her brow, as if about to swoon.

"Are you okay?" Nicky says. He feels a rush of confidence. "Here, sit."

"Just a little drunk, is all."

Nicky offers Stacy the adjacent stool he's been saving for himself, knowing he'll have to evacuate the corner spot once Victor arrives—and, speak of the devil, here's Victor now, an enormous beast of a man in an orange polo shirt, lumbering across the barroom, muttering to himself, it seems, until he adjusts what looks like the chrome husk of a locust in his ear and barks a familiar threat to one of his fourteen managers stationed throughout the city, each prepared for at least one such nightly call—and one such personal visit. Before Nicky can relinquish his seat, Victor is already bearing down on him, stabbing his thumb in the air, delivering his graceless eviction notice.

"Good boy," Victor mutters to Nicky, his wad of keys spraying on the bar top. He reaches for the bulging back pocket of his madras pants and plants his sixteen-ounce wallet next to his BlackBerry, which his immense finger resumes pounding.

Heart in his throat, Nicky rotates and stands, now, over Stacy Fredericks, who doesn't seem to have heard a thing, and in fact appears charmed by his spontaneous generosity. "A lawyer *and* a gentleman," she says—the compliment penetrating like a poisoned arrow.

Janet delivers Victor's sparkling water with lime, along with a refill on the Inquisition Fizz and a smirk Nicky can't help interpreting as more baffled than impressed.

"I'm done with lawyers, by the way," Stacy says.

"I didn't mean anything by that," Nicky huffs, trying to forget about Victor, who coughs and growls, his back to the world. Nicky imagines himself mid-flight, roundhouse kick about to split that pumpkin head in two.

"Divorce lawyers, I mean—though I don't plan on needing a personal injury lawyer anytime soon either."

"Let's hope not." Nicky takes a deep breath and tries to mirror Stacy's smile. "What are you drinking?"

She shakes her head. "I almost didn't recognize you with the spiky hair and makeup."

Nicky nudges his full glass. "Try mine."

Her eyes expand as she sips. "That's *good*."

There is silence for a moment, and he is spellbound—not just by her obvious beauty, but by her vitality; her luscious flesh, bound in black leather, seems imbued with optimism, her taut skin humming with intelligence. Beyond her, Victor Gold has transformed—Nicky sees him as not just monstrous, but miserable, doomed. A mere minute in the presence of Stacy Fredericks, and for the first time in his life Nicky believes that the world is nothing but what one makes of it, and that he is, or could be, a man of extraordinary potential.

"So tell me about a case," she says, setting down the glass, "your most interesting one, or one you're working on now."

"Sure," he says, with a confidence he doesn't feel. But then, in a flash, he sees himself at a table with a dozen Amish men in Lancaster County, he in an Armani suit, they in straw hats and beards, all there to discuss a fair settlement on the case of the kid whose head was rammed by the hoof of a horse that smashed through the windshield of his father's car on a certain rainy Wednesday night last March. He paints the picture for Stacy. "See, the Amish don't buy insurance," he explains. "They don't believe in damages for pain and suffering. So I have to go in there and make them understand that this kid was in the hospital for a month with his skull literally sawed off so that his swollen brain could return to its normal size. I show them pictures, and I explain that any jury who saw these pictures would award a million, minimum. I'm asking half a mil. And this old Amish guy starts saying how pain and suffering is part of life, God's plan for the human race."

"This is amazing. They really sawed off his skull? It sounds like a million-dollar case to me."

"Problem is," Nicky says, "the kid's practically retarded to begin with . . ."

On the bar, Nicky's vibrating cell phone moves in place. He sees that it's Chris calling, just as Stacy says, "Is that a problem?"

He should answer the phone, tell Chris he's ready to be his own man—or that he's *not* ready, that he's a hopeless case after all.

"I mean, isn't that good for your case?" she asks. "Doesn't that add sympathy, if he's, you know, mentally challenged?" She's looking at him as if he has something to say worth listening to.

"See, you have to prove real loss," he says.

Stacy sips, her eyes unflinching. "The whole thing is unbelievable. I could never do what you do."

Again, Nicky's cell phone vibrates. He turns it to silent mode.

"So I say to the father, 'Go get your son,' and at first he refuses, but then he comes back in twenty minutes with his kid, who's smart enough to know he can't fake being stupid. So we're all standing there, and I ask the kid, 'Who's the president of the United States?' and the kid just stares at me, clueless. Then I ask the kid, 'Who's the football team in Philadelphia?' and the kid says, 'Eagles!' I say, 'Who's the quarterback of the Eagles?' and the kid says, 'Donovan McNabb!' and I say, 'That's right.' The old Amish guy interrupts and says, 'We don't know football. We wouldn't know if these are the correct answers or not. What does any of this prove?'" Nicky stops. He can't remember where his brother was heading with all of this.

"So?"

"So? Well, I say, 'You're right. They are the right answers, Mr. Stoltzfus, and what it proves is that I'm not a liar, and I'm not lying when I tell you that this case is worth at least the half-million we're asking for, because your horse went through this man's windshield and his son was in the hospital for a month with his skull sawed off so that his brain could return to normal—and it's only right that your people take responsibility for what happened.'"

Stacy is grinning, anticipating the jackpot finish. Nicky wishes that there were more to the story—or that he could remember the rest of it. He remembers Chris explaining how the Amish collected the money from the community, how, when Chris asked why they didn't buy insurance, the old Amish guy told him, *We believe in two things: God and each other.*

"So did you *win?*"

"Yeah," he blurts, takes a deep breath. "Five hundred thousand dollars."

The bluish face of Nicky's phone lights up a third time.

"Someone's trying to track you down," Stacy says.

"My brother," Nicky says, shaking his head. He turns the phone over.

"You have a brother?"

Nicky goes silent, his thoughts tangled.

"Older or younger?" She's nearly finished the drink. She offers him the rest before polishing it off.

"Younger."

"Is he as cute as you?"

Behind her, Victor Gold sets his glass down. The drone of his furious rattle goes on. Stacy seems suddenly flushed again, perhaps embarrassed for her compliment, which has gone unanswered. Nicky wants to say something, but he's lost in the space of her exposed neck, pinkish in the shadow of her flared collar.

"Is everything all right?" she says.

"Of course, no, it's fine," he stutters. "My brother, that's all. He's, uh, he's a bit of a fuckhead. Good-looking, yes, cute, handsome as hell, actually, but a fuckhead. He calls a lot—or *I* call *him*, check in on him a lot, make sure he's not doing anything stupid." He can hear his brother's sympathetic voice in his own, and he chokes up. "A man needs to move forward in life. He doesn't get it."

"I'm sorry. You want to call him back? I don't mind—"

"No, no. He's just—it's hard to explain—or, it's actually kind of easy to explain. He smokes a lot of weed and has a shitty job. That's his life. He wasn't always that way. He was a good kid, smart. He could have been whatever he wanted. And then my mom died, and then a few years ago my dad shot himself. And he just stopped. And started being a fuckhead. I'm afraid, you know . . ."

Victor Gold hisses, "Fucking shit," as he rises from his stool and heads for the kitchen, his shoulder brushing Nicky's.

Stacy says, "I'm so sorry," and bows her head into her hand. Nicky is surprised by this sudden display of pity. She reaches for his elbow, offers her tenderness, which is not for him, Nicky understands, but for Chris, who must endure the burden of this faceless brother.

Nicky contemplates the empty stool, the brazenly discarded items on the bar.

He wants to fly from his body. He doesn't want to be Chris or Victor—just anyone but himself, anyone but the fucked-up son of the ultimate fuck-up.

"You want to go?" he says.

She takes his arm and the moment they hit the sidewalk takes his face into her hands. "I'm so, so sorry," she says.

"Fuck it," he mumbles to himself, just as he spots the yellow car whose insides glow when he presses the button on the key he's aiming toward the street, the silver bunch jangling.

On cue, she turns. "Is that your Maserati?"

They drift toward the brightness under the canopy of birches across the street.

"You have to let me drive," she says, beaming now.

With a last glance back, he says, "Why not?"

Inside, he imagines the two of them united on a mission to create some new future for themselves. Her smile grows increasingly luminescent, as if draining the light from the overhead lamp. They are ensconced in black leather. As she feels for the ignition, he taps his foot, glares out the window. He flicks open the glove compartment to find the mother lode of dope, rolling papers and all, sealed in a Ziploc bag. At first he doesn't recognize the blunt silver barrel of a gun, until he reaches for the twinkling Zippo and a finger hooks the trigger guard.

The engine rumbles. The glove compartment door clicks shut. Stacy leans forward, then settles back with arms outstretched and hands gripping the wheel. With a few deft, seemingly practiced maneuvers, she manages to exit the curbside spot and enter the open lane, which appears, in a suspended moment of pure potential, to lead straightaway toward a positively magnificent, if shadowy, future, lined with inferior automobiles.

There is an explosion of force, and they are sailing forward. It is not long before the car veers vaguely right and Nicky leans left, as if to counteract this unfortunate detour. A faint, feminine yelp—followed by the snap, like a mushroom cap, of a sideview mirror—signals the beginning of the end.

The rest feels patently catastrophic, these seconds an eternity of unending metallic screeching. It is as if Nicky is poised at the crotch of a giant zipper, its teeth off kilter, some stubborn force willing these two discordant halves to unite, only so that they can be free of each other once and for all. It makes no sense that they haven't yet come to a stop, in spite of this rib-curling resistance. How many have they already sideswiped? Three? Ten? She must be gassing it, in spite of the mounting disaster, as if to race toward the inevitable, or from it.

At last, they have come to the T at the end of the road, an instinctive foot on a brake, with the help of the curb, having saved them from the profile of the oblivious brownstone straight ahead. They are heaving in unison, taking in the common air. "I'm bleeding." Her eyes are locked on her reflection in the rearview mirror. She dabs a fingertip to her forehead. Outside, the world has stopped, while inside, their hearts and thoughts become entwined in mutual terror—albeit born of independent fears.

"I can't get a D.U.I.," she utters.

"I have to go back," he says.

The sidewalks are empty, the windows of the surrounding houses dark or, if lit, free of shadows.

"I make $750,000 a year." She seems to be in a trance. "I'm the lead anchor on a major network in the fourth largest market in the country." She sets her hollow gaze on Nicky and asks, apparently in earnest, "What the fuck am I thinking?" After a pause, she screams, "I'm asking you! What the fuck am I doing here?"

"In Philly, you mean?"

"No! With you! Here! Now! Why do I keep letting asshole men ruin my life?"

"I don't know," Nicky says. "Just—go."

In this merciful moment in time, there is no one in sight, not even through the rear windshield.

"What do you mean?" Her voice softens. "Walk away?"

"Run." He means it. "I'll take the heat. Forget this. Me."

Her lips quiver. She blinks out waves of tears that tumble down her cheeks. It's too late. In the distance, light spills from doorways, onto stoops, as slumped silhouettes make their way toward the wreckage.

"I'm sorry," she whispers. "I didn't mean what I said—about you."

"Get in the back," he hisses.

Her grace has returned. She understands the plan. In one swift, elegant gymnastic feat, she becomes one with the leather, heaving herself through the narrow gap between seats, hips twisting, legs and heels and toes all pointed in their mission to clear the way for Nicky, who with undramatic haste removes them from the scene of the crime.

Even in these dark streets, there is no way for this car to be discreet. Curious, envious eyes flash from the sidewalk, as Nicky wraps around a corner or two before quietly pulling over.

"Why are you stopping?" Stacy whispers nervously.

"We won't get far in this thing," Nicky states. "We'll go to my brother's. It's right around the corner." He gets out and offers his hand, scanning the empty sidewalk, as one stiletto boot follows another onto the concrete.

When she takes his arm, crossing the street, a shiver of recognition shoots up his spine, his chivalry tainted.

She looks back, puzzled. "What about your car?"

He forgot that the car is his. "I'll call it in as stolen."

She seems to consider this. "Okay," she says softly.

He nods and remembers what a real thief would remember. "Wait here."

The passenger side is wounded with depressed streaks of ugliness and, at the shoulder, an awful black spot—an absolute absence of something that once existed, severed at the root—marking the trajectory of that brief ride. Inside, the light dissolves around him. He glances at the beautiful woman waiting by the trunk of a tree, cupped hands at her elbows. She could run, as he'd urged her, but she is waiting for him—and this is something good, he tells himself. There may be hope. He stuffs the bag of dope into the puffy pocket at his knee, a perfect fit, slips the gun into the slim pocket at his hip, along with the keys—he adds the Zippo and alights.

When he reaches her, a distant siren pops and goes silent. She squeezes his arm and pulls herself close. "Did you call?" she asks.

"That car is officially stolen," he assures her.

Two more blocks, and they ascend the stoop and stairs to his apartment. Inside, she heads straight for the living room. When he comes from the kitchen with a damp washcloth, she's facing the window, legs tightly sealed, poised steadily on those two impossibly tall, thin pedestals he hadn't noticed give her at least an inch on him. She appears unsure at first, until he gestures toward her forehead. Her whole body sinks, softens, under the warm pressure, and just like that the thin line of dried blood has vanished.

"It's gone," he says, and for a moment pretends he has erased their troubles. He can see a million miles in her eyes, infinite stretches of sun-baked highways and yellow-ribboned roads that go on forever. She must feel discovered. Her eyes close and lips descend. When her tongue meets his, he finds the bare small of her back and pulls her against him. He travels to her neck, her shoulder, the hidden downy hair behind her ear. There is a line, he imagines, joining his two hands, and that line is the golden zipper he delicately fingers. As they shift toward the couch, he thinks, I can die now, just as she whispers, "Stop."

"What is it?"

They sit, fingers entwined on their adjoining thighs.

"What about your brother?" she says.

He shakes his head. "God knows where he sleeps every

night." He frees a hand and touches her cheek, her forehead.

"I can't," she says, and turns away. "Not like this. Not tonight. I should go."

"You can't go out there."

"I don't live far." She's already up. "Please don't get the wrong idea—I am so grateful. You saved my life tonight."

"I'll walk you." He follows her to the door, where she pauses.

"Please . . ." She touches his face, takes his hand. "Thank you."

"You want to get high?"

"No," she laughs. She must think he's joking—one last crack for the road. "I'll call you," she grins, dabs bashfully at her forehead, "1-800-INJURED, right?" and slips from his fingers.

Her smile lingers in the room, the memory of it tangible, like molecules of goodness dissipating in the air, as dingy reality returns and he sinks into the couch. 1-800-INJURED. He contemplates the implications of a single phone call. God knows how Chris will work his magic once the sordid tale unfolds.

Nicky hits the lights, lies back on the couch, unloads the weighty goods from his pockets. He rolls a fat one, sparks the Zippo.

In a dream, it's Nicky's office. She's in her anchorwoman skirt suit; he's in Armani. They are just back from lunch, from a real restaurant, one with no theme. He closes the door. She pulls him by the tie toward the big desk. This is their routine.

A knocking wakes him. The light from his phone glows. Sirens ring out. Windows and walls flash. He sits up, stares at the door.

Phone in one hand, gun in the other.

"Open the door, Nicky!"

"They're coming for me," he mumbles.

"Everything's gonna be fine."

"I'm sorry," he whispers.

"Don't be stupid, fuckhead. Listen to me. It's your brother, who loves you."

In his mind he can see him out there, pounding, head against the door, and then it's as if he's out there himself, feeling what it might be like to be left alone. "I love you too," he blurts, and when he leaps for the door, to let his brother in, it's as though he's racing to save them both.

"CANNOT EASY NORMAL DIE"

BY CARLIN ROMANO

University City

I f every block in Philadelphia had only one resident, Isaac figured, lots of things would be different.

Parking would be easier. Mail carriers would stop screwing up. Next-door neighbors too dumb to pack their garbage in plastic bags might disappear, because you wouldn't have a next-door neighbor.

Isaac saw the downside too. Infrequent block parties. A pathetic neighborhood association. Ratcheting up of that lonely feeling Isaac used to get when he lived in Vermont and wondered how people in isolated houses survived the big snowstorms.

One-person blocks might even stir up aristocratic leanings, a sense of "to the manor born" that might lead people to consider getting their streets closed off, and their fiefdoms turned into separate municipalities.

Anyway, it was just empty, abstract theorizing, because so far as Isaac knew, he was the only person—at least in University City—with a block of his own. And even the neighborhood historian couldn't tell him exactly how St. Irenaeus Square—not that it was a square—had turned out that way.

"There used to be a stable there, where your house is, in the late nineteenth century," ventured Mildred, the old woman with semi-encyclopedic knowledge of Spruce Hill, at the last block event to which she'd limped her way. "I think that put some potential builders off."

Another theory, ventured by Irina Butova, the realtor who'd first showed the structure to Isaac years ago, was that his unique, detached, slope-roofed oddity of a house had been built in defiance of neighborhood logic.

401 St. Irenaeus Square, after all, sat surrounded by backyards. To Isaac's right, when he exited his house, lay the well-maintained yards of the celebrated Queen Anne homes on Spruce Street, the area's architectural gems. To his left, beyond his own impressive yard with sixteen trees, loomed the leafy expanse formed by the backs of Pine Street's solid row houses, the first two being the lovingly manicured creations of Derek Gombrowicz, the friendly architect who owned them.

In front of him, as he opened his door, sat the back of the mighty twin that ended the string of Queen Anne houses along Spruce Street as it headed west. Behind him, outside his bedroom window, lay the backyards of South 42nd Street, several of them regular venues for frat parties, on which Isaac sometimes eavesdropped during slow nights.

"Is quiet and full of peace like cemetery," Irina had joked when she'd shown it to him three years before, right after it had been cleared of its student tenants. They'd messed up the house so badly, Irina explained, that it remained on the market for a year before Christy Greenfield, one of Isaac's old lovers (he'd always liked realtors), referred Isaac to Irina as a match made in heaven. Irina had been in one of Christy's courses at Temple's Real Estate Institute, and then been a trainee at Plumer when Christy was still there. They'd kept in touch.

Christy knew both her client and colleague well. Isaac, a former foreign correspondent for the *Inquirer* in Russia, came with no wife, no kids, lots of boxes, papers, and books, and a complete indifference to interior design. His ideal look was used bookstore, circa 1950. He wanted a house with a porch or veranda so he could, like literary heroes from the past, sit on it in a chair made of natural materials and look literary. He preferred weeds and overgrowth to a regularly landscaped yard, thinking (incorrectly) that onlookers would mistake its choked anarchy for a lush Italian garden. He refused to do housework or gardening of any kind, remarking once to Christy that such impulses had died with his father's generation.

Irina, for reasons Christy didn't understand, had ended up with the 401 St. Irenaeus listing even though she mainly worked Russian neighborhoods in Northeast Philadelphia. It had something to do with the owner two back being Russian before it had been sold to the University of Pennsylvania. As listing arrangements went, it struck Christy as a bit of an odd match.

Most buyers in Spruce Hill fell into two categories. First came the mid-thirtyish academic couples new to junior teaching posts at Penn, eager to get into the catchment area so their not-yet or barely bred kids could go to Penn's appealing new community school. For them 401 looked like a major fixer-upper, the expense of which might be funded by converting 401's unusual side garden—one of the largest in University City—into the site for another house.

The second category of buyers was the older Wharton or med-school types, often full professors or moneyed professionals who'd settle for nothing less than *Architectural Digest* perfection and were willing to pay for contractors to accomplish it. One couple of the sort had purchased the first Queen Anne west of 42nd Street a few years back for about $700,000, torn it up inside, created a huge atrium perfect for a glossy-magazine shoot, then put it back on the market for $950,000.

Both types seemed perfect for 401 St. Irenaeus. But Irina, to Christy's surprise, couldn't unload it that first year. According to Irina, Christy told Isaac, something had gone wrong every time it looked as if she had a buyer—financing that fell through, cold feet, fear of crime, whatever.

Christy, of course, knew it had to be more complicated than that—it always is when selling houses. One couple that had bid on 401, before Isaac came into the picture, told Christy that Irina grew belligerent when they asked about the legality of building a second house on the side yard, which was wider than 401 itself. "You buy sixteen fantastic trees to kill sixteen fantastic trees?" Irina had said to them. "Believe me, for you I can find house without trees! Not this house!"

That's the story that first made Christy think of Isaac, who she knew was house-hunting. True, he'd been house-hunting for more than twenty years, since he'd come to Philly from New York. And Isaac had long since admitted to Christy that while he was, in principle, looking for a house, house-hunting was also one of his tried and true methods for picking up new lovers. Isaac knew how to charm real-estate agents, even the crusty cynics, and, Christy had to admit, his strata-gem had worked with her.

From Isaac's point of view, visiting open houses always beat Internet dating or bar-hopping (though it came a distant second to chatting up women at academic conferences). First, all real-estate agents had their photos and first and last names right there in the Sunday ads. You could research them, nar-row the field to the most appealing, then go to their open houses and see how they stacked up in the harsh setting of real life. You couldn't do that with the Internet unless you had a spare decade to spend on coffee dates.

Nothing beat an open house for inviting friendly conversation, self-revelatory or inquisitive, free of all activity clumsily designed to bring boys and girls together. When Isaac felt he'd clicked with an agent, he followed up by making some excuse about the house itself, while dangling an overture about a meal or coffee sometime. And so something would or wouldn't begin. And every affair that did begin, he explained to Christy, far outweighed—on the scale of pure pleasure—any number that didn't.

Had Christy known Isaac's MO the day he came to see a trinity she was handling on Waverly Street years ago, their seven-month thing would never have happened. She'd thought he liked the house, not her headshot in the Sunday *Inquirer* real-estate section. But he let on only years later, long after they'd climbed back from the breakup to be solid if irregular pals, able to talk about his or her latest romantic disasters.

Because Isaac couldn't commit to anything beyond his next piece or foreign trip, Christy knew he'd never commit to building on 401's side yard. He fit Irina's oddly proprietary criteria for 401. Irina wanted someone who wouldn't endanger the overgrown yard. She quickly discouraged would-be buyers who eyed the property as a twofer—one unique detached house, one enormous lot where you could build a second structure and make a killing.

"Is like Russian forest," Irina had joked to Isaac the first time she showed him how 401's side yard, and Gombrowicz's backyard, combined to form a veritable mini-park of soaring evergreens and overlapping foliage. The only difference was that Gombrowicz's yard had neatly cut grass on its ground. The vines and weeds to the side of 401 made it look like a house that had landed, *Wizard of Oz* style, on a jungle floor, with terra firma at least six inches below the sight line.

Christy knew her biz. The sale and closing happened fast. Christy even suspected that Isaac and Irina might have slept together preclosing, despite Irina's being a few years older than Isaac, which put her about twenty years outside his routine demographic. The only time the three of them had drinks together, she'd seen the flirtation between them, Isaac dropping more than necessary of the fifty words that had gotten him around Russia, and Irina looking overamused at his anecdotes about St. Petersburg.

In the two years since the closing, Christy had seen Isaac about six or seven times for one of their friendly meals or coffees. The conversations took their usual pre-401 course. First they'd gossip about the *Inquirer* (where Isaac now found himself bored as the paper spiraled downward to irrelevance), City Hall sorts they both knew, what was in the news.

At some point, Isaac would send a signal that he'd still happily sleep with Christy and Christy would gracefully rebuff him. Then they'd share recent romantic wins and losses. The new part, which Christy disliked but also found professionally flattering, were Isaac's questions about his rights and possibilities as the sole owner and resident on the 400 block of St. Irenaeus.

At dinner the previous Friday, Isaac, oddly, seemed ready for a commitment.

"Seriously," he'd said, "I know Irina would kill me, but would it really be so hard to get the permission and variances to build a small house in the yard, one that would still leave some greenery and trees?"

"I told you already, Isaac," Christy replied, "it's not a big deal. You own that lot. There are no covenants or restrictions on it. Your neighbors and Irina might go apeshit, but it's a pretty clear path."

"I'm more afraid of Irina than Derek," Isaac said. "I'm beginning to think real-estate women have a harder time pulling away from houses they sell than from men they, so to speak, handle—"

"Nice try," Christy cut it. "But I hear a new form of whining just around the corner. Let's not go there."

"The last time she dropped by," Isaac said, taking Christy's cue and dropping the "Poor me" tone, "I was watching Larry King do his latest Michael Jackson show, about the endless wait for the funeral. At first Irina was funny. She listened to it for about a minute, then uttered one of those Irina-isms I love." Isaac shifted into his heavily Russian Irina impersonation and accent. *Poor Michael Jackson! Cannot easy normal die!*

"So I was feeling obnoxious," Isaac continued, dropping the accent, "and said, 'Right, Irina, you can only *easy normal die* in Russia. You just sit in your car after offending someone powerful, or write the wrong story, and *pow*—you're gone.'"

"That *was* nasty!" Christy said. "You know she loves that whole Russian tough-guy thing, and Putin. Plus she really doesn't like anyone even noticing her accent, let alone making fun of it."

"I know, I know," Isaac said, a little too knowingly for Christy's taste, "and, yeah, she did act strange, weird, after that. She just looked at me in a way she never has before. Really cold, as if she didn't recognize me."

"Have you slept with her?" Christy asked with a chirp in her voice.

"What does that have to do with anything?" Isaac shot back. "I've told you before—no."

"Yes, but you've also told me 'No' about other women in real estate, then changed it to 'Yes.'"

"What's the point?" Isaac asked.

"The point is," Christy said, her sarcasm getting the best

of her, "if she wants to share that unique feeling of being with you, and you haven't gotten there yet, don't jerk her chain."

"I guess I can't say I've never slept with my realtor," Isaac offered, hoping for a smile.

"No, you can't," Christy replied, not granting one.

A week later, Isaac made clear to Christy that he wasn't kidding about the side yard. His 401K had dropped 40 percent in the recession. His bridge loan on 401 would come due in two more years. Isaac wanted to know if, at least, the second-house idea was feasible.

In the eleven years since they'd stopped sleeping together, Christy had never made a dime off Isaac. Now, she thought, she should.

"Look, Isaac, if you're really serious about this," she told him on the phone, "let's deal. The first thing you have to do is to see if it's even possible to lay a foundation and build there. If you're serious, for a $5,000 retainer, with you bearing the costs, I'll arrange for the initial testing."

"Five thousand is pretty steep," said Isaac. "How much would the testing cost?"

"Probably a couple of thousand."

"Five thousand is too high," Isaac said. "What would you think of doing it as a team, with you taking a commission if I build the little house? You said all along that this was a unique property and situation—sort of 'Own your own block right smack in University City.' You could sell both together for over a million. I'd give you 10 percent on the whole thing."

Christy liked the idea. She'd never seen a Philadelphia city block with only one house. A wild notion that she'd had before about 401 came back. It could be her signature project. She could explore that craziest of all inner-city ideas: trying to turn the 400 block of St. Irenaeus Square into a private street. Or a gated area like one of those suburban enclaves she'd long admired. Isaac's prominence as an *Inky* writer might get her coverage as an innovator.

"Okay, let's do it," Christy replied after a long pause. "I mean, the project—the house!"

"You can't tell Irina," Isaac said.

"Of course not," agreed Christy.

Isaac gave Christy a set of keys—he traveled half the time anyway, and trusted her. Christy arranged for Eric Busby, who'd worked on some of the town houses that replaced the imploded Southwark Towers, to do the initial research, checking city records on underground lines and obstacles, checking out the yard. Isaac would be off in Europe for three weeks right after the semester ended in May. She might get things off the ground by then. She told Isaac as much.

It didn't turn out as Christy planned. Most of the time, when she thinks of Isaac and 401—and, occasionally, when she sleeps there (deals often leading to other deals)—she's glad about that. The sixteen trees make it feel like someplace else, not Philadelphia. Isaac's sudden avaricious side—the instant developer eager to make a profit and let nature be damned—didn't become him. When they both realized they had to stop cold on the second-house idea, Isaac seemed vulnerable again, even sexy, as he had when they first met. Just a writer, and a dreamer, in a house full of books.

Christy broke it to him pretty quickly after he came back from Europe in June. They were sitting in Isaac's living room, on the old Imperial couch.

"There's not going to be a second house," she began. "It can't happen."

"What's wrong?"

"Eric dug down into the yard about forty feet back from the sidewalk."

"So?"

"So, he hit something. An obstruction."

"An obstruction?"

Christy got up, walked over to her travel bag, and took out something wrapped in old pages of the *Daily News*.

It was a matryoshka doll.

"*That's* what Eric hit in the yard?" Isaac asked, his eyes riveted on it.

"That's not all he hit," Christy answered, with an efficient air that suggested—this thing is over: game, set, match.

"Try part of a rib cage next to it, not quite separated from its accessories."

Isaac looked at Christy as if she'd just told him that she'd gotten pregnant by him years ago, given birth, and now it was time for Isaac to meet his daughter. Christy looked at Isaac with an expression that said: *You owe me for the rest of your life.*

"Don't worry," Christy said quickly, "Eric was just as scared and worried and in shock as I was. He's totally trustworthy on this—he's fine. He filled up the hole again, and spread the weeds and leaves over it. You'd have to look really close at it, standing right there, to even know it's been disturbed."

"I want to show you something," Isaac said. He got up and went to the attic, where he kept the papers and souvenirs of his three years reporting and teaching in Russia. When he returned, he showed Christy the larger matryoshka doll he'd brought back from Russia—a gift from one of his students there, the daughter of a prominent St. Petersburg businessman.

"Doesn't the whole doll-inside-a-doll thing stand for the,

uh, endless similarity of the human spirit?" asked Christy, repeating something she thought she'd once heard.

"It does," Isaac replied. "Katya, my student, told me all about them when she gave it to me. Apparently, Russian mafia sometimes bury one of them with a body."

"What does it mean?"

"According to Katya," Isaac said, looking impassively at Christy, "it means there are more bodies nearby."

They peered at each other. Isaac shook his head. He started to say something, but Christy spoke first.

"It never happened. Eric and I never saw anything. So don't worry."

Isaac nodded.

"Isaac Lalli," he said, in a self-mocking tone, "sole master and resident of the 400 block of St. Irenaeus Square."

Christy gave him a look of solidarity. She came over to the couch, sat beside him, and leaned against him as she hadn't for years.

"It's an amazing yard, beautiful just the way it is," she said.

SEEING NOTHING

BY DIANE AYRES

Bella Vista

I don't know what shocked me most: the way my foul-mouthed neighbor screamed and cursed his hoary mother to the grave—when she already appeared to have gone and returned from it—or the way she screamed back. Especially when she was holding the meat cleaver, standing at the kitchen table whacking the wings and legs off a chicken, always with a cigarette stuck to her lower lip.

I actually heard a mob hit one evening while working in my home office, which I found less disturbing than the sound of that woman—somebody's grandmother—shrieking the F-word at the top of her two-packs-a-day-for-fifty-year lungs. Hardcore.

The side of our house overlooked the back of their house, where they fought in the kitchen in front of a picture window with blinds they never closed, yellowed by tobacco smoke and splattered grease. When windows were open in this corner of old row homes, voices blasted from below, amplified, between brick and stucco, directly into the window beside my desk as I was trying to work.

My husband and I lived on a side street off a side street, off a side street, which brought to mind a feudal town in Tuscany with passages through a maze too narrow to drive. On a map, our neighborhood, lovely Bella Vista, looks like the border between gentrified Center City and the old-time neighborhoods of South Philly. But at the street level, it felt like a funky residential oasis between noisy, once-hip South Street, where nobody told the kids from Lancaster that Sid Vicious and his haircut were dead, and the inimitable Italian Market, where Rocky Balboa once ran, oozing sweat and punching meat to a really loud and rousing song. And, mostly, Bella Vista life was quiet, except for the Freudian nightmare next door.

I wasn't one to spy on my neighbors. I only glimpsed them down there, at an extremely sharp diagonal, inadvertently, when I got up to adjust the window, depending on the season and the volume of their noxious spew. When I spotted them, my instinct was to avert my eyes because I found them hideous—like some incarnation of the monster Grendel and his mother, in their lair down below. But I was no Beowulf to slay them, or even to ask them, nicely, to use their indoor voices. I was unnerved by the prospect that they would even spot me up here.

Grendel was a walking case study of vitamin D deprivation, termite-white in a dingy white sleeveless undershirt, sprouting black body hair like a mass of horseflies crawling all over his back and shoulders and up his neck, where they got trapped in his coarse black, greasy hair. He had a matching unibrow, and a Fu Manchu that had taken root in the 1970s and never been weeded. Revolting.

He frightened all of the Bella Vista womenfolk and small children who passed him on the sidewalk as he went to or from his job at our friendly neighborhood corporate chainstore pharmacy, wearing a logo-emblazoned uniform and visor. Though what the visor was for was anybody's guess. He walked with an elongated stride, as if he were imitating *Homo erectus*—and badly—swinging his brown bag lunch stiffly, grinning weirdly to no one in particular. There wasn't a woman who wouldn't shudder instinctively at his sight, assuming he was a serial killer until proven innocent. Imagine our spine-crawling response when we found out that he was the guy behind the counter who developed our personal family snapshots. For us, the Digital Age couldn't come too soon.

Grendel's Mother was almost as strange to behold when she emerged from the back door on shopping day, barely a head taller than the grocery cart she stole from the Superfresh on 11th Street. A sturdy woman, she wore the black widow's housedress of the Old Country, with her white hair pulled straight back in a bun. The crone drove that rusty piece of junk to and from the market with such road rage that innocent bystanders could only pray she wasn't packing her meat cleaver. The top-heavy wire basket nearly tipped over at times as she pushed on, having no respect for obstacles she couldn't see, oblivious to the unpredictable cobblestones, crooked sidewalks, and crumbling curbs, making such an unholy racket I could hear her two blocks away.

It was hard enough trying to concentrate while she was threatening to chop up her son like poultry—I kept thinking, *Eeewwww . . . she'll have to pluck him.*

One day their homicidal promises were so convincing that I actually picked up the phone to call 911.

I'll stab you in your sleep!

Not if I smother you first—you crazy old bitch. Gimme the money. I know you got it, Ma.

I could hear him rifling through kitchen cupboards, popping the lids off of old tin flour canisters, throwing cereal boxes and canned goods hither and yon.

Where'd ja hide it, damnit?!

Holding the phone, I hesitated, wondering if callers were required to identify themselves. *Hmm.* I had to think about this. After all, it's a big deal to call the cops on your neighbors. Did I really want to get involved? Obviously, some families just yelled a lot and said awful things. That's just how they "communicated." And I had never actually witnessed any physical abuse.

I decided to defer to the collective wisdom of my Bella Vista elders, whose official word on the street was invariably: *I didn't see nuthin.*

But I sure did hear a lot: and it was mostly from colorful characters who charmed the hell out of me. The Happy Guy who strolled down our street every day at lunchtime, for instance, belting out a respectable version of "Volare." Or the trio of highly seasoned bookies who worked our block and the local convenience store, assuming their positions every day on this or that corner, in rotation. Aging wiseguys with chewy old skin like the Italian dry sausages hanging on strings from the ceiling of Claudio's in the market. The way they made themselves laugh at their own jokes never failed to crack me up from afar.

When I passed these bookies on the street, they were flirty, but always respectful, and they took to greeting me playfully with a nickname: *Hey, Smiley.*

Between these guys and the nosey neighbor ladies (of which I soon became one, being home all day), I felt relatively secure. *Not to worry, hon,* one of the native grandmas reassured me when we first moved in as newlyweds. *They only kill each other.*

Good to know, I humbly thanked her.

And then she asked me why I wasn't pregnant yet—a question she continued to ask every time she saw me for the rest of her life, which she lived out mostly sitting in her folding lawn chair in front of her house. I would just play the blushing bride—Smiley—although after several years she eyeballed me suspiciously, and then sympathetically, and finally in complete senility, at which point I could only pat her hand gently and say: *Not to worry, hon.*

I had to wonder at my own tendency to be blasé about the wiseguy-on-wiseguy crime that made our neighborhood legendary. We got our slices at Lorenzo's on the corner of 9th and Christian, and ate them just down the street under the two-story mural of the late Mayor Frank Rizzo looking vaguely off. It didn't disturb my appetite for splashy red tomato pie to know that mob boss Sal Testa almost got his arm blown off in this same spot, eating a bucket of raw clams.

And then there was the night Nicky Scarfo, Jr. got hit at Dante & Luigi's, a beloved old family restaurant two small blocks away from us. I actually heard that one. October 31, 1989, a balmy Halloween evening, perfect for trick-or-treating, and the kids were skipping and squealing in the streets below, all hopped up on sugar, while my husband was downstairs manning the candy bowl at the front door—also hopped up on sugar. I was in my office when I heard an unusually loud: *Pop pop . . . Pop pop pop . . . Pop pop pop.*

I assumed some older kids—hooligans!—were setting off firecrackers over in Palumbo Park. But within a minute I heard the sirens descending from all directions, their strobes overreaching the rooftops.

Urban dwellers are nonchalant about sirens, as long as they keep on moving—*Nothing to see here*—farther and farther away. We live for this Doppler effect, and only drop whatever task at hand when we hear the sirens stop, followed by that dreadful sound of police cars, ambulances, and, scariest of all, the fire engines coming to a breakneck halt. It's way too close to home if you can hear the static-y radio dispatchers talking about your neighbors.

Nicky, Jr., a big baby-faced kid in his mid-twenties, was dining at Dante & Luigi's, enjoying a plate of his favorite white clam sauce (always the clams—what's with the clams?), when he was approached by a grown man in a Batman mask, carrying a plastic trick-or-treat bag emblazoned with a fiendish pumpkin. Batman reached into his candy bag and pulled out a MAC-10 machine pistol, shooting Nicky, Jr. eight times about the head and neck.

Batman took flight, eluding capture.

And Nicky, Jr. was lucky he had a very thick neck. Nine days later, he walked out of the hospital, shrugging off the assassination attempt for the local TV cameras.

As for my neighbors, everybody saw nothing.

Curious, considering so many people were always watching: mostly grandmas and great-grandmas looking out their windows and doors, or tending to their pretty flower boxes or elaborate seasonal decorations, when they weren't sitting in their lawn chairs in yards of concrete.

Some Saturdays these ladies—in their floral-patterned house dresses, rolled Supp-Hose, and sensible nun shoes— would appear in the street with buckets of soapy water to clean their stoops and sidewalks.

The wiriest grandma, who lived in one of the houses across from us, would wash her front window standing on a stepladder, making me nervous, afraid that she would fall "on my watch." I couldn't concentrate on my work when she was out there. I would carry my phone around the house, peeking constantly out my own front windows just in case I had to call 911.

And yes, of course, I offered to help her. But she appeared to take this as some kind of insult, because she gave me the stink-eye. I figured it was probably because I didn't feel compelled to give my house a bath every month. I like to think that's why Mother Nature provided us with weather.

But I did sweep occasionally, and the first time I ventured out with a broom, I was love-bombed by the whole lot of them. Ladies I had never even seen before poked their heads out their front doors to wave and wish me a good morning. One grandma actually crossed herself. Another kissed the crucifix on her rosary beads in my general direction.

The solidarity I felt with them as a result, not to mention my appreciation for the spontaneous benediction, increased my empathy when I heard the horror story about the last young couple that had moved into the neighborhood, around the corner on 9th Street. The husband, an untalented stockbroker who wasn't much better at dealing drugs, stabbed a guy to death—twenty-seven times—in his row house during a cocaine deal gone bad. The panicky killer rolled the profusely bloody body in a drop cloth and dragged it outside, in the darkest hours, down our block—only yards from our front stoop—to deposit it in Cianfrani Park on the corner of 8th Street, where dozens of residents would be walking their dogs at dawn. So it was immediately discovered.

When the cops arrived at the park, they literally just looked down at the sidewalk and followed the bloody trail on foot, back to the murderer's house, right up the marble steps to his front door, where they rang the bell and the homicidal imbecile answered. Case closed.

But it wasn't the shocking murder that disgusted my neighbors—since the victim was dealing cocaine, *he got what he deserved*. It was the thought of that unholy mess the murderer left all over the sidewalk, and who the hell was going to clean it up? And what about the killer's own stoop around the corner? Did he have a wife who would get out there and put a scrub brush with Clorox and Lysol to those blood-stained steps?

The sound of my neighbor ladies' collective outrage re-bounded off the houses.

Fortunately, their cleaning concerns were washed down the storm drains thanks to a deluge that lasted for days. I re-frained from saying I told you so.

But it was only because I got out there with a broom that I heard the illicit history of our own house, which had been a front for a still during Prohibition. This explained why the center of our basement was walled in with concrete. For some inexplicable reason, previous owners had decided to brick in the whole contraption instead of removing it. The walls were so excessively reinforced you would have thought they con-tained a radioactive core. I couldn't help but think that maybe it also served as the final resting place of a bootlegger or two, who got what they deserved in a booze deal gone bad.

During the fifteen years we lived in that house, I was al-ways looking for "the body"—or some hidden treasure. Up-stairs, I found a secret hiding place in the floorboards, and used it to stash a small metal lockbox of valuables. While in-stalling the air-conditioning ducts, our contractor discovered an amber beer bottle still sealed with an old-fashioned wire and rubber stopper, sunk into disintegrating cheesecloth, the beer having evaporated down to dust. Holding that bottle up to the light, I had to wonder at the idiots who made alcoholic beverages illegal. Imagine being compelled to hide a bottle of beer in your wall because it could get you arrested.

When spring came one year, I was anxious to let in some fresh air, and during that first week of mild days, working by my window, I became aware of a creeping uneasiness. And then

I realized, bolting upright from my desk and going to the window—listening.

Nothing. I heard nothing.

Not even a snarl from Grendel's lair. I looked down at their house, taken aback to see that their kitchen blinds were shut tight.

Sometime later, I heard a noisy old diesel truck with squeaky brakes parking over on their street, followed by the sound of yo-dudes hollering to each other as they jumped out. *Hmm.* Seemed like a furniture delivery to me. When it went on longer than a typical delivery, I grabbed my trusty broom and stepped outside to do some investigative sweeping.

I swept beyond our section of sidewalk—affecting the aspect of an exceptionally good neighbor—all the way to the corner, about forty feet, where I could see the front of the Grendel house.

A medium-size truck belonging to a junk-hauling business was parked there, and two beefy yo-dudes were hoisting a beat-up old washing machine from the basement through the bulkhead doors opening up onto the sidewalk. No sooner did they set down their unwieldy load than another old appliance came floating eerily upward, like a spooky stage apparition through a trapdoor, elevated by a couple more yo-dudes from down below.

Since I was standing in front of my friend's house, knowing she was at work, I decided to tidy up her sidewalk too, going about it quite methodically so I could keep an eye on the scene, exchanging greetings with passersby. My neighbors were especially curious, looking puzzled regarding the sheer number of discarded washers and dryers lining up on the sidewalk, a half-dozen or more, all of which were wrapped excessively with duct tape.

The appliances were also covered with sticky contact paper designating four decades of decorative patterns and styles: dainty Williamsburg prints of the '50s, psychedelic op art of the '60s, metallic disco dazzle of the '70s. *Good Lord*, I muttered to myself, laundry day at the Grendels must've been confusing.

Why in the world would somebody have so many broken washers and dryers? It didn't seem possible any one family could go through so many of them, not even in a lifetime. And why get rid of them now? Why not just wall them up in the middle of the basement like the nitwits did with our still? Were they moving? Were they dead?

Later that day, I strolled over to the market to get some provisions and saw that the truck was gone. Grendel's Mother was out front with a bucket of soapy water and a scrub brush, scouring her stoop.

I couldn't believe my ears at first, but as I got closer I confirmed that was she was, indeed, listening to Louis Prima. I had never heard a pleasing sound emanating from that house before, and felt myself grinning at her when she looked up. She was squinting against the setting sun and the smoke of a cigarette that was jammed in her crinkly, chubby cheek.

Remarkably, she kind of grinned back, as if she had forgotten for a moment to appear freakish, and I felt triumphant for having overcome my revulsion. Those bookies didn't call me Smiley for nothing.

A week later my husband heard from a neighbor that Grendel had left his job sometime back in winter, and soon after, skipped town. One theory had him hopelessly beholden to a loanshark for gambling debts. Another had him caught red-handed trying to sell snapshots of kids he had stolen from customers.

I had my own theory, of course, but I didn't share it with anyone—just minding my own Bella Vista business—because what do I know anyway?

I didn't see nuthin.

PART IV

THOSE WHO FORGET THE PAST . . .

LONERGAN'S GIRL

BY DUANE SWIERCZYNSKI

Frankford

S omewhere out there, in the dark, was a noise. Lonergan twitched and tried to roll over but something blocked his way. He rolled the other way then stopped, sensing a huge void. *Don't fall in*, he warned himself. He jerked back—

And woke up on the Frankford El.

The train thundered down a set of rails one story above the street, the whole works supported by a green skeleton of steel. Lonergan was in a middle car, sitting on the end of a bench near the center door. There were about a dozen passengers with him, almost all of them reeking of beer and cigarettes and gin. Everyone spaced themselves apart on the bench so they wouldn't have to stare at a stranger across the way. Or watch a stranger vomit.

Lonergan briefly wondered where the El was now, how long he'd been asleep.

Outside the tops of dark buildings sped by, the sun having long vanished behind them. Best Lonergan could guess, it was around eleven p.m. The El slowed and began to screech. He recognized the sound. This was where the green skeleton curved from Front Street to Kensington Avenue. The Dauphin-York station. He was halfway there.

When the El first opened a little over a year ago, it was

the eighth wonder of the Quaker City. Imagine—riding a new, arch-roofed Brill car from City Hall to the outskirts of Frankford in less than twenty-five minutes—a trip that ordinarily took close to an hour by other means! Thousands lined up to try it out, squeezing onto the benches and clutching the leather straps that hung from the ceiling.

Lonergan had been one of them, along with Marie and the boy one bitter Saturday in early December '22. They didn't mind the lack of heat, or the way the cars tossed their bodies around like dice in a cup. Riding the El was a thrill like no other. The boy's eyes were wide the entire trip.

"Papa, look! There's a giant milk bottle on top of that building!"

"Papa, what if the train tips over and falls off the track?"

"Where will this take us, Papa? Can we ride it again?"

Lonergan had no idea that in less than a year he'd be riding the El all the time. And now he actively hated the damned thing.

It froze him, the night wind chilled by the Delaware before it blasted into the cars. It carried him past neighborhoods he didn't know, and didn't care to know. It jolted his body before and after each stop. Worst of all, the Frankford El constantly reminded him how badly things had gone since the elections.

The El pulled away from Dauphin-York. Lonergan's body tipped to the left. He wasn't fully awake yet. Where had he nodded off? Somewhere under City Hall? Jesus, he was tired.

A hard chill cut through his coat. He should have worn a warmer shirt. Lonergan's city-issue bluecoat was warm, but he wasn't wearing it. The City liked their cops in uniform as they made their way to their stations—the more bluecoats, the more citizens enjoyed the illusion of a well-protected place. Well, Lonergan decided he wasn't wearing it any longer than the required seven hours. That's all the City deserved for its $5.50 a day.

Huntingdon now. The same stops, day after day, night and morning. He had them memorized. Sometimes it helped make the trip go faster, sometimes it didn't. He should have picked up a pulp at the newsstand. He'd forgotten. The doors opened. A gust of frigid air whipped through the car. Rush hour was long over. The only people who rode the El this late on a Sunday were returning from a night at the cider saloons, the gambling dens, and the rowdy houses in the Tenderloin. The lack of body heat made the cars even colder.

Officer John Lonergan, out in the cold, now and forever after.

Political exile had come swiftly. The Vare boys had won in November, but by that time Lonergan had already broken with the Vares in a very messy fashion. One minute he was their prize enforcer; the next, their ultimate betrayer. At the time, Lonergan thought he'd played it smart by aligning himself with the competition. Not so smart, after all.

Ward leaders don't have the authority to fire cops, but they can strongly recommend to your captain that a transfer is in the best interests of the Department. It took less than forty-eight hours to have him reassigned to a station so far across the city it almost qualified as Bucks County.

Lonergan used to be able to make it to work at the West Philadelphia station in seven minutes flat—or three minutes on a streetcar when he didn't mind spending the nickel. Now his trip meant a streetcar to Market, a long haul on the Frankford El beneath Center City and out past the river wards, and then a second streetcar out to the hinterlands of Northeast Philly just in time to make midnight roll call.

Ninety minutes, one way. Three hours round trip. Three hours wasted out of twenty-four, every working day.

That was how they punished cops in this city.

Somerset now. As the El stopped Lonergan tumbled slightly to the left, and threw out a hand to support himself. After he stabilized, Lonergan rubbed his eyes with his knuckles. He shouldn't be on this freezing train. Not this late on a Sunday night, breathing other people's gin fumes. He should be home in a warm bed with Marie. He was already exhausted and his shift didn't even begin for another hour. It would be a struggle to stay awake through the night.

And then he had the return trip. The same stations, in reverse, early-morning sun stabbing him in the eyes. Pitying looks from the buttoned-up people making their way downtown to real jobs. Another small piece of his life erased.

Lonergan wanted to quit the force. But he couldn't do that to Marie and the boy. They were all trapped, just like he was trapped on this damned freezing El car.

Just after Allegheny, Lonergan noticed that the green-eyed girl was on the car too.

He saw her often, and wondered about her. She was pretty, but her clothes were worn and frayed. She wasn't a flapper or a hooker. But clearly she worked for a living. Her hands were gloveless and rough. Lonergan never saw the station she used to enter the train. He hoped it wasn't the Tenderloin. There were very few good reasons for a young girl to be out riding the El this time of night.

Lonergan pretended to glance at the advertisements above the girl's head and saw that she glanced at him—briefly. Had she recognized him too, from previous trips? Maybe she saw the blue slacks with the yellow stripe and realized he was a cop. Maybe she felt safer making a night journey with a cop sitting nearby.

A short while later the El pulled into the Torresdale station. Lonergan steadied himself and this time anticipated the jolt. When the train stopped, he was able to keep his body perfectly still.

Lonergan stole another glance at the girl and wondered if they'd ever talk, or acknowledge each other's presence. Or maybe they'd just keep each other company in polite silence.

He decided he'd be her guardian angel. He'd protect her, even if she never spoke a word to him. She wouldn't have to ask him, or thank him. He'd be looking out for her, though, from now on. Lonergan would stay awake and find out where she got on the train. She'd ride the El unmolested.

At the very least, it was something for an off-duty cop to keep his mind occupied with in a rumbling car full of drunks.

The doors opened. The green-eyed girl looked to her right. Lonergan followed her gaze to the concrete platform. No one there. The door closed. The El jerked forward and began making the steep incline to the Church Street station. The green-eyed girl looked to her left and nodded.

Maybe that wasn't a nod. Maybe it was just the jolt of the El.

Lonergan heard movement further down the car. A man in a black duster stood up from the bench. Something heavy fell at his feet, like a length of rope. Lonergan followed its length up to the man's hand and realized what it was. A whip.

"Wallets and purses," the man barked.

Lonergan stared at him, unbelieving.

The man handed a small sack to the bleary-eyed passenger sitting closest to him. "Put them in there. Nobody do anything or I'll cut your face open."

Was this man trying honestly to pull a hold-up on the Frankford El with a blacksnake whip?

Then Lonergan thought about it. Relatively few people on the train, but one or two of them might even be flush from a night in the Tenderloin. And they were all captive. The incline to Church Street was probably the longest stretch between stations—there was enough time to do what he wanted, and nobody could run away. And then at Church Street, he could run down the stairs to street level and disappear into Frankford.

"Don't you hear me? I will cut your faces open!"

For a few long seconds nobody moved. The passengers were either too drunk or stunned to react. It probably seemed like a lousy fusel oil fever dream. The El chugged its way up the incline. The entire world seemed to tilt a few degrees.

Lonergan instinctively reached for his hip and felt the space where his holster should be. He stopped carrying his gun too—Marie had forced him to keep it locked up at the station, against regulation. She didn't want the boy to find it. Too many stories in the newspapers about children shooting themselves with their fathers' guns.

"Shall I show you?"

No gun meant that Lonergan should just sit tight. Let this man take what he wanted and leave.

The bandit pumped his arm. The whip was a dark blur as it traveled a quarter-length of the length of the car and ripped into a passenger's chest. His body convulsed. The Stetson fell from the top of his head. He screamed, and then the girl sitting next to him—the green-eyed girl—slid a few inches away. The whip had almost hit her.

Everyone got busy opening wallets after that. The man

who'd been whipped was holding his hands to his torn coat, rocking and moaning incoherently.

The El was close to Church now.

"You."

The bandit was staring at Lonergan. He had hard little black points for eyes and a soft mouth.

"You too, big fella. Your roll in the bag—now."

The next passenger, a small man in a crooked bow tie, shoved the bag forward, waiting for Lonergan to take it.

Lonergan said nothing. They'd be at the Church station soon. There were two dollars in Lonergan's front pocket, and he'd be damned if this son of a bitch was taking it. If he tried to use the whip Lonergan would get up and knock him on his backside.

"Now!"

He glanced over at the green-eyed girl, who was staring at him with a puzzled expression. She seemed to be wondering, *Why aren't you giving him what he wants?*

Lonergan thought: *I'll show you why.*

He stood up and reached toward his hip, mimicking a draw. "Police officer," he said. "Drop the whip or I'll shoot you down."

The bandit shook his head as he took long steps backward. "I'll cut off your head before you even—"

Before the bandit could finish, Lonergan pumped his legs and started to lunge. Then a violent jolt as the El pulled into Church Street made Lonergan stumble. The bandit retreated a few steps. The center door slammed opened. Lonergan looked up just in time for the bandit to give him a face full of the whip.

Someone screamed—it may have been Lonergan. He didn't know. All he felt was searing numbness followed by the intense heat of the slash. Around him the shock-sobered passengers gathered themselves together and fled the car, crying out for the operator to stop the train. Either he didn't hear them or didn't care, because soon after the center door slammed shut again.

Lonergan heard the bandit cry: "MY MONEY!"

The little man with the crooked bow tie—he must have walked off with the sack. Maybe bow tie would do the right thing and return the stolen items to his fellow drunken passengers. Or maybe he'd toddle down to the street level and do his own disappearing act.

The El jolted forward. Lonergan watched as drops of his own blood began to streak across the floor of the car.

"I'm going to cut you apart," the bandit said.

A woman's voice cried out: "Clayton, *no!*"

Lonergan glanced to the right. It was the green-eyed girl, still here, perched on the rattan bench. Why hadn't she left with the others?

Then all at once he knew.

The bandit was coming at Lonergan now, cracking the whip across the seats. Lonergan didn't have a strategy. He merely reacted. Whip be damned—he lunged for the bastard.

The two of them stumbled backwards into the center door. Made impact. Glass spiderwebbed behind Lonergan's body. Lonergan could smell beer on the man's fevered breath. He was skinny but strong. The El start to slow down again. Orthodox-Margaret station, coming up.

Lonergan gathered a fistful of the bandit's duster, put his foot against the wood, and pushed forward. They spun until they collided with the center door opposite. The glass, again, cracked—and the bandit went partially through it. Shards rained down on the track. Lonergan drove a fist into the bandit's face. Then again. And again. And again. The train stopped, jolting both of them to the left. The center door opened.

The bandit pulled himself free, crashed to the ground, and then scrambled backwards on the platform, leaving the whip in Lonergan's hand. Lonergan took two steps back then fell to the floor of the car. His face was no longer numb. The pain was starting to appear in deep, angry throbs. He felt nauseous and dizzy.

By this time the conductor had gotten the hint something was wrong. Maybe he saw the bandit scrambling for the concrete steps leading to the street. The El idled at the station, doors open. Night air blast-freezing the interior of the car.

Lonergan glanced up at the green-eyed girl, who'd been left behind. He felt hot blood run over his jaw and down his neck.

"Seems Clayton's left you," he said.

The girl appeared afraid now.

"So you're the lookout, I suppose. Did you follow someone from one of the gambling houses? Did one of them hit it big tonight?"

She wasn't looking at Lonergan. She was looking at the whip in his big hands. If Lonergan peeled off her shirt and saw her bare naked, what would he see? *You ride that train or I'll hide you again, you bitch.*

"What are you going to do?" she asked softly.

It was a good question. What should he do? He wasn't wearing the bluecoat. He didn't have his gun. He wasn't in his district. He still had his two bucks in his front pocket. He didn't have to do a thing.

After a while the operator, a florid-faced man, came rushing into the car, asking what had happened. The green-eyed girl made a small cry as she rushed out of the car and ran across the platform. Lonergan said nothing. He listened to the rapid clicking of her shoes on concrete as they faded away.

But he wanted to tell her, *Stay with me.*

He wanted to tell her: *You don't understand. I'm your guardian angel.*

REALITY

BY CORDELIA FRANCES BIDDLE

Old City

I should explain that I write historical dramas, so as I wander the streets of Philadelphia I ponder how they looked before the curse of the internal combustion machine, and what vile secrets lurked behind the brick façades that now appear so *H&G* perfect. My theory (unproven) is that stone, being porous, is capable of retaining energy from the souls of the damned and despairing in the same manner that sponges hold water. Concentrate hard enough, and long-buried crimes will leach out.

I take my dog on these exploratory jaunts. I figure she adds an air of respectability to what otherwise might be mistaken for a stalker's prowl—my beady glance measuring eyebrow windows hidden under the eaves, or mismatched brick work where once were doors.

Our route is simple: 6th Street (6th and Lombard was a red-light district a century and a half ago, the "fancy houses" now converted to upscale residences—or so local realtors insist), through Washington Square (frisbees zooming over the unmarked graves of Revolutionary War soldiers—Americans planted feet-first, Brits buried head-down in retribution), past the rear entrance of Independence Hall (oft-promulgated tales of Colonial derring-do). After that I cross 5th Street toward the Second Bank of the United States where I customarily pause to parlay with Nicholas Biddle, ancestor and financial wizard, before continuing my journey into the alleys and courtyards the tourists avoid. Nick died in 1844, so it's a one-sided conversation, but I envision him standing there lordly and a trifle vain (Byron would have admired the long, wavy locks) amidst the marble columns that mark his particular temple to Mammon.

Now isn't the moment for a diatribe against that snake-in-the-grass Andrew Jackson and the fiscal ruin he visited upon the nation, but let's just say I bear the ex-pres a colossal grudge. The root of my wrath is lucre, not the noblest of motives for revenge, but there you have it. At any rate, as I stop, I ask old Nick (or old Nick's spectral self) to find a miraculous means to shower me with money—which would permanently cure my writer's block. I figure an ex-banker should have ready access to the celestial till. I do this while the dog noses around looking for the perfect place to pee. At least *her* prayers are answered.

I've digressed.

It was during a late afternoon at the end of September, a day that had been unremittingly dreary and depressing, and while I was nearing the Second Bank I heard them—the reenactors, that is. If you've ever strolled the city's landmarks, you've encountered these ubiquitous street performers. They dress exclusively in period garb and bombard passersby with tales of eighteenth-century moxie. Don't misunderstand; I have nothing against idealism, or spunk either, but I become suspicious when the Founding Fathers are portrayed as action heroes. It makes me want to canvass the Founding Mothers for their opinions.

These particular actors weren't the predictable for-God-and-country types, however. For one thing, despite the advanced hour and waning light, they'd attracted a large, enthusiastic crowd, big enough and noisy enough that I couldn't get near the players who stood on the pebblestone road fronting the bank. For another, the script was more trenchant than the usual family-style (read: Disney-fied) entertainment. The change of pace was a welcome variation to the traditional bell-ringing and saber-rattling. I decided to listen in. Besides, old Nick needs the cold shoulder treatment once in a while. Most captains of finance and industry do.

"He keeps slaves on his Southern plantation—which doubtless you're aware. The crimes perpetrated upon them are demonic: floggings until their flesh comes away in bloody strips, children snatched from their mothers and sold—"

"You tell 'em, sister!" a female audience member yodeled at the actress delivering the lines. Other voices sprang into action, attempting to shush the interruption.

"I've a right to my opinion," the provocateur shot back. Naturally, this was met with more orders to cease and desist.

"Let the gal finish, why don'tcha? The wife and I didn't come to Philly to listen to you."

"This is a free country, bro. In case you haven't heard."

"Just shut up, okay?"

"You gonna make me? You and *the wife*? Doesn't she have a name?"

"What's that crack supposed ta mean?"

"Whaddaya think?"

"Hey, c'mon, you two. Take it elsewhere."

As additional members of the crowd joined the enlightening argument and then settled into a tenuous peace, they—and I—pressed closer to the improvised arena. I couldn't see the performers yet, but the initial actress's vocal quality and range was impressive, a professionally trained instrument that could hit the back of any theater. I wondered what she was doing hustling tourists for tips.

"This isn't merely abolitionist fervor. My entire life is affected by his shameful philosophy." She paused to let the dramatic tension build. As I mentioned, she knew her stuff. "For I must also consider the mulatto bastards his seed has produced—"

A gasp from two protective parents arose. The crowd opened to let them and their children scurry through, the boy and girl lagging behind, eyes glued to the ground lest anyone assume the totally dorky choice to vamoose was theirs.

"I thought these dramas were supposed to be clean and wholesome," the mother muttered while the son, who looked to be about eight, demanded: "What's seed? It's not like grass stuff, is it? I know what a bastard is." In the silence, his falsetto voice boomed.

"Hush, Anthony, we'll talk about it later—"

"That's what you always say, Mom!"

"At least the play's educational," the father offered with a wary chuckle. "That's what we wanted, wasn't it? American history made fun—"

"Paul, how can you?" Having registered her disapproval, Mom spun away from Dad and bent down to her son. "Don't use the word *bastard*, honey."

"Dad does—"

"What your father says and does isn't always suitable. You may as well learn that right now."

"Like when he—"

"That's enough, Junior." This time it was Dad who did the scolding. He was now carrying the boy's sister, a yellow-haired girl of four or five who clung to his neck and stuck out her tongue at her earthbound brother. As the father held his daughter aloft, a grin of false indulgence spread across his face. It didn't begin to conceal his dismay at being the focal point of a bunch of tittering strangers.

"But you do, Dad. When we watch the Phillies, you—"

"Anthony, that's enough."

"Bastard, bastard," the little girl sang out.

"Look what you made your sister do, Junior. I want an apology. Now."

"What do you expect, Paul, if you set the kind of examp—?"

"Drop it, Sheila."

"I'm not allowed to tell the truth, is that it?"

"Now. Drop it now."

With the audience torn between eavesdropping on a family meltdown and watching professional performers, a space became free for me to slip forward (dog in tow) until the actors were in sight. Two women and a man, dressed not in homespun and breeches and tricorne hats but in full Victorian regalia: the women draped in silks and expensive paisley shawls, the man in a fitted coat and tall beaver hat. He had his back to me; the women were also turned away, their faces concealed by their bonnets' wide beribboned brims. All three might as well have stepped from the fashion plates in *Godey's Lady's Book*, the period's answer to an amalgam of *Cosmo* and *Redbook*. I shouldn't have been surprised at their outfits; reenactors are obsessive people. They don corsets and crinolines, tight wool trousers and tighter cravats, whether the heat index measures a hundred degrees Fahrenheit or sleet is slinging itself sideways. In my opinion that's odd.

"All the while, he struts around the metropolis, esteemed by his peers as if the gentleman farmer from the Carolinas were unconnected to the God-fearing churchman dwelling in Society Hill," Actress Number One continued. Her tone had grown more strident; her posture (or what I could see within her voluminous clothes) was rigid. "How can this be? Wasn't the transatlantic slave trade abolished in 1808? Then why does the government allow this evil to persist?"

The argument hit a chord with the audience. There were cheers; several people clapped. It seemed a likely time for an educational interlude, a Q&A during which the cast traditionally breaks character and engages in a group discussion, encouraging onlookers to air their views on whatever political message is up for debate. I took this as a cue to vacate my spot. Besides, I figured the dog was growing bored standing in one place while a lot of human types made noises that had nothing to do with food. However, the actress who'd taken the lead wasn't about to relinquish her soapbox. I opted to linger a bit longer.

"It's not merely the Southerners who are to blame. Here in our own city the textile mills supply fabric, so-called *cottonade*, for those despicable slave owners—"

"Haven't I experienced that abominable situation myself?" the second actress interjected, her tone also incensed, although her interpretation was subtler than Actress One. "And our calico is traded for human cargo along Africa's Niger River. But, I repeat, what's to be done in your case? Your husband's within his rights. As demonic as it—"

"Within his rights? Oh, where's your sense of decency and equality? What about the burning of Pennsylvania Hall during the Anti-Slavery Convention, or the rioting that ensued? Entire blocks of houses set on fire. Men and women dying in the conflagration and their homes reduced to ashes. And this the City of Brotherly Love!"

Louder applause followed the bellicose speech. A few people whistled and stamped, their shoes drumming a tattoo against the stones. The instructive vignette was taking on the rowdy passions of an Eagles game. I began worrying for my dog's safety. The team's reputation as being pooch-friendly is a sullied one, but that's another story.

"What you say is true," the male actor picked up the cue. "Now we face riots over laborers' rights, which increase the civil unrest. But men and women—and children—must be paid fairly for their work." There was authority in his delivery, and sorrow that sounded genuine. I was sorry I couldn't see his expression. I was also impressed at the amount of research the playwright had done. I know this period well. The facts were solid.

"But what about your husband?" Actress Number Two persisted. I watched her lay a gloved hand on the man's sleeve, an indication that the scene was about to shift focus. Attentive though the audience was, the encroaching dusk, combined with the siren call of Geno's Steaks, would soon take its toll. It was time to address another topic. "I assume you haven't mentioned your critiques to him."

"Oh, I have. Naturally, he repudiates my arguments. No matter. I intend to divorce him, and desert his bed and wicked habits forever. Indeed, I should never have wed him, but I think you know that well enough."

"Well, duh!" two female audience members whooped in unison, although their advice might as well have been whispered. The performers never reacted to the commotion.

"You say nothing in response," Actress One eventually sighed. "But what other choice have I? I can't continue as I have been. Turning a blind eye to his numerous peccadilloes. Feigning devotion when what I feel is abhorrence. I see no other solution but to sunder our marriage bonds. Speak, please. I know you'll support me in my plight. I must divorce him, mustn't I, Martha?"

"Martha?" This time I was the one who attempted to interrupt the proceedings. *Martha . . . ? It couldn't be. Or could it? Had the unimaginable happened? Had people I believed I'd never encounter miraculously materialized? No. No, it was inconceivable. Fictional characters don't leap out of the pages of books and confront their authors.* I studied the actress called Martha: the narrow waist and fashionably full sleeves, the cameo eardrops and brooch, the reticule held in a gloved hand. *Of course, she was a reenactor. A good one, certainly, and wearing more costly accoutrements than most, but that didn't mean she was the genuine article, a resident of 1840s Philadelphia transferred to the modern city. Probably the name was pure happenstance. Or perhaps I'd misunderstood. And yet . . . And yet, what if truly it were she? What if fantasy had turned into fact?* "Martha . . . Beale?"

She made no sign of having heard my words, but she turned and faced me. Despite the fading daylight, I knew in an instant that this was no counterfeit. It was Martha Beale in the flesh. Her aquiline nose and proud jaw, her pensive eyes, the tall, stoic frame: who else could it have been but she? Practical, resolute Martha who'd finally broken free of her dictatorial father's troubling legacy. And there she was, gazing in my direction as though the encounter was a commonplace occurrence.

How to explain what I felt seeing her standing before me after all these years? Shock is too pallid a word; I was utterly confounded. It simply wasn't possible that she was living and breathing, but somehow she was. I stared at the broad steps leading up to the bank; pollution had cut runnels in the marble; the columns were streaked and crumbling, so I knew the time wasn't 1843 but the present. And then there were my fellow audience members: exposed bellies bulging over hip-huggers, facial piercings, flip-flops despite the season, the

sartorial trappings of the twenty-first century. This was no fig-
ment of my imagination. Martha was alive. Now. I reached
out my hand. I couldn't help myself. "I'm—"

"Hey, no touching the actors," a nearby participant ordered. "That's like harassment or something."

"But she's my—"

"Gab all you want after the show. For now, ya shut yer yap,
capisce?"

"She's not an actr—"

"Lady. Shut the hell up."

I examined the other supposed performers. Of course, it
was Thomas Kelman and Becky Grey Taitt, two other person-
alities from my newest novel. How could they have been ab-
sent if Martha was present? Kelman with the scar that traced a
silver line diagonally across his cheek, and the somber expression that turned to joy whenever he looked at Martha; Becky,
quixotic, effusive, temperamental, and a celebrated beauty.

You'll wonder why I hadn't recognized them immediately.
These three are the products of my brain, after all. Without
my fingers and keyboard they wouldn't exist. When I tell their
stories, I don't write them, I live them. Each of my fictitious
persons has its doppelganger in me, and I in them, and in
the other characters in my books too. Villain or victim, they
and I share one soul, one heart, one mind. Think what you
will about the consequences of multiple personality disorder;
I embrace the condition.

"Oh, my friends." Tears filled my eyes; I dispensed with all
doubts. How Martha and the others had conjured themselves
out of fiction and into reality was too stupendous a question
to pose. Besides, I'm no scientist. I stretched out my arms.

"Shut. The. Hell. Up," a burly guy with thick, hairy forearms snarled. His calves, visible beneath hip-hop length shorts

were hairy too. *Hirsute* might be a better literary description. Or *simian*, perhaps. His legs bowed like an orangutan's. "You made the actors clam up. My kid was really into this. You like that, spoiling things for kids?"

He was right about the lack of conversation emanating from the impromptu stage. The boon companions of my days and nights had fallen silent, although I was certain the cause was Becky's declaration that she intended to divorce William Taitt. I decided to rectify the situation. There, with evening fast approaching, with the background rumble of horse-drawn tourist carriages and the drone of the drivers spewing out far-fetched data about the birthplace of liberty, I would do my part as a patriotic citizen. I would welcome each and every stranger, and give them the benefit of my insights into our city and its customs.

"That's because Becky—Mrs. Taitt—announced she was going to leave her husband. Martha and Kelman are mulling over her words. Divorce is commonplace now. It was scandalous in the mid-1800s. Unheard of, actually."

The man glowered, moving his mouth in wordless spasms as if he were trying to lip-read. I realized a dissertation on Victorian-era mores was reaching a trifle higher than desired.

"Let me back up and explain the situation. I'm an author, *their* author. These are my characters. I specialize in historical novels. You may not read that genre, but it's what I write. And I'm guessing you're here because you enjoy learning about history, isn't that correct? You like drama blended with fact." I smiled at the confrontational creep and all the other playgoers who were now viewing me with a mixture of hostility and confusion. Despite their antipathy, I beamed. Showing off your creation(s), even when the moment is improvisational and the audience unreceptive, is a heady experience.

"This is Martha Beale, a Philadelphia heiress, and Thomas Kelman, her suitor. He wasn't born into her social sphere, but never mind about that at the moment. More important is the fact that he has a special political appointment to the city's mayor. I should explain that there was no centralized police force at the time in which my novels are set. Kelman solves crimes. That's his *raison d'être*. And Becky, well, she really is an actress. Or she was. A famous one. From England. She's retired from the stage at the moment; her husband's a member of the aristocracy. As you just heard, he owns a plantation in the South, which wasn't uncommon. Many upper-class Philadelphians were married into Southern families. Our commerce was also closely intertwined. That's why the city was bitterly divided at the onset of the Civil War. You have only to read S.G. Fisher's treatise on race to appreciate how impassioned sentiments were, though I warn you his views are alarming. I'm getting ahead of myself. I apologize. The period in question, which Becky, Martha, and Thomas are presently discussing, is twenty years prior. You heard mention of the riots in—"

"Christ, lady, you're a regular nut job."

I studied the faces peering at me through the gloom. That seemed to be the general consensus. I also got the impression everyone wanted me to pipe down, so they could get back to watching the scripted drama instead of a disagreement between two audience members. The problem was that it wasn't scripted. Not by me, at any rate.

At that moment, Martha turned her back on us all, took Becky's arm, and began to stroll away. Kelman brought up the rear of the trio, keeping a slight distance between himself and the ladies so they could discuss Becky's future in private. At least that's the way the tableau appeared.

"You bitch. See what you done? All this woo-woo shit? The actors think you're a loony-tunes too. They put court orders or somethin' on weirdos like you. You better hope they're not headin' off to find a cop."

I would have argued with the jerk, but I was worried he might take out his anger on my dog. Besides, he had a child with him. He began to trot after Thomas Kelman.

"Hey, buddy, I'll make it worth your while. All of yous. The kid likes this stage-type shit, what can I say? Just finish up what you started before that kooky dame started bustin' your chops. I'm no sensitive Sally; if your friend wants to off her hubby, that's fine by me. Hey, maybe I could help yous out with that . . . Audience input, you know? I know some guys . . . Hey, what can I say? Connected. Know what I mean?"

Kelman didn't answer, which tickled the hairy charmer to no end. "Yous guys are *good*! It's like you don't even hear me. I could use that on the missus. I can't yak now, hon, I'm acting." He chortled as he and his kid chugged to keep pace. Then the boy, who was half as tall as his father and a quarter his heft, began to complain about being hungry. "All right already. So we'll quit. You wanna quit? Let's do it." There was kindness in his voice. Playfully, he cuffed his son on his skinny shoulder. "Who's the boss?"

It wasn't a question, but the boy replied with a pleased and chirpy: "Me, Pop."

"You bet."

The pair started to amble south toward Walnut Street while the remainder of the audience dispersed, rebuking both me and the cast with varying levels of indignation. There's nothing like canceling a free performance to get people's dander up. My failed effort at city boosterism made me want to slog home and return to the pitiless computer screen. It may be a harsh critic, but it's a silent one. Despite my bruised ego, I stuck close to my mystical pals, waiting for an opportunity for a private dialogue. Which, if you think about it, could have turned into a ventriloquist's monologue/pantomime.

I didn't get the chance for a confab, though, because William Taitt rushed onto the scene, charging in from 4th Street and almost barreling into the parent-child duo. The electric streetlamps hadn't yet winked on, so visibility was reduced. Fortunately, Dad spotted Taitt as he strode forward, oblivious to anyone but himself. It was clear that Becky's husband was infuriated, and that decorum had been thrown to the winds. As he drew closer, it was equally apparent that he was inebriated. I'm sorry to say that's sometimes the case with William Taitt. I blame myself.

Becky, my brave Becky, blanched and turned her head away as if expecting a blow. Martha squared her shoulders, preparing to give Taitt a piece of her mind. Kelman stepped forward to block the man's approach.

"Kee-rist," the father gushed while his son burbled an impressed: "Cool."

"Didja see the guy's shoes? High heels. Like a dame's. I'm tellin' you, this is somethin' you'll never forget. Them dopes that left early are missing a real good show. NYC don't have nothin' like this. You'd pay big bucks up there for an act like this."

Parent and child returned to the center of the action while Taitt bore down upon his wife. As always, he was dressed in the latest style: the shoes that had caught the dad's attention as well as a plum-colored jacket and trousers the hue of a fawn's soft hide. The piping around his coat's lapels was syenite-blue. Were he a few years younger, Taitt would have been viewed as a dandy. His hair beneath his hat was wild, however, and his shirt and cravat askew.

"You make a mockery of me, wife," he seethed. "I won't permit it. And hiding behind your Amazon warrior. Mistress Martha Beale's no mythic queen who'll guard you from—"

"Have done, Mr. Taitt," was Kelman's quiet command, which drew immediate ire from Becky's drunken husband.

"Do you dare to countermand me, sir? This is a private matter. I insist you—"

"And I insist you behave in a civil manner toward your wife and Miss Beale—"

"*Civil*, Mr. Kelman. I doubt you understand the meaning of the word. You, a mere Johnny-jump-up who hopes to pluck golden coins from your heiress while laying her in your feathered nest. Here hen, hen, hen. Produce some shiny eggs for me, pray do." He attempted to push past Kelman, who stood his ground. The scar on his left cheek twitched; his hands curled themselves into fists.

"William, please. Desist. I'll come home presently—"

Naturally, Martha objected. "Becky, what did you just tell us? Besides, remember the pain he has inflicted in the past under similar circumstances. I won't allow you to be battered again." She put a protective arm around her friend's shoulder, which further enraged Taitt.

"You three can go to the devil! I'm William Taitt. My family built this city. I won't be denied my conjugal rights."

"Your rights don't include assault, sir." This from Martha, which drew a sneering condemnation from Taitt: "How would you, a spinster, know anything about marital rights, madam? Or fornication, unless it's with a—?"

"Taitt. Silence—"

"Lay a hand on me, Kelman, and I'll make certain you're hounded from the city. I am aware that you are in the mayor's employ, but his relationship with me is one of friendship and camaraderie."

You may wonder where was I while this altercation unfolded. The truth is that I stood stock-still and slack-jawed. My characters speaking for themselves? Carried along by their own volition? Like the father and son, I watched the scene in silence.

"I'm waiting, wife. You have a child at home, in case you've forgotten."

"I haven't, William. How could I?"

"Ah, contrition, Becky . . . A new guise. But I think not spoken with sufficient sorrow."

"My sorrow is in seeing you under the influence of drink. You make a spectacle of yourself in front of our friends—"

"You call these people friends? Well, I do not. And I won't have my spouse hectoring me." He held her arm tightly as he spoke.

Martha snatched at his sleeve when he attempted to lead Becky away; Kelman grabbed Taitt's shoulder. Kelman's fingers may be as long and tapered as a pianist's, but he's accustomed to using force when necessary. He's also tall; when roused he appears taller and even more imposing. Becky's husband looked puny beside him, as if his fine garments were sturdier than his limbs.

"Let her go, Taitt. Your threats have run their course. She told you she'd return in due time."

"I ordered you not to touch me, Kelman." At that, William Taitt yanked a pistol from his jacket, a new derringer manufactured in the Northern Liberties. If you're a history buff, you're familiar with the weapon and its eponymous inventor. If not, this is no time for an aside on the Gold Rush of '49, or the romance of the Old West. *Deringer, Henry.* Look him up.

When the gun was whipped out, everyone except Taitt froze. This included the dad and kid. I was already doing my zombie impression.

"Not quite the cock-of-the-walk, are you now, *Mister* Kelman? Unhand me at once, or I'll do some damage." Taitt waved the shiny weapon aloft, pointing randomly at the purplish sky. "This is no fowling piece, I assure you. Oh, I know, gentlemen don't arm themselves on our city streets, but you see, I'm in the vanguard of taste. I set style, I don't follow it. Who knows, someday derringers like mine may become *de rigueur* accessories like hats or walking sticks or ladies' parasols. I intend to have my wife obey me." He lowered the gun to shoulder height and smiled. "Don't think I'm not sincere. The pistol's loaded."

With that he discharged it, the retort so loud that even the pigeons accustomed to backfiring motorcycles and belching city buses flapped upward in alarm. Above the bank, the starless air filled with the frantic flutterings of their wings. I watched them circling, as black and swift as bats; then I heard a groan and the thud of a body falling while Becky implored: "William, don't." Her voice was now whisper-soft, an echo of what it had been. "I'll do as you say."

My focus returned to earth, but she and my embattled creations had vanished. In their place was nothing, no muzzy wavering of ectoplasmic matter, no faint entreaties from on high. Night had descended, but it wasn't darkness that hid my friends from view. They were simply gone, as if they'd never stood on the soil in front of me.

"Don't leave," I whispered, but my plea was too late. However those four had managed to materialize, they'd chosen the same means of escape.

"Coo-ool," the boy said. "Dad, that was waaay cool." He

stood beside his father, who was now lying on the pebble-stones, facedown, his head inches from the entrance steps to the Second Bank. The child's expression as he gazed at his father's prone form couldn't have been prouder. Reflecting the glow of an exterior floodlight, the boy's eyes shone white and enormous.

"Blood and everything. Wow. Just like on TV. It's on the dirt too. How'd you guys do that? Like, how'd you know he was gonna shoot you, and not the other dude? Wait'll I tell the kids on the block. Wow. Mom's gonna be pissed about your shirt, but hey, it's like reality TV. Or something, right? I'll tell her the badass dude with the gun did it. All right? That's what we'll tell her, okay? I mean, she won't care if it's like a famous person who made a mess. Dad? You can get up now. The other actors left. It's just the crazy lady and me. Dad? Hey, Dad."

THE RATCATCHER

BY GERALD KOLPAN

South Street

F inlayson blinked in the sun. He would normally be asleep at close to ten in the morning, but old Mitford had told him to make the sacrifice. Whoever it was that wanted him was willing to pay, and as Finlayson needed to pay Mitford, he was keeping the appointment in both their interests.

Standing outside the Hippodrome, Finlayson realized he had never been inside it, or any other theater. But then, entertainment cost money and there wasn't much of that in his line of work. He figured that any week he could keep his belly from talking and get drunk enough to stand his life, he was on velvet. Play-actors and Chautauqua speakers were for Rittenhouse Square ladies and fairy boys, anyway. Besides, he did his business at night when they did theirs, and his quarry wasn't about to wait around while he sat through the last act of *Alice Sit-by-the-Fire*.

Until today, Finlayson's routine had seldom varied: he woke at three in the afternoon, made up his pallet on the floor of Mitford's stable, and ate a buttered roll purchased from Kelem's delicatessen the night before. Then he grabbed his canvas duck bag and headed for the Franklin Refinery docks. This was, in his opinion, the place to find the city's best rats, fed on the sugar that came in from Cuba until their small eyes fairly crusted over.

Last night had been good. His traps contained four large brown captives, all alive and fit to kill. The average Norway weighed about a pound, but you could always count on a Franklin rat to go four to eight ounces more than that. They were lively fellows too: full of sugar for energy and fresh vegetables for strength and stamina. He always said that a Franklin rat was the king of the Delaware, able to jump right from the river to a ship's deck or swim across to Camden using only its tail as an engine. Putting one end of each trap into the bag, he tripped a spring to open its gate and dumped the screaming occupants inside. The sack vibrating like a saloon on election night, he walked down Delaware Avenue to Pemberton Street and turned left into Pier 34. Once inside, he made his way to the office of Jimmy O'Mara.

Jimmy ran what was probably the last rat-baiting operation in Pennsylvania, maybe the last in America. On Wednesday nights, he would welcome between fifty and sixty diehards to his pit in an unused storeroom. The first hour was devoted to beer and whiskey, so by the time the trainers arrived, they were greeted with whistles and applause. As the men cursed and cheered, each trainer would place his dog on a cargo scale to be weighed. Jimmy would then step to the edge of the pit and deposit a corresponding number of rats onto its dirt floor. If the dog weighed fifteen pounds, he would fight fifteen rats; twenty pounds, twenty rats, and so on. Based on each dog's reputation and breeding, the spectators would place bets on the amount of time it would take for the dog to kill all the rats. The man who came closest won.

Finlayson's rats were highly prized for their size and ferocity and Jimmy could always count on them to go down fighting, lunging at an eye or tearing at an ear.

Ordinarily there was not a word exchanged between

O'Mara and Finlayson. The ratcatcher unloaded his prisoners into a large barrel and Jimmy counted them. He paid twenty-five cents for each one, thirty-five if a rat was particularly large and aggressive.

His earnings in his pocket, Finlayson nodded and left. He crossed Delaware Avenue and walked up Kenilworth Street to Front, arriving at the Schooner Tavern just as Henry Kulky was opening up. He sat down at the bar, downed two double whiskeys and a beer, and ate whatever sandwich Kulky felt like making. He paid, walked up Bainbridge to 3rd, and returned to the stable. Mitford usually just grunted at him and collected the twenty cents that was his night's rent. But today, the old man actually spoke to him.

"You know where the Hippodrome the-a-ter is?"

"Who doesn't?"

"Don't crack wise with me, Fin," Mitford said. "I'll shovel you out of here with the rest of the horseshit."

"Yeah, I know where it is," Finlayson said, "up 6th and South."

"Well, that bum Bobby Monoldo was in here last night. I figured he was gonna try and put the bite on me so I was ready to chuck him into the street, but he said he had some info for you. That you was to show up at the Hippodrome 'round ten in the a.m. and that if you did, a guy there would make it worth your while."

"He say who this guy was?"

"Didn't I just get finished tellin' ya what he tol' me? That's what he said. No names, no numbers, no angels singing alleluia. And if that's not enough, mebbe you should hire a secretary."

"Okay," Fin said. "I guess I ain't got time to clean up."

Mitford laughed. "Ten o'clock's in ten minutes. Cleaning you up would take until St. Patty's. No, I'd say you ain't got time to get dainty. I'd say you should get the fuck out of here."

Now, Finlayson looked up at the huge marquee. It was the kind that had giant letters bolted to a framework attached to the building's archway. He figured that the letters spelled out *Hippodrome*, but the only word he could read was printed boldly on all of the exterior posters: *RATS*.

He walked up to a tired-looking woman sitting inside the box office. She was reading a copy of *Aunt Sally's Policy Player's Dream Book*.

"My name's Finlayson," he said. "Somebody here wants to see me."

The woman glanced up from the book and immediately remembered the days when someone like this would never have been allowed near the Hippodrome, not even to haul away the garbage. Her mouth turned down in disgust at the torn coat and blackened shirt collar, the matted red hair and filthy hands. She could smell him through the glass of the booth.

"Yeah," she said. "You's expected. Go t'ru the lobby and where it says *Lounge*, head downstairs. Make a right and you'll see another sign says, *Artistes*. Walk t'ru that and it's the first door. Don't talk to none of the patrons."

Fin did as instructed. He walked quickly past the few customers milling about, waiting for the eleven o'clock matinee. When he got to the bottom of the steps he spotted the sign and opened the heavy iron door.

The first thing he saw in the corridor was a rat. It was dressed in what looked like red and gold silk. Almost by instinct, Finlayson jumped toward it. In the old days before he could afford traps, he caught hundreds of rats with his bare hands. Terrified, the rodent scurried through the first door on the left. Fin followed it into what appeared to be a dingy dressing room, just in time to watch it vault into the lap of a man sitting in an old caned chair.

Had he been standing, the guy probably would have measured only five-three or -four, but he had the confident air of a man twice his size. He wore a splendid suit of brown gabardine intersected with thick chalk stripes. His pale blue waistcoat was of silk floral brocade and his dark blue necktie was stuck with a good-sized sapphire. Black patent leather shoes peeked out from gray buttoned spats and his left hand rested on a silver-headed cane. Sitting on his shoulder, his arm, both his thighs, and the crown of his cream-colored Stetson were rats; each one attired similarly to the first, in shining silks of multiple colors. On closer inspection Finlayson noticed that every tiny outfit bore a number on its back.

"Ah, thank you for coming. I see you've already met Commodore Dutch. My name is Professor Alois Swain. If you are indeed Mr. Finlayson, then I am the one who sent for you."

Commodore Dutch peeked out from beneath Swain's jacket and then turned and ducked inside.

"You, sir, come highly recommended," Swain continued. "I have been told in every saloon along this fine thoroughfare that you are Philadelphia's finest rat man."

"Thanks, mister, " Finlayson said, "but it looks like you're doing pretty well along that line."

Swain frowned. "As of now, yes. But these few little fellows may not always be sufficient for the daily practice of my art."

"Art? What, do you draw them or something?"

Swain laughed. "No, Mr. Finlayson, I am not that kind of artist. But even though I do not sculpt or paint, the adage remains true—one picture is worth a thousand words. So if you will be kind enough to accompany me onto the spacious stage of the Hippodrome, I will be only too happy to illustrate for you that which has made me and my little charges a household name amongst those who demand the unusual in their entertainment."

Fin nodded and Swain rose from his chair. As he did, the gaily dressed rats scampered up his suit and onto his shoulders and arms. They clung with their claws to his back and one even dangled by its teeth from his tie. Finlayson could no longer see Commodore Dutch and guessed that he had taken refuge in one of the professor's interior pockets.

Fin could hardly see through the gloom of the theater's wing. He could hear grit crush beneath his boots as he followed Swain through a long black corridor. When they passed through an archway the professor flipped a large switch attached to a gun-metal box. The stage illuminated.

"Electricity," the professor said. "The greatest boon to the performer since the theatrical brothel."

Finlayson squinted at the sudden brightness and looked out at the many rows of worn seats. He was amazed at the sheer size of the auditorium and the grandeur of its pilasters and carvings. Women's heads, men's heads, and the heads of various animals were sprinkled across the two long balconies, and the stained carpet was in the pattern of a *fleur-de-lis*. In the far corner of the orchestra section a man was snoring in his seat. Fin recognized him as Stewie Barnes, the fry cook at Bolc's Tavern. If he knew anything about Stewie, the guy had been here all night. Fin didn't blame him for wanting to sleep in such a magnificent place.

Swain took Finlayson by the arm and led him to the center of the stage. There, beneath a huge canvas cover, sat an enormous object, flat on the sides and top. Swain grabbed the cover and with a single yank, pulled it to the floor.

As if on cue, the rats jumped from his arms and shoulders and on to what looked for all the world like a miniature version of a racetrack. It was oval, had a flocked "lawn" at its center, and was surrounded by tiny banners representing many nations. In the middle of the greenery and largest of all was an American flag, stiffened by glue into an eternal wave.

Swain reached beneath the track and began to remove a series of small wooden cages, six in all. From each, he produced a large cat. Like the rodents, they were bedecked in silks of varying color and number. On their backs were tiny leather replicas of English saddles. At the appearance of the cats, the rats each took up positions equidistant around the ring and stood on their hind legs.

One by one, Swain placed the cats in the center of the ring; then he snapped his fingers.

At the sound, each rat ran for the cat whose colors and number matched its own and leaped into the saddle. Swain snapped again and the cats began to race around the track in single file. After a few moments the professor clapped his hands and the cats turned toward the center of the ring. They zoomed past each other at top speed and then began running around the track again, now occupying each other's positions. Swain clapped twice and the cats reared up. As they did, each rat leaned in toward the neck of its mount like a cowboy whooping it up on a western plain.

Swain struck the side of the track with his fist and the rats dismounted, returning to their original positions. The cats turned toward the little grass "lawn," bunched together, and lay down, stock-still. The professor turned to his guest and grinned.

"It's better with an orchestra."

Finlayson stood quiet and amazed.

"I see you cannot speak," Swain said. "Your reaction is a common one and typical of those who first experience our little exhibition. It has taken me many years to produce the zoological marvel you have just witnessed. As a result, we have topped the bill across this great land and in the capitals of Europe. I daresay that nowhere in the world is there an amusement remotely similar to Swain's Rats and Cats."

Fin tried to speak but his mouth was dry. Swain took a pitcher of water from a nearby stand and poured it into a thumb-marked glass. The ratcatcher took a long draught and wiped his mouth on his dirty sleeve.

"What's this got to do with me?"

Swain's brow knitted tightly. "Way back when, I had time to haunt the wharfs and alleys, seeking out the finest specimens. I found number six there, Romulus, in an infested theater in Brooklyn when he frightened Miss Fanny Brice into leaping on to the nearest chair."

He reached beneath the platform again. From a large paper bag, he produced several handfuls of dried corn and sprinkled it on the floor. Immediately the rats leaped from the platform and began to gorge themselves. The cats remained in place.

"As an expert, you likely know that, even with the finest of care, the lifespan of *Rattus norvegicus* rarely exceeds four years, and I am far too occupied with travel and performance and training to seek out new members of my cast. Like the rest of my small charges, Romulus is aging, and in a year, perhaps two, certainly by 1915, he and his colleagues will enter our Lord's own sewers. This, sir, as they say, is where you come in."

"You want some rats?"

"Mr. Finlayson, I am asking far more than that. I am proposing that you become the official ratcatcher for Swain's Rats and Cats. In this capacity, you will perform the duties such as have been your living, but that living shall be far more comfortable. I will pay you the sum of thirty dollars per capture, up to forty dollars for a swollen female of fine size. Once our business is established and mutual trust confirmed, I propose to rent a facility here in which you will breed new stars for me. New Romuluses! New Dutches! New Esmeraldas and Kittys and Whiskers!"

Fin eyed the little man suspiciously. "Thirty dollars for a rat?"

"Thirty dollars for the *right* rat, sir. He must be young and strong and of sufficient proportion to be seen from the rear of the mezzanine. He must be hale and smart and fecund, well able to reproduce himself *ad infinitum* in the cause of family diversion."

Finlayson looked pained. "Do you want me to sign a paper? I can't read or write."

"No, no, my boy. All I want is for you catch me big, fat, healthy rats. Rats that will honor your skill as they delight and amaze theatergoers the world over."

Swain whistled the first six notes of "Liebestraum" and the rats immediately stopped eating and took up their positions on the track. Then he reached into his watch pocket.

"Our first performance begins in five minutes. Here's a ducket for the show. What you have seen is only a portion of what my little friends can do. I'm sure that once you've absorbed the complete performance, you'll wish to be a part of their success. Afterward, we'll repair to Wexler's for the poison of your choice and a toast to your fortune and mine own."

* * *

Jimmy O'Mara jammed his cigar in his mouth, puffing on it hard. Finlayson had only just come in from his nightly rounds and Jimmy was ready to pour some arsenic in his ear. His customers had begun to complain.

Only last night, Fatso Eagan, the owner of a particularly nasty fox terrier named Billy, had bitched him out royal over the declining quality of his bouts.

"May's well pick posies as bring Billy here," he said. "These rats what yous've been getting act like ladies at a ice-cream social. It's six weeks in a row Billy's kilt 'em all in under one-thirty. Nobody's layin' down shit for wagers and I'm losin' money. Now I know they didn't close down the refinery. Where'd all them nice, big sugar rats go, Baltimore?"

"Mebbe they croaked a' the diabetes," Jimmy said.

Fatso's eyes narrowed beneath his huge brows. He shifted the chew in his cheeks from left to right and hocked. The spittoon rang like a new telephone.

"G'head and laugh," Fatso said, "but I can count. Last week they was twenty guys in here. Week before was thirty, week before that, near fifty. You're shrinkin' like balls in a blizzard, palsy-walsy. And until you get some rats in here wanna kill my dog, guess I'll hie me over the Camden side. I hear they got a pit there, one dog fights the other."

Jimmy's hollow cheeks lengthened in disgust. "Fuckin' barbaric."

Now he nearly bit through the cigar as Finlayson stood before him and emptied his sack into the pit. Twenty-odd rats spilled out and ran squealing for the ring's edges. They were small and thin, cowards each not more than six months old. O'Mara surveyed them for a few seconds.

"Mice," he said.

"I'm real sorry, Jimmy," Fin said. "I don't know if they've

shut the sugar lockers tighter or they finally brought in their own catchers, but it's like I've told ya—these past few months the pickins has been slim."

"Mebbe," Jimmy said, "or mebbe anymore, you're not a proper ratcatcher."

Finlayson's face became a wound. "Whadaya mean, Jimmy? Ain't I spent most my life bringin' you the best?"

"Yesterday and a nickel rides the horse car, m'boy. Look at you. You used to be the pitcher of your occupation—dressed in rags with that stable's manure attached. Same shirt and collar every day. Never could tell if it was gray from dye or dirt. And the stink! I could always tell you was comin' before you ever hit the door. That popcorn smell of rats mixed with your own sweat and the blood from where you'd been bit. It did a man's heart good to inhale that smell and know there was a true professional about the premises, a man you could trust. Now look at you."

"What's wrong with me?"

"I was up Big Hearted John's on Tuesday to buy a shirt and John tells me you been in. He says you bought that new coat and tie you're wearin' and what a bargain it was. Then I go to pay my bill at Mitford's and the old man tells me you lit out and were holed up at the Caledonia Hotel. Now, the Cal's a flea circus and them clothes are just what some guinea didn't pick up after alteration. But for a ratcatcher, it's like rentin' out Vair-sye and wearin' soup and fish. You ain't dressin' the part no more, bucko, nor actin' it neither."

Jimmy took the cigar from his mouth and crushed it on the floor. Then he turned to the poor excuse for vermin Fin had spent the night collecting.

"I can't use these," he said. "You can either drown 'em or I'll set Blackie on 'em just for practice. Besides, it looks like the game's dead. I'm sure as hell outta business."

Finlayson made to say something but the words stuck sideways like fish bones. He certainly couldn't tell O'Mara that twenty of the refinery's finest specimens were presently in training to replace and enlarge Swain's current troupe, or that thirty more were at this moment rutting in a series of breeding cages in the basement of Knox's Triangle Saloon. In the preceding six months, Swain had paid him nearly one thousand dollars for his rats: more than he usually earned in five years. As for his clothing, it reflected his new station, as would the clothes of any man who's come up in the world. Yes, he was still a ratcatcher, filthy and despised by the decent. But now, instead of being a supplier to a dying sport, he was a man of show business, a talent scout as it were, bringing new performers to a public blessed by a six-day work week and a hunger for amusement in the leisure time between factory and church. Finlayson took the canvas bag and turned toward the door. Jimmy O'Mara had already lit another cigar and turned to his ledgers.

Outside, autumn had come. The clouds gathering all night had broken into a gentle rain. Fin turned up his collar and crossed Delaware Avenue. He made a right onto Kenilworth and found the Schooner already open.

Without a word, Henry Kulky placed two shots on the bar and then pulled the tap for Fin's Esslinger. Except for the two men, the bar was empty. It wouldn't begin to fill until eleven when the dockworkers came off graveyard. As Fin downed the whiskeys he measured Henry's silence. After all these years he knew his good quiet from his bad.

"Hey, Kulk. Wanna see something new?"

"I already seen your suit," Kulky said.

"No, this ain't the suit. This is something so new, nobody except me's ever seen it. So when you see it, you'll be the second."

"Take much time? I'm busy."

"A minute."

"Cost me anything?"

"No."

"Okay."

Finlayson reached into his inside coat pocket. From it, he pulled a good-sized rat.

"Get that fuckin' thing outta here!" Kulky snapped. "Ya want me to lose my license?"

"Just wait a second, Henry boy, please."

Kulky reached beneath the bar for his bat but before he could grab it, Fin placed the rat on the worn wood and clapped his hands. The rat stood at attention like a rookie cop.

"Hut!"

With a squeak, the rat ran over his right hand, up his coat sleeve, across his shoulders, and down his left arm. Finlayson again shouted, "Hut," and the rat stopped cold.

Kulky brought the bat from beneath the bar but didn't raise it.

"Hut, hut!"

Fin held his arms a few inches above the bar and the rat jumped over them both and then returned, jumping to and fro until he whistled for it to stop. He took an old baseball from his pocket, placed it on the bar, and clapped again. The rat leaped onto the ball, rolling it across the bar like an elephant in the circus. He double-clapped and the rat turned, rotating the ball back toward him. Finlayson opened his coat and whistled once more. With a powerful spring, the rat leaped from the bar and back into the pocket, where it disappeared.

"Hey," Kulky said, "that's pretty good."

"It'll be better," Finlayson said, "with an orchestra."

GHOST WALK

BY CARY HOLLADAY

Chestnut Hill

I.

September 1899

In a basement in a stone house in Chestnut Hill, Frances Watkins, aged seventeen, and her mother are treated to a tour of an unusual collection: a group of preserved bodies owned by Vaughan Beverly, who is the widowed Mrs. Watkins's fiancé.

Vaughan gestures to a glass-topped casket and says, "This woman turned to soap."

Frances feels sick. The dinner at the restaurant where Vaughan took them was rich and heavy, and she drank too much champagne. She wishes her mother had never met Vaughan Beverly on his mysterious trips to Baltimore, where Frances and her mother resided. Tomorrow, her mother will marry Vaughan Beverly, and this is the house where they will live together. I won't stay here, Frances vows. Not with dead people in the basement. She and her mother have known about them: Vaughan boasted of them at the party where Frances and her mother first met him, at the home of wealthy relatives. Vaughan is a man of science, everyone says.

Her mother acts as if it's a grand joke, these bodies. Maybe after the wedding, her mother will come to her senses and have them taken away. Surely it is wrong to have them here, as if they are of no more consequence than Vaughan's display cases of butterflies and beetles, with their carefully printed labels. Vaughan collects many things—guns, knives, and trophies of exotic animals. Last night, Frances stayed up late in his extraordinary library, reading about birds.

The basement is furnished as beautifully as the rest of the house, with electric lights, upholstered couches, and paintings on the walls. Frances can't help but be intrigued. "She turned to soap?" she asks, peering through the glass. The cadaver is naked except for strips of cloth over its breasts and loins, and it appears whitish-gray.

"Tell us about her, Vaughan," says Mrs. Watkins gleefully. She sips from a glass of wine and places a hand confidingly on her fiancé's arm.

Vaughan pats her hand and says, "She died of yellow fever, probably in the epidemic of 1792, and was buried near the river. Some of those old cemeteries filled up with water. This woman, being rather rotund, well, her fat combined with chemicals in the wet earth. The substance is called adipocere. It's much like lye soap."

Frances's mother repeats, "Adipocere. What a lovely word. It sounds French. Like an exclamation, *au contraire. Adipocere!*" she says in mock dismay, waving her hand.

To look at a dead body is shocking, Frances thinks. To look at a person dead more than a hundred years is astonishing. She asks Vaughan, "How do you know she's soap?" She imagines Vaughan in a bathtub, humming and lathering. She heard him humming last night, while she searched for towels in a cupboard in the hallway outside his lavatory. Strange that in a house so ornate and well-appointed, there are no servants.

"I have washed with her," says Vaughan. He laughs, and Frances's mother joins in. Vaughan adds, "If you mix a bit of this body with some crushed lavender, it's the finest soap you'll ever have. I can open the case, Frances, and you can pinch off a piece."

"Oh, no, that's all right," Frances says.

Frances feels light-headed, and she assumes it's from the company of the dead. Vaughan's collection includes a mummified woman and baby, a pickled horror of indeterminate gender floating in formaldehyde, and a remarkably fresh-looking boy about Frances's age.

Vaughan thumps the glass cover of the casket holding the boy. "Meet the Young Master," he says. "He was almost certainly a soldier. He turned up near the site of the Mower Hospital, a Civil War hospital in this neighborhood which was torn down after the war."

"Turned up?" asks Frances, determined to challenge him. "Did you dig for him?"

"He was brought to me," says Vaughan, "and I have given him a home. He was already embalmed. Someone did a first-rate job. All I had to do was clean him up and put clothes on him. He was naked. I found this uniform in the attic, and it fits as if made for him."

Frances dares to ask, "Does the constable know these people are here?"

Frances's mother frowns at her.

"The authorities have enjoyed this same tour," says Vaughan. He points to a table pushed into a corner. "We've played poker here, with the soap lady and the Young Master looking on."

Frances feels Vaughan's fingers on her back, just the lightest pressure. She has felt the fingertips before, and has assumed the touch was an accident. Does her mother see? No, her mother is absorbed by the Young Master. Vaughan takes the empty wine glass from her mother's hand and slips an arm about her shoulders.

He says, "He's one of those people who just don't rot."

"Who brought him to you?" Frances asks.

"An old fellow who used to be a guard at the hospital. I'll introduce you to him, if you like. He has wonderful stories. The hospital was the best in the nation. If you got shot or got sick, it was where you hoped to go. We'll stroll over to the grounds some time."

Frances returns to the soap woman and gazes at the mute face, its closed, webbed-looking eyes, the dark pit of the slightly open lips. The glass is cloudy over the mouth, as if the soap woman breathes now and again. Frances feels she's in the presence of a marvel. To think that this woman lived and spoke and ate, perhaps loved a man and bore children, then fell ill and suffered and died. And her body, without her soul in it, went on to have a separate life of its own, somehow being brought to this mansion in the northwestern part of the City of Brotherly Love.

For the past three days, Vaughan has entertained them. They rode in his carriage through the leafy avenues of Chestnut Hill, with Vaughan calling out in a clarion voice: "Shawnee Street! Mermaid Lane!" They explored the cool splendor of Fairmount Park. Vaughan's horses pulled to the edge of a ravine, and Frances held her breath as she looked down into Wissahickon Gorge.

It is the end of summer, the last year of the century. Frances felt a keen nostalgia as she breathed in the unfamiliar scent of the northern forest. Today, they took the trolley down Germantown Avenue, fast, faster than Frances ever moved before, flying over the Belgian-block cobblestones of the swerving street, while pedestrians ran pell-mell out of the way. Down and down the trolley plunged, with the passengers holding their hats during the steep careening slide, as if from the top of the world. Vaughan pointed out great houses that belong to friends of his, mansions where they will dine and dance, where Frances will meet young people "who will be congenial," he promised. Frances couldn't help but thrill to the thought, even though she knows she must run away from Vaughan's house, away from these bodies that Vaughan waited until tonight to show them, as a *pièce de résistance*.

She and her mother are being saved by Vaughan, and all three of them know it, saved from a wretched district of Baltimore where laundry flaps on lines and streets smell of garbage. Frances's mother has never allowed Vaughan to visit them there; in the three months they have known him, he has courted her mother in the homes of the prosperous Watkins relations who have kindly pretended that Frances and her mother are closer kin than is the case. Frances can't remember her father, who died when she was young. She feels like an old woman, as if she and her mother have switched places in a fairy tale. It should be Frances marrying a prince, not her mother marrying strange, compelling Vaughan Beverly.

Yes, Frances is in love with him, she admits to herself as she regards the soap woman's ravaged face. Frances keeps a tiny photograph of Vaughan in a locket around her neck, and when she is alone, she examines it, admiring his dark golden eyes, his Roman nose and high cheekbones, the slight puffiness of his lips. In Frances's fantasies, something happens to her mother—oh, not anything bad, but something clean and painless that simply takes her mother away—and then it's Frances whom Vaughan falls in love with, and they marry and live happily in this cavernous house on West Evergreen Avenue, and when she steps into this basement as Mrs. Vaughan

Beverly, it's like any other basement, holding only damp bricks and piles of ashes. She would make him wait until they were actually married—unlike her mother, who has occupied his bedroom these past three nights. It was not only Vaughan humming in the lavatory last night, it was her mother too: Frances heard them both. In the mornings, there have been plates piled high with eggs that Vaughan scrambles in his enormous kitchen in a great iron skillet, and the three of them in dressing gowns have eaten the eggs with butter and thick slices of toast that Vaughan pulls from his blazing oven. Maybe there are servants after all, because Frances never sees a dirty dish from one morning to the next.

Frances consults the soap woman silently about her dream: Can it be? Will I be with him? The glass of the casket fogs a little, as if the soap woman has answered. No, it's just her own breath, condensing there. She takes out her handkerchief and rubs at the spot. How can she long to stay with him, yet know that she must run away? Where will she go? Back to Baltimore? No. She's in a new place now. In Chestnut Hill. The very name rings in her mind like a bell. *When I was seventeen, I came to Chestnut Hill*, she imagines telling the soap woman. Then the story in her head stops, because she can't imagine what might be next. Probably nothing will ever happen to her, and she will always be her same plump self, with freckles.

When she looks up again, her mother and Vaughan are kissing.

"But the question is why?" Frances demands. "Why would someone bring you a dead body? Why would you take it, and keep it? And why do you have so many?"

"Francie," her mother scolds, from within the circle of her fiancé's arms. "Vaughan's a man of science. You know that."

Science seems to represent all that Frances will never understand. She bursts into tears.

"Would it make you happy, Frances," Vaughan asks, "if I buried them? There's a cemetery at Gravers Lane and Bowery, the Old Free Burying Ground. I've spent enough time there to learn names on tombstones: Frederick Detwiler, Alexander Parks, Catharine Antieg."

Frances stares at him. Will it be this easy? To object, to cry, and thus to get her way?

"There's no need, Vaughan," her mother says, but he lifts a hand to silence her.

"Yes," Frances declares. "They ought to be buried."

Vaughan looks from Frances to her mother. "Then they shall be," he says.

Frances feels her tears dry on her cheeks. *Her face was wreathed in smiles*—she read that line somewhere, and it comes back to her as she beams at Vaughan.

"Any objection to the dead butterflies, Frances?" her mother asks sarcastically.

"No," Frances says. What has come over her mother? This woman in the lacy white dress—*Thank heavens for this dress*, her mother confided during the courtship. *One nice dress and my good complexion*. Is this the same woman who struggled to keep their house clean, who sewed clothing for the rich relatives, who made Frances say her prayers every night?

"They can go to a museum, Vaughan," her mother says. "Aren't they valuable examples for science?"

"Yes, and I'll miss them." Vaughan strolls over to the soap woman to stand beside Frances. "This one, of course, we could just use her up," he says and laughs.

"Keep her, at least," Frances's mother urges him.

Vaughan says, "No, I've had their acquaintance long enough. I'll see that each one is decently interred."

"Thank you," Frances says. Generosity has always embarrassed her. "If you'll excuse me, I think I'll go to bed."

"Of course," replies her mother coldly, and Vaughan nods.

Then Frances realizes something else that is amiss, aside from a basement full of bodies. With a wedding tomorrow, shouldn't there be neighbors and friends calling to wish them well? She and her mother don't know anyone here, but Vaughan has lived in Philadelphia all his life. Where is his own family? He is not old; he is possibly younger than her mother. Is he alone in the world? She is overcome by the sudden conviction that the wedding will not take place, that this is all some ruse.

"Goodnight," she says and turns. She hurries up the stairs, to the first floor. She flings open the door that connects the basement with the rest of the house, runs across the deep carpet of the central hallway, and dashes up another staircase and another, to reach the guest room with the high feather bed and the cheval mirror.

There she opens the mullioned windows and breathes in the fresh air that smells of pine and spruce. The window overlooks a dark terraced garden. She hears little peepers that must be tree frogs, insects buzzing, and some low, croaking call from an animal or a bird of prey. Their songs and cries are old familiar ones of summer ending, of autumn beginning. The nighttime emits a glow, as if starlight is catching on blades of grass.

She is alone, like the soap woman. She has no friend to tell her fears to, no one to write a letter to. Since leaving school two years ago, she has kept close company only with her mother, assisting with the sewing, anticipating and dreading the invitations from relatives, when she and her mother would go forth bravely, in hopes that someone like Vaughan would rescue them. Her mother, donning the lace dress, once asked in anguish, *How many times must we do this?*

"And here I am," says a voice behind her, and Frances whirls from the window.

There stands Vaughan. In the light of the wall sconce, he looks taller than ever, his face ruddy, hair golden, brow smooth. He asks, "May I sit down?"

She nods, and he takes a seat on a slipper chair. She remains standing, awkwardly. She wonders whose room this was, who chose the rose-colored damask for the chair, whose face has been reflected in the mirror.

Vaughan says, "You're scared, Frances. How can I set your mind at ease?"

"Do you love my mother?" she asks.

"I love you," he says. "You knew tonight. Didn't you?"

She has longed to hear these words, yet now she feels only alarm. He rises from the chair and reaches for her hand. His fingers are warm and strong.

"It's not too late," he says. "You and I can be married."

"What of Mother? Would she live here, with us?" Frances's head spins. She can't believe she's saying these things.

Vaughan says, "I've been trying to figure it out. Things have moved rather fast. And just now, I'm sorry to say . . ." His voice trails off.

"What happened?" Frances asks. She pulls her hand out of his grasp. "Where's Mother?"

He looks at her with an expression of great gravity. After a pause, he speaks softly and urgently about her mother, saying she felt ill, then began clutching at her heart, then collapsed. "She seemed to recover a little, and staggered. She got as far as the Young Master, and then she, well, died. She's dead."

Terror ripples along Frances's spine. She tries to scream,

but only a sigh comes out. Vaughan pulls her to him and settles onto the slipper chair with Frances on his lap. He says, "A young woman and her mother travel north. The mother is to marry a scientist. On the eve of her wedding, she suddenly dies. The man marries the lovely, innocent daughter instead. It was just as well, since he'd begun to find the mother tiresome, with a ghoulish streak."

"She was angry with me," Frances murmurs, stunned. "This wouldn't have happened if I hadn't made her mad."

"You wanted to do the decent thing," he says. "Bury those bodies. A man wants a woman who'll make him do the proper thing."

"Is this a horrible joke?" Frances asks.

"This house knows no jokes," says Vaughan.

She leaps from his lap and runs for the door. He says, "Think it over, Frances."

She hurtles down the stairs, into the basement, and spies the still form of her mother.

"Mother," she cries, and touches her mother's cheek, which is already cool. She pulls at her shoulders, but the body sags in her arms.

She takes the steps again, two at a time. If she can reach the door, she can get outside, to some safe place. She can almost feel the dew on the grass, the distance she'll have to cover.

II.

"So that concludes the Ghost Walk," Annie says, as her tour group applauds. "The Beverly mansion used to be right here. It was torn down a long time ago, but that's a true story." She adds the capper: "And Frances was my great-great-grandmother."

The group gasps, and Annie savors the effect of her tale.

Where the Beverly mansion used to stand, there's only a depression in the ground. Across the street, there's a massive Victorian-style apartment house, where Annie herself lives, with towering sycamores out front. Annie has heard the tree frogs, just like she said. Besides, this is the perfect place to wind up the Ghost Walk, because the Irish-themed bar where Annie works is a five-minute walk away. She went on too long about Frances and Vaughan, though. She doesn't have time to return her oil lantern to the Chestnut Hill Welcome Center.

"I think he murdered Frances's mother. He was a serial killer," a woman in a trench coat says. "Is that what we're supposed to believe?"

Annie's legs hurt. It was a mistake to wear platform sandals to traipse around these sidewalks in the dark. She says, "Frances died before I was born, but the story was handed down. She did escape, and she married somebody else."

"Did she tell the police?" asks the trench-coated woman. "If she didn't, then she let him get away with killing her own mother."

Annie feels her authority fading. It would be so much better if the house were still here. "I don't know all the details. The Beverly mansion stood empty for years, and people claimed to hear screams coming from the basement."

"It's a legend," a bearded man tells the woman. "Ghost stories are supposed to leave you hanging. They're not about closure."

"Well, I'm disappointed," the trench coat says flatly. "If it's true, she ought to know the rest of it."

Annie is chilled to hear herself spoken of in third person. And she wants to say, *It's not just a legend.*

A child pipes up: "I saw leeches at the other place."

The child's mother, a young woman in a pink tracksuit,

says, "We went to the Ebenezer Maxwell Mansion. He's talked about leeches all day."

"Have you ever eaten eyeballs?" the child asks Annie.

"No," Annie says. "How do they taste?"

The mother says hastily, "They were gumdrops, with M&Ms stuck in."

"And there was brains!" the child gloats. "All red and squishy."

"Cold spaghetti," the mother explains. "They turned off the lights and let the kids stick their hands in it."

"Well, I want a latte," the woman in the trench coat says. "Join me, anyone?" and she looks pointedly at the bearded man, who edges away.

Annie says, "You can get apple cider and cookies at the Welcome Center. It's free."

She feels a tug of regret as her little group disperses, heading for cars or hiking north to Germantown Avenue. She forgot to ask their names. What's the matter with her? She was with them for an hour, ever since they gathered at the side entrance of the Chestnut Hill Library and paid five dollars each to benefit a youth group. She volunteers because she loves to tell the stories of these old streets, the old churches, and especially the tale of Frances and Vaughan. She grew up with it; her mother remembered seeing the Beverly mansion as a child. The story makes Annie proud. It's her heritage.

It's practically all she has, she admits to herself. She grew up in the neighborhood, on Highland Avenue, went to college in Altoona for two years, came back, and allowed the job at the bar to become her career.

For one spooky, lively evening every October, she's a star.

She hurries toward Germantown Avenue, wondering if anyone ever guesses that pieces of her own life, not only her great-great-grandmother's, are embedded in the story. An old boyfriend had seen a soap woman at a museum. Captivated, Annie worked her into the spiel. She has no idea what Vaughan Beverly looked like, so she made up a description. Her own widowed mother can be maddening and oblivious, like Frances's mother. Yet Annie feels she has not found the right ending. It's not enough, somehow, that Frances gets away.

Annie and her mother used to entertain each other by embellishing the few known facts. Then her mother left Chestnut Hill for a retirement home in Jenkintown. The last time Annie brought up the Frances story, her mother gave a sheepish smile and said, "It's bunk, for all I know. I've forgotten what's true and what isn't." Annie went cold, for if the story is bunk, then her whole life feels like a lie.

When Annie reaches the corner, one platform sandal twists loose. She trips, falls, and skins her knee. The lantern flies out of her grip and smashes on the sidewalk. Its light sputters out, and she smells the spilled kerosene.

"Are you all right?" someone asks.

She looks up. A streetlight illuminates the bearded man from her tour.

"Here," he says, taking her hand and helping her to her feet.

"Thanks," she says, feeling shaky. "These stupid shoes."

How quickly he vanishes. Her knee stings, and there was that brief panic of losing her balance. She gathers the shards of the lantern and tosses them in a trash can. Another Ghost Walk group passes by. Annie doesn't recognize the guide, a woman with a booming voice and silver eye shadow. This group looks jollier than Annie's was.

The bearded man is gone, but Annie's hand still tingles from his touch.

She has given the Ghost Walk for ten years, and she suddenly feels too old, at thirty-nine, to speak in the exaggerated cadences she uses for drama, and to wear navy-blue nail polish and a tight black dress: her witch outfit. Did the man even recognize her? She hurries along, her ankle aching. Trees and restaurants along the avenue twinkle with strands of tiny white lights. Every store, every bank, has a glowing jack-o'-lantern out front, or cornstalks and baskets of gourds. She smells the raw squash of pumpkins and the potpourri of candles. Fake cobwebs drape the doorway of the Irish bar. She lifts them up and ducks inside.

It's a busy night, but Dale, the manager, seeks her out to talk.

"It's like this," Dale says. "Everywhere we go, people give my wife pigs. Knickknacks and stuff. Always pigs. She don't even like them. She don't know how it all got started."

Dale never talks to her, not like this. Annie can't get rid of him, because he's her boss, so she has to listen and keep busy, cleaning the bar, wiping it down with a towel until it shines.

Dale says, "It started when she was little. She had a birthday party, and all the kids brought toy pigs. My wife thought her mother told them to, but her ma said no, she didn't. So my wife grows up and meets me, and we get engaged, and her friends give her a shower."

A customer signals for another beer, and Annie gets it.

Dale goes on: "And at the shower, everything's pigs. Salt and pepper shakers. Pig bookends. A clock that's a pig's face, and a curly tail going tick-tock underneath. She busted out crying, and they said, *What'sa matter? Don't you collect 'em?* That was in Pittsburgh. So we move to Philadelphia, and we don't tell a soul about the pigs. And then yesterday was her birthday, and the people she works with, they give her a party. And guess what."

Dale slaps his hand on the bar and Annie jumps.

"How far do we have to go?" Dale asks. His mouth opens, but it's not a laugh, it's a soundless, slack droop.

Suddenly, Annie is frightened. This is her life. She lives alone; there's a screamer in the neighborhood—somebody who shrieks in the night for no apparent reason, as if there really is a captive in a basement, as if Frances never got out. A *screamer*, the police say when she calls to report it. She has sat up clutching the covers, heart pounding, fingers slippery on the phone. There have been burglaries in adjacent apartments; she has smelled cigarette smoke and heard gravel crunch in the alley behind her bedroom window, as if some intruder is staking her out. Robbery she can deal with, but please God, keep rape and murder away.

"You look scared, Annie. What's the matter?" Dale asks.

She shakes her head.

"Come outside," he says.

She follows him out the back door, into the humid evening.

There, they are surrounded by sounds of invisible revelers. Laughter, chatter, ring tones. She hears with keen uncanny clarity: dogs' nails scraping the sidewalk, a sneeze from the direction of the old water tower. Yet she and Dale are alone. A weathered fence separates the backyard of the bar from the parking lot of the farmers' market.

Inhaling, Dale says, "Tell me what you smell."

Annie breathes in and out. "Garlic, shrimp, wine, leather, perfume."

"It's the smell of happiness," Dale says. "People who live here, they go out to eat every night, buy stuff in all these stores.

Me, I came up the hard way. Still coming up." He shrugs. "But tell me what's wrong."

They might be in a movie, Annie thinks. A harsh bulb over the bar's rear door backlights Dale's head. They're a man and a woman having the first real conversation they have ever had.

"I'm scared of getting old," she says, "and there've been break-ins close by. Nothing feels safe anymore. I don't feel safe."

"What if I gave you this bar?" Dale says. "What would you do?"

She pauses, considering. "I'd take the Irish stew off the menu. It sucks."

"Okay," he says. "What else?"

"Keep the windows open during the day. Air it out."

"How would you manage the rowdies?" he asks.

"Same as I do now. Cut 'em off."

"What do you do when you're not working here?"

"I just gave a Ghost Walk," Annie says. "Have you ever gone on that?"

"No," he replies, moving closer.

"You're not going to give me this bar," she says, meaning: *What would your wife say?*

Then he kisses her, planting his lips on hers slowly, so that she has time to think the word *lingering,* and all she has to do is stand there and feel how much taller he is, how big, and how she must feel like an escape to him. If this were a movie, she'd lay her head on his shoulder, curl into the embrace. But she can taste Dale's worries on his lips, the dry breath of another's fear. She steps away.

"Do you give good ghost?" he asks.

"It's funny," she says, "the way people want to be scared.

The Ghost Walk, horror movies. Why? When there's so much real stuff to be afraid of?"

Something like anger flickers in his eyes. He says, "That pig stuff. That's what's scary. My wife's going out of her freakin' mind."

"Get her to collect something completely different," Annie suggests, "to throw people off the scent."

"You think we didn't try that already?" Dale snaps.

He jerks open the door and goes inside, and Annie follows.

Costumed celebrants stream into the bar for food and drink: devil, clown, cowboy, pirate. Annie takes their orders. The pirate grins when she hands him a plate of fried mozzarella, and hope shoots through her. His teeth and his earring catch the light. She imagines lying in bed with him, telling him about the woman who turned into soap.

Her twisted ankle throbs, and she kicks off her shoes. The floor of the bar feels ice cold, and every passing car on the cobblestones outside sends a tremor beneath her feet.

ABOUT THE CONTRIBUTORS

MEREDITH ANTHONY is a Pennsylvania native who spent considerable time on Philadelphia's Main Line with her beloved mother-in-law, the late Nancy Light. She is the co-author of the thriller *Ladykiller*, which received many rave reviews and was nominated for the year's best mystery by *ForeWord Magazine*. Her short stories appear in *Ellery Queen Mystery Magazine*. She currently lives in New York City and is working on a new thriller.

DIANE AYRES is the author of *Other Girls*, a widely praised satirical novel. She also does editorial consulting, and her "Fiction Addiction" workshops, developed at the University of Pennsylvania, have inspired many students and professional writers. Ayres has lived in the Bella Vista neighborhood of Philadelphia with her husband, author Stephen Fried, for over twenty years, so they are still considered newcomers. For more information, visit www.dianeayres.com.

CORDELIA FRANCES BIDDLE is the author of the Martha Beale novels *Without Fear, Deception's Daughter*, and *The Conjurer*, set in Victorian-era Philadelphia. The series was inspired by research into two ancestors: Nicholas Biddle, president of the Second Bank of the U.S., and Francis Martin Drexel, whose brokerage house helped finance the government during the Civil War. Biddle also penned the historical novel *Beneath the Wind*. For more information, visit www.CordeliaFrancesBiddle.com.

KEITH GILMAN's debut novel, *Father's Day*, was awarded Best First Novel by the Private Eye Writers of America. Gilman is also a cop, on the job in the Philadelphia area for over fifteen years. The second book in Gilman's series of detective novels is due out in 2011. For more information, visit www.keithgilman.com.

CARY HOLLADAY, a native of Virginia, lived in Chestnut Hill, Philadelphia, in the early 1990s and still misses the cobblestoned streets and the cheese shop. She is the author of five volumes of fiction, including *The Quick-Change Artist: Stories*. She teaches at the University of Memphis.

Milton Perry

SOLOMON JONES is the best-selling author of six novels, including *The Last Confession, The Bridge,* and his critically acclaimed debut, *Pipe Dream.* Jones is an adjunct professor at Temple University's College of Liberal Arts, an award-winning columnist for the *Philadelphia Daily News,* and an aide to U.S. Congressman Chaka Fattah. He is a member of The Liar's Club, a Philadelphia-area writers group. For more information, visit solomonjones.com.

Jonathan Rubin/Studio Nine

GERALD KOLPAN lives in Philadelphia's Queen Village neighborhood. He has been an illustrator, graphic designer, and rock musician, as well as a print and broadcast journalist. In the 1980s, Kolpan was a contributor to NPR's *All Things Considered,* and for over twenty years he was the Emmy Award–winning features reporter for Philly's WXTF-TV. Ballantine Books published his first novel, *Etta,* in 2009 (www.ettathenovel.com).

Nick Kelsh

AIMEE LABRIE received her MA in writing from DePaul University in 2000 and her MFA in fiction from Penn State in 2003. Her collection of short stories, *Wonderful Girl,* won the Katherine Anne Porter Prize in Short Fiction in 2007. Her short stories have also been published in *Minnesota Review, Pleiades, Quarter After Eight, Iron Horse Literary Review,* and other literary journals. Currently, she is the director of marketing and communications for alumni relations at the University of Pennsylvania.

Emily J. Kovach

HALIMAH MARCUS was born in Philadelphia and grew up in Narberth, a western suburb of the city. After receiving her BA in English at Vassar College, she returned to live and work in West Philadelphia. She currently attends Brooklyn College's MFA Program in Creative Writing for fiction.

CARLIN ROMANO, Critic-at-Large of the *Chronicle of Higher Education* and Literary Critic of the *Philadelphia Inquirer* for twenty-five years (1984–2009), is now Professor of Philosophy and Humanities at Ursinus College. In 2006, he was a finalist for the Pulitzer Prize in Criticism, cited by the Pulitzer Board for "bringing new vitality to the classic essay across a formidable array of topics." He lives in University City.

Patrick Hinely

ASALI SOLOMON was born and raised in West Philadelphia. She received a Rona Jaffe Foundation Writers' Award and was selected as one of the National Book Foundation's "5 Under 35" for her first book of short stories, *Get Down*. After nearly twenty years of wandering, she once again lives in West Philadelphia, with her husband and son.

Mark Breedlove

LAURA SPAGNOLI lived in various apartments in Philadelphia's Rittenhouse Square area for twelve years before moving to the Italian Market neighborhood. Her poetry has appeared in ONandOnScreen.net, *New Millennium Writings*, and *Philadelphia Stories*, among other places. She works as an associate professor of French instruction at Temple University, where she founded a magazine featuring students' original writing translated into and out of English.

Duane Swierczynski

DUANE SWIERCZYNSKI is the author of several best-selling Philadelphia-based crime thrillers, most recently *Expiration Date* and *Severance Package*. He also writes for Marvel Comics, and is especially proud that he once brought Frank Castle, a.k.a. the Punisher, to the mean streets of Philly. He's the former editor-in-chief of the *Philadelphia City Paper*, and lives with his family in the so-called "Great Northeast."

Rachel Tafoya

DENNIS TAFOYA was born in Philadelphia and lives in Bucks County, Pennsylvania. His first novel, *Dope Thief*, was published by St. Martin's Minotaur in 2009. He is a member of the Mystery Writers of America, the International Thriller Writers, and the Liars Club, a Philadelphia-area writers group. His second novel, *The Wolves of Fairmount Park*, was published by St. Martin's in June 2010.

Jonathan Rubin

JIM ZERVANOS is the author of the novel *LOVE Park*, which was hailed as "a love letter to Philadelphia" and a "tribute to the power of brotherly love." His fiction has appeared in numerous publications, including the story anthology *Philly Fiction*. He is a graduate of Bucknell University and the Warren Wilson MFA Program. An English and creative-writing teacher, he lives with his wife in the city's art-museum area.